P9-EKY-448

Red Hawk's Trail

OTHER FIVE STAR WESTERNS BY MAX BRAND:

In the Hills of Monterey (1998); *The Lost Valley* (1998); *Chinook* (1998); *The Gauntlet* (1998); *The Survival of Juan Oro* (1999); *Stolen Gold* (1999); *The Geraldi Trail* (1999); *Timber Line* (1999); *The Gold Trail* (1999); *Gunman's Goal* (2000); *The Overland Kid* (2000); *The Masterman* (2000); *The Outlaw Redeemer* (2000); *The Peril Trek* (2000); *The Bright Face of Danger* (2000); *Don Diablo* (2001); *The Welding Quirt* (2001); *The Tyrant* (2001); *The House of Gold* (2001); *The Lone Rider* (2002); *Crusader* (2002); *Smoking Guns* (2002); *Jokers Extra Wild* (2002); *Flaming Fortune* (2003); *Blue Kingdom* (2003); *The Runaways* (2003); *Peter Blue* (2003); *The Golden Cat* (2004); *The Range Finder* (2004); *Mountain Storms* (2004); *Hawks and Eagles* (2004); *Trouble's Messenger* (2005); *Bad Man's Gulch* (2005); *Twisted Bars* (2005); *The Crystal Game* (2005); *Dogs of the Captain* (2006); *Red Rock's Secret* (2006); *Wheel of Fortune* (2006); *Treasure Well* (2006); *Acres of Unrest* (2007); *Rifle Pass* (2007); *Melody and Cordoba* (2007); *Outlaws From Afar* (2007); *Rancher's Legacy* (2008); *The Good Badman* (2008); *Love of Danger* (2008) *Nine Lives* (2008); *Silver Trail* (2009); *The Quest* (2009); *Mountain Made* (2009); *Black Thunder* (2009); *Iron Dust* (2010); *The Black Muldoon* (2010); *The Lightning Runner* (2010); *Legend of the Golden Coyote* (2010); *Sky Blue* (2011); *Outcast Breed* (2011) *Train's Trust* (2011); *The Red Well* (2011); *Son of an Outlaw* (2012); *Lightning of Gold* (2012); *Comanche* (2012); *Gunfighters in Hell* (2012)

Red Hawk's Trail

A Western Story

Max Brand®

FIVE STAR
A part of Gale, Cengage Learning

Detroit • New York • San Francisco • New Haven, Conn • Waterville, Maine • London

Five Star™ Publishing, a part of Gale, Cengage Learning.

LIBRARY OF CONGRESS CATALOGING-IN-PUBLICATION DATA

Brand, Max, 1892–1944.
Red hawks trail : a western story / by Max Brand.
p. cm.
ISBN 978-1-4328-2627-7 (hardcover) – ISBN 1-4328-2627-1 (hardcover)
1. Western stories. I. Title.
PS3511.A87R39 2013
813'.52—dc23 2012037259

Published in conjunction with Golden West Literary Agency.
Find us on Facebook– https://www.facebook.com/FiveStarCengage
Visit our website– http://www.gale.cengage.com/fivestar/
Contact Five Star™ Publishing at FiveStar@cengage.com

Printed in the United States of America
4 5 6 7 17 16 15 14 13

ADDITIONAL COPYRIGHT INFORMATION

Chapter One

Amityville looked good to me. It was partly the name and perhaps it was even mostly the name, because my life had been a long war from the time I was three years old and fell out of the second-story window trying to catch a bird. There was a tree under the window and that kept me from breaking my neck, but the branches whipped me and cut me up a lot. I still have some of the scars. That day was prophetic, you might say. Because though I have lived through a good many things, most of them have left their mark upon me.

So Amityville looked to me like a real place.

I had headed for the Far West in a hurry. A gentleman in Fort Worth had mistaken my back for a pincushion and tried to stick a Bowie knife through me when I wasn't looking. That led to quite a conversation, and before the end of our little talk, he looked rather depressed. I was afraid that he wasn't going to live, in fact. And a lot of other people felt the same way that I did about it.

They decided that the law would have to take a hand with me, and just as the law got ready to do that very thing, I found an open window and dived for the ground. Luckily there was soft sand underneath that saved me from a smashed spinal column. I got up and dodged half a dozen slugs of .45-caliber lead. Then I got to a horse and pulled out for parts more distant.

That was two months ago. I have changed horses five times in the interim. I have changed clothes three times. Not for disguise, but because I had to. Bad luck kept spoiling my clothes. But when I came through the gap in the mountains and looked down on Amityville, I was in pretty good shape. The last change had been for the best. The night before, I had met up with a man who was traveling in style, with a fine horse and a good set of togs. He had a bulging wallet, too, and he wanted to make it more bulging, by way of a poker game.

Poker isn't a habit with me—it's an instinct. He kept losing. The more he lost, the more he wanted to play for higher stakes. I told him I didn't want to eat his bacon and his money, too, and that made him mad and all the more determined. Before I knew it, he had his last $100 in on the game, and I won that.

The next minute he called me a crook and dived for his gun. He was one of those bad actors who keep a gun handy under an armpit. And I had laid aside mine when I eased myself of my belt. There was nothing for me to do except to grab his arm and freeze onto it.

God gave me a queer lot of power in my hands, my father used to say, so that I could get a good grip on trouble and keep attached no matter how fortune tried to shake me loose. Anyway, I kept attached to the gun arm of my friend until I got a chance to jam my other fist into his ribs. It took his wind and flattened him, and by the time he got his breath I had his gun.

After that, I had a right to look on myself as the conqueror and to the victor belongs the spoils, as somebody said who ought to have known better. Well, I sat myself down and made myself into a court of justice, and considered things. What I decided was that, since we were about the same size, I'd take his togs and his horse and saddle, which were all prime. To even things up, I left him my worn-out nag and my tattered clothes, and then I halved the money that I had won from him. There were $612, and that gave us $306 apiece.

Take it by and large, I suppose that that was a pretty fair division. You see, I could have taken everything. He sat there watching me with poison in his eye, but, when I offered to fight him fist to fist, he had nothing to say. He had had enough of that game. So I went on. When a man won't fight for his rights, you can put it down that he doesn't deserve to have any rights.

So I hit the mountain gap in style and looked down at a little town that curved along the bank of a stream—a shack of a town, of course, because western Texas didn't have towns of any other kind in those days. But it was early spring. And Texas was all massed over with desert flowers. They only last a little while, you know. They only come out for a few days, and then they are wiped away by the heat and the seeds mature on little dry stalks, and then drop back into the sand to cook and cook all the late spring, all the summer, all the blazing autumn. Then through the winter they drink up a shower here and there—and so they have strength to make the world beautiful for one more moment in the next year. It was beautiful now. The bald sides of the mountains that ripped into the sky all around the town were soft with color—the sort of color that runs into your eyes like perfumed air into your lungs. It made me smile to see that valley and that town.

A fellow with a pair of burros before him and the looks of a prospector's outfit packed on the backs of them came up the bend of the road and waved a hand at me through his own dust cloud.

"What town might that be?" I sang out to him.

He looked at me as though I had asked him the name of a continent. "Amityville, of course," he said.

Amityville. I turned that name back and forth in my mind and I liked the taste of it. Amityville, and me with a quarter of a century of battle behind me. All at once it seemed to me that every scar on my body ached for rest.

"It sounds good to me," I said. "Where did it collect a name like that, partner?"

The dust cloud had blown away, now, and I could see him leaning a big elbow on the sharp hip bone of the burro. His face was all red with heat and the work of the upgrade.

"I'll tell you," he said. "That town got its name because when it was burned down the third time after gunfightin' riots, the folks figured that its old name wouldn't do. So they raked around and give it this here new name of Amityville. It's sort of long to spell, and I never can remember exactly where the Y comes in the name."

"Well," I said, "it looks pretty peaceable to me, just now."

"Sure it's peaceable," he said. "There ain't been a killin' for over twenty days. Big Pete Gresham has took the town in hand and he's keepin' down crime."

"Is he the boss?"

"Sure. He's the mayor and the sheriff and the saloonkeeper, and the Society for the Prevention of Cruelty to Tenderfeet all rolled into one. Besides, them that come to town wantin' to raise the devil, never want to raise the one that's inside of big Gresham."

"He's real, eh?" I said.

"He's real," answered the big fellow, grinning, and I heard a ring of good enthusiasm in his voice. "But outside of Gresham, the town is sure restin' nice and soft on cactus thorns."

"What's wrong?"

"You find out for yourself, young man. I ain't a newspaper dealin' out facts about Amityville. Besides, there ain't more'n one man in the world that *can* explain what's wrong with her. But I say," he went on, turning and looking gloomily back at the little place, "that not even a Gresham like Peter can save Amityville from goin' to hell. It's wrong. It was made wrong. It growed up on the wrong sort of ground. And it means poison for them that try to live comfortable and quiet in it."

He gave a point to this little speech by thumping the burros and plodding off up the trail muttering to himself, and I had an impression that he was making tracks to get as far and as fast from Amityville as the good Lord would let him go. For my part I would have liked to talk with him a good deal longer about the town, because, of course, what he had to say upset me a good deal—in the frame of mind that I was in that morning.

However, when I looked for another while on the valley and the town and the mountains, all the warnings of the prospector slid out of my memory. There was nothing but peace in the look of that hollow, believe you me. The river lazed around the bend as smooth as a lake, and I could see the big green reflections of the trees even from away up where I was. There were trees in the street of the town, too. There was the green look of gardens in front of the houses that promised flowers to see and smell, and there was a green look behind the houses that promised fresh vegetables for chuck. And it all looked pretty good to me, and better and better the longer that I stared down at it.

Another few days and the color would be brushed off the edges of the mountains, and the summer sun would be baking and burning. However, I didn't picture that or I would never have gone nearer to the place. The beautiful part about it was that I started for the town in order to get *peace*.

Well, I got down to the bottom of the valley and flipped some of the dust off my togs and off my horse, and then I went sashaying into Amityville as proud as a picture.

Although, between you and me, I was never planned beforehand to do duty as a picture. The Lord made my nose too small and my jaw too big. My father used to say that I was composed to stand a good pounding without showing it. And I suppose that he was right. He generally was, when he was talking about me, because he felt that the right way to take me was the *worst* way of taking me. He used to say that he never could wish me any harm because he knew that flocks of it were flying my way all the time. This, by way of showing you that my father was a good deal of a prophet in a minor way.

However, I was feeling pretty happy when I slid into Amityville. And it's a queer thing that a homely fellow like me can forget his face and think so easily of nothing except his clothes. I knew that my new outfit hit me off as neat as though it had been made for me, and I couldn't keep from swelling out my chest as I pranced that horse down the main street.

The first thing that I saw was a big sign across the best-looking building in the town: *GRESHAM'S HOTEL.* Right under that sign, and a little to the side, there was another sign just as big that said: *GRESHAM'S SALOON.* And over on the far corner of the building there was a third sign: *GRESHAM'S GAMBLING PARLORS.*

I said to myself that Mr. Gresham was certainly making a good job of it, and while he cleaned up the town and made it safe on the one hand, on the other hand he was calmly picking the pockets of the citizens. Anyone could see that was good business. On the whole, I decided that I would have to see Gresham for myself and make up my own mind about him. So I dismounted and started for the door of the saloon.

Chapter Two

Frankly I was prepared to find Gresham an out-and-out hypocrite and sham, and there is nothing that makes my fighting blood rise more than the thought of such a person. I was almost disappointed when I got into the room and found that there was nobody who looked official behind the bar except a big Negro. There were half a dozen fellows sitting at little tables in the end of the room, drinking. And everything was quiet.

Everything was clean, too, and a lot different from the usual Western bar. The floor was paved with green flags of stone, still dark from a recent scrubbing. And the tables at the end of the room were yellow, and freshly painted. There was a painting of the fighter, Heenan, hanging on the wall and showing itself again in the great big mirror behind the bar, and there were pictures of race horses—and particularly of the great Lexington.

Well, when you consider that most Western bars, in that day and age, were just a plank laid on a couple of standing barrels, and the room was a tent or a shaky lean-to, you'll understand that I was sort of awed. I looked around me a couple of times, and then stepped up to the bar.

"Gimme a drink," I ordered, and I looked around again at the picture of Heenan. Just the name of Heenan was enough to make me rage. The idea that an American of his bulk had stood up to a little shifty lightweight like Sayers and been held to a draw—yes, or probably licked, if it had not been for the rowdies who broke up the fight before the finish—and the idea that an

American could not represent his country even in the prize ring any better than that, always maddened me. But the picture of him was alone enough to show the reason. He stood on his heels—not on his toes. He looked as solid as a bronze statue—but just about as agile. And he had one weak place—his right arm was held like a bar across the front of it—and that weak place was his stomach. The painter had tried to do Heenan a good turn by painting in a few muscles, but even with that addition he was a flabby-looking creature in the midsection. And no doubt every time one of the lean, hard fists of Sayers struck the stomach of the big man they must have sunk in almost wrist-deep. I studied the picture and grew hotter, and more and more I wished that I been in the shoes of Heenan for that fight. I would have shown the Englishman! At least at rough-and-tumble!

A voice seeped into my attention from the outside. "What'll you have to drink, stranger?"

It was the Negro barkeeper, and I whirled on him and glared. There was something easy-going and familiar in the voice of the barkeeper that made me hot and hotter.

"What'll I have to drink?" I yelled at him. "Why I'll have whiskey . . . what else *would* I be having? Water?"

He shrugged a broad pair of shoulders and squinted at me in a hostile way, as though he were not used to accepting such language from anyone.

"We got a good many different sorts of things here, sir," he said. "We can give you what you want in the way of a couple of good clarets, and some fine old port, and a bit of sherry that's not so good, and then we have a line of brandy, old and new, and. . . ."

"My Lord," I said. "Have I gone to New Orleans in a dream? Did you say claret . . . and brandy?"

He nodded and grinned at me.

"I'll have brandy then . . . the old kind," I told him, "and if the stuff that you give me is new, I'll wring your neck, Sambo!"

He tried to smile, but he only made a grimace. He was growing a little angry. And that pleased me.

"My name is plain Sam," he said.

"Your name is Sambo," I said. And then I exploded at the impudence of him. "Because," I said, "I come from Louisiana, friend, and down in that part of the world a Negro is anything that a white gentleman chooses to call him."

"Askin' your pardon, sir," said Sam behind the bar, "but I don't think that a white gentleman would talk to a colored man like the way you're doin'."

"The devil he wouldn't," I said. "Are you talking back to me, you black trash?"

The bartender walled his eyes and slid a hand under the bar.

"Keep your hand clear," I said. "Lemme see that hand of yours."

And I got ready to tip a gun out of a holster in case of need. And there might have *been* need, in fact, because it turned out that Sambo was as game as any white man. He did *not* remove his hand from its place of hiding and he repaid me with a fighting glare. However, he did not have to fight his own battles. For here a man stood up from one of the tables in the rear of the room.

"Look here, stranger," he began. "We don't allow that sort of talk in this here town. Keep off that Negro, will you?"

It was a good deal to say, you have to admit. I had been all in the wrong with poor Sambo, I have to confess. But when that man stood up and handed me that sort of talk—well, it drove me mad. I walked to the back of the room and stood over him.

"Partner," I said, "I dunno what sort of a town this here may be. I come down here right peaceable and looking for no trouble. But if this here town is made up of the likes of you, I'm gonna start reforming you-all. You hear me talk?"

That was paying him back $2 for every one that he had loaned me. But I was always liberal with that sort of money. The man didn't make a move at me, for a moment. I thought that he was going to take water, but he wasn't. He answered me in a second with a very cool sort of a voice.

"I'm not here to pick quarrels with strangers," he said. "I simply have given you warning that we won't have Sam bullied."

I felt that he was in the right; I felt, too, that I had been acting and talking like a ruffian. And I was weak with shame. Morally weak, I should say, because the weakness didn't come within miles of my muscles.

"Will you tell me your name?" I said.

"My name is Tom Kenyon," he answered.

"Kenyon," I said, "you've said more than I'll swallow."

His answer sounded very queer to me. He turned his back partially toward me. "Boys," he said to his friends, "do you think that this fellow has been sent in here purposely to pick a fight with me?"

"It don't make much difference whether he was or not," said another of the crowd, looking at me with hungry eyes as though he would have liked to take a hand in the party.

"I know." Kenyon sighed. "I suppose that I have to." He stepped out in front of me. "What do you want with me?" he asked.

"I want," I said, "to find out the color of the lining of you. And I figger on finding out what it is."

"You low hound," said Kenyon, and struck me across the face with his left hand.

I suppose the regular thing would have been for me to recoil a step or two, damn his ancestors, and then we would both go for our guns. But in a pinch, I've formed the habit of what my father used to call: thinking with my hands. I answered Kenyon with a left-hander that nearly tore the head from his shoulders. I stepped in to follow with a right that I planned to shove clean through his ribs, but he was already down on the floor, his head resting against the end of the bar and his eyes looking seasick. That fight was finished before it had more than got started. And that made me play the fool worse than ever.

I stood up before the crowd and told them in a wild riot of words that I would welcome a chance to take on the entire group, that I was in need of a bit of work, and that nothing would please me more than to take on the entire town of Amityville!

I got about halfway through the speech that I intended, when something in the face of the others made me pull in my horses a little. One of the men had gone to help Kenyon back to his feet. The others regarded me pretty steadily and calmly.

When I made a pause, the oldest said: "What'll we do with him, boys?"

"I'm asking for no advice," I assured them.

"You young fool," said the old chap, "you'll stay put until we've made up our minds about you. Don't move a step. Don't move a half step."

They meant what they said, and they meant it with the most profound sincerity. I saw, at a glance, that, if tried to rough it with them any more, they would answer me with four or five fairly accurate guns. Moreover, I saw that they were men of the upper class, self-respecting, grave, and deliberate. They were out here to mine or to ranch—they were not of the adventure-hunting type. Amityville had reason to want peace if she possessed many of this type.

I cursed myself silently for falling out with people of this type. I had been hunting for months to find a few unadulterated white men, and the moment I found them I had to conduct myself like a hoodlum. I wished Sambo and the entire Negro problem at the bottom of a great pit.

"Well," I said, "you gentlemen seem to be holding quite a few cards."

"We have them, and we intend to play them," said a second man. "And most of all, my young friend, you may thank the Lord that Peter Gresham is not in town, for, if he were, he would make such an example of you that would sting the rest of your life."

The first speaker said: "If you were drunk, there would be a partial excuse. But you were simply drunk with meanness. I think that we'll let you off if you'll get out of Amityville and get out of it quick."

"And never start back in this direction," said a second speaker.

"Gents," I said, "you have me beat. I've made a wrong start. And I admit that you're in the right. So long."

I turned on my heel, but I was stopped by a call from Kenyon. "Don't let the cur get away. He slugged me with a club, Jerry."

I stopped, and I half turned. "Do you want me to finish that job?" I asked him.

"A gun, you rat!" shouted Kenyon.

But a man took him on either side. "Let him go," they said. "Why should you throw yourself away on scum? You . . . get out!"

I got.

Chapter Three

Well, I was pretty well disgusted with myself that day. I told myself that I was a barbarian, that I had been born a barbarian, and that I would still be a barbarian when my death day came. There was no possible good excuse for the way I had acted in the Gresham saloon. I had to go out from the place so fast that I couldn't even stop to curse the Negro for the smile with which he was looking on. He was pleased, of course. And that made me fairly foam, because, down in Louisiana in those days, a man was raised to look at a Negro in only one way. I've changed a little since that time. But not a great deal. It's a hard thing to get away from one's boyhood training.

Anyway, I got out of the saloon fast and took my bronco and rode on through Amityville. That name had seemed mighty fine to me when I first heard it. Peace after a long war, and that sort of thing, you know. But now I was ready to move. There was no *amity* in the world for me. I was an outcast.

I suppose that the worst mood in the world is a sulky mood, and that was my humor as I rode out of town. A sulky, sullen fit will turn a man into a thing that is closer to the devil than any other mood that I know of. Because, when a fellow is sulky, he thinks and does things that will torment himself as much as they hurt and torment others. I have seen a man beat a dog he loved when he was sulky, simply because it gave him an exquisite torture to harm the dog and himself at the same stroke. I've actually seen a husband quarrel and fuss with his wife simply because *he* was in the wrong—and knew it.

That was my state of mind as I left Amityville. I knew, of course, that it was dangerous to go into a section of the country that was strange to me without learning the proper trails to take, but just then I didn't care what came of me. I had decided that I was a useless failure; I hated the world because I felt that the world had good reason to hate me. And so I struck away blindly through the mountains.

I went along for a couple of hours fairly oblivious to where I was headed. My head was down, and I didn't pay any attention to the heat of the sun. The first thing that pulled me together a little was the sight of a loafer wolf that came out on a jutting rock on the wall of the valley opposite to me—half a mile away. Those big wolves know guns and their ranges, I'm pretty sure. If I had had a rifle along with me, I never would have seen that brute. But I have nothing but my pair of Colts. And I swear that the tramp knew it.

There he stood as big and brave as you please. And in that wonderfully clear, bright air, I could see every detail of him. I pulled in the bronco and took a long look at the big fellow, just as he was having a long look at me. For I decided that I would have done better under the hide of a wolf than under the skin of a man. Where it was a case of sharp tooth and fighting heart, I would have done very well, no doubt. But as a man. . . .

I mention this to you to let you know that I was really very low. And here I tried my canteen of water and found that there was no water in it except half of a lukewarm mouthful. It was a paralyzing thing to me, because that canteen had been with me so long that I looked on it as a sort of personal friend on which I could depend. There was a good iron body to the container and around that body I had wrapped a lot of fine flannel, sheet by sheet, and sewed every sheet separately. I had fitted the shoulders of that flask like a tailor making a coat, and when the job was finished up—it took me the evenings of two weeks!—I had a canteen that any buckaroo would be proud to own. The advantage of the flannel wrappings, of course, was that I could drench them down with water and they'd hold the moisture for a great part of a long ride, and so long as there was outside moisture to evaporate, the contents of the canteen would be kept drinkably cool.

I tell you about that canteen in detail because the emptying of the water can struck me, at that moment, as a particularly vital blow. Just as though even inanimate things had turned their backs on me in a time of need. Of course, there was a simple explanation. That was an old, old canteen, and rust had finally worked a way through a lower corner of the iron. On this very day it happened to work a hole the size of a pin head through the metal and the water had leaked out. That was all there was to it—logically, but a man isn't logical when he is in the humor that I was in that day.

There was no danger. All I had to do was to turn that mustang around and he would probably follow the trails over which we had just ridden until he came to the town of Amityville where I could get a new water can. But at that moment the thought of returning to Amityville was purest poison. I couldn't stand it. I couldn't go back there and let the people who had seen me in the saloon point their fingers at me and smile. I wasn't so much afraid of their guns. But what would they say of a fellow who came in looking for trouble—he was so hard—and yet such a fool that he rode out of town with a leaking canteen?

So I looked far ahead of me to the point where the mountains began to turn blue with distance. *There's water some place,* I told myself. *And I'll get to it. And if I don't, what the devil difference does it make.*

This may sound like madness, particularly coming from a

man who knew the West and thirst horrors intimately well. But that was exactly what I said to myself, and again I say that a sullen mind is really a mind half crazed.

I rode straight ahead for I don't know how long. I decided that I would forget that there was such a thing in the world as thirst, such a thing in the world as water, such a thing in the world as bubbling, babbling fountains that ripple, iced, out of the cool caverns of the earth. I said that I would not think of any of those things, and the moment I made that decision, of course a torment began.

The best temperament to withstand such agonies is the temperament of a fool or at least of a sluggard. A fellow with imagination goes through ten hells before a dullard feels any suffering whatever. I made a vast effort to close the scene of trouble out of my head, and for that very reason the sense of trouble became my terrible and intimate neighbor. For another hour I kept pegging away, and at the end of that hour I stopped my horse and sat trembling in the saddle with sweat of heat and of fear coursing down my face. For I realized that I had deliberately ridden myself into a deathtrap.

You will say that having journeyed out from the town in three hours, I could simply turn around and ride back again—and a total of six hours without water would surely not be fatal to any man. But, of course, my horse was about as badly off for the lack of water as I was. He had come three hours out of the morning. He had to turn around and go back through the fire-hot middle of the day. And his strength was not what it had been in the morning. No, it was far from that. So you will see why it was that I sat for a long time in my saddle, trying to swallow my fear and finding my throat too dry to succeed.

Oh, in any climate east of the Alleghenies I should not have cared. But the Western air was different. This was not a flower-softened landscape like that beautiful one around Amityville.

This valley in which I was riding was cunningly composed of hewn and polished rock so that the force of the sun would be multiplied by ten. One never came to a cool stratum of air. One simply occasionally struck a layer that was less burning than the rule. What was not rock in cliffs and boulders were rock clippings, and valley floorings of roughest sand—the sort of sand that nothing but a dry storm wind could ever pick up and whirl along. But when it *is* in the blast, it cuts like a stream of chisel edges.

It was a mighty arid valley, I can tell you. But do you know what aridity can mean? It sounds like part of a geography lesson. But there is a dryness in the air that can be dangerous. They tell stories of air so dry that continual drinking can hardly satisfy thirst, so swift and steady is the drain of the sun upon the body—so mortally does that doubly dried air thirst for moisture.

So when I say that was a mighty arid valley, you'll know what I mean, and perhaps you'll even understand when I say that I was pretty badly scared. More than scared. The sullenness dropped away from me. The chilling certainty that I had made an overwhelming ass of myself gripped my mind. And then I saw with a perfect clearness that I was inevitably doomed to die. Nothing in the world could have saved me.

If I needed a strong proof, I had only to try my bronco with the spur. Usually one hint of the sharp steel made him leap away like an antelope from a panther. But now he merely tossed his head with a grunt and started into a slow trot.

What did I do first? Well, for a whole minute or two I sat quietly in the saddle fighting back a panic, and perfectly convinced that, if the terror once got over the wall of my good sense, I should become a maniac in no time whatever. I had seen fellows brought in from the desert like that—babbling. It wasn't nice to see. And I closed my hands until the nails bit into my palms.

Twice I hesitated about turning back toward Amityville, and twice I determined to ride on. I could not face three hours of backward journey, but I *might* be able to find some luck by traveling straight ahead. So on I went.

Imagination? I thought of what I should be in a few hours hence. I thought of a swollen, blackened tongue as big as a baseball. And as I thought of it, a stream of fiery pain ran down to the roots of my tongue and seared the hollow of my throat. Imagination? I began to die every half mile—and every step of the horse was matched by a step in my thoughts. In my mind, I allowed myself to shrivel and dry just like a green leaf in a great furnace.

I am ashamed of this. I don't want to write down everything that happened in my head during that journey. But I may as well freely confess, in the beginning, that I haven't that sort of courage that thoughtful men call the highest kind—the sort of courage that lies in the brain. When I see danger, I don't mind it so much, and particularly if there is a chance for me to fight back, I almost like it better than anything else in life. But to face fire, or drowning, or—thirst—well, that's different. And I shrivel up and turn into nothing mighty quick.

I went on with the horse until I felt him staggering under me. Then I got off and took a long look at him. He wasn't much of a nag. When he was running free he had looked like a great animal, but after he was saddled, he hadn't amounted to much. He wasn't even very tough. But I told myself that he might have a chance to save himself if he were unburdened of me and the saddle and the bridle.

I dismounted and stripped him of everything. And he stood there with his head hanging and his lower lips pendent, which gave him a very foolish look. But, after a moment, seeing that I stepped away from him, and feeling that there was no bight of a rope on him, he tossed up his head and went off with sagging knees.

Chapter Four

When I saw that poor beggar of a horse throw his nose into the wind and then start off at that weak-kneed trot, I knew that he had the scent of water, or thought he had it. And so the best thing that I could do was to make him my leader and follow him. Perhaps you will wonder why I hadn't simply given him his head and let him *carry* me on the same trail. But anyone who knows mustangs understands that they refuse to think for themselves as long as a bit is between their teeth.

This nag looked at first, as he started away from me, as though he would drop at any step, but he seemed to gather strength of body as well as spirit when he realized that he was actually free, and now I saw him positively rock into a canter and go swaying out of my sight around a tumbling junk heap of hills that had fallen from the higher wall of the valley through which we had been passing.

By the time I got around the same corner, he was out of sight, and the ground over which he had passed was a double-tempered quartzite on which even the shod hoof of a running horse made no more impression than a tapped fingertip makes on armor plate. The mustang was no good to me even as a guide.

And now I saw that what had looked like a tragedy—nine chances out of ten—was now a tragedy ten chances out of ten. Whatever hope I might have had, I threw it away. I stood for a moment turning chances over for the last time. There was nothing left. I realized that the easiest way was simply to pull my gun out of the holster and send a bullet through my head. Because there was nothing in the world that could save me except the miraculous appearance of a spring in the midst of the desert, or the still more miraculous appearance of a human being. But what human being would travel this untracked waste? Unless it were, perhaps, some random Comanche out praying for scalps.

However, I did not shoot myself for the simple reason that I felt it was a sort of miserable cowardice to give up the fight while there was still any strength in me. And, without hope, I turned up the valley once more and plodded along, head down.

What made me look to the side, suddenly, I don't know. But there I saw a horse and rider in the very act of turning a corner of the valley and away from my sight. I had a weird feeling, for a moment, that it was a specter come to haunt me—or a desert mirage. But something in the way the sun glittered on some silverwork on the bridle of that horse made me realize that I was seeing facts—blessed facts. So I began stumbling toward that happy apparition and waving my arms and trying frantically to shout.

He was not two hundred yards away at that moment, I suppose, but I couldn't make a sound. Utter thirst had caked my throat and the breath merely came whistling and crackling up through it without a vocal sound.

I tried again, but a horrible panic had hold of me now and finished what the thirst had begun. To my exquisite torture, I saw that horseman vanish around a pile of rocks out of which half a dozen great cities could have been quarried. My savior was gone!

I almost dropped at that. When I stumbled, if I had gone down, I think that I should have stayed down, with a ton's weight of despair to press me flat into the sands. But I managed to maintain a reeling balance and now I struck into a rickety run, lurching toward that point where I had seen the rider disappear. He had gone around that point of rocks at a slow trot. If that trot continued, he would still be within my hearing. If he freshened the trot to a canter, he would be beyond all but eyeshot of me.

I turned the edge of that granite junk heap and there he was, swinging across the floor of the valley with a strong gallop, far, far beyond the reach of my voice unless it had been at its loudest. For all voices sound faint in the thin air of the mountains, and when I strove to scream at the fugitive, there was only a faint, high-pitched moan. My voice broke like the voice of a fourteen-year-old boy.

I was ended, then. For he was riding straight away from me with his back turned—when something made him turn fairly in the saddle. The next instant he had seen my waving arms. I was leaping into the air and waving my hands the better to attract him. Then he whirled his horse about and came straight forward.

Like an angel out of blue heaven—that's how he looked to me. No poet has ever said anything good enough to describe him as he came zooming along. No poetry set to any sort of music would be any use.

What made him turn in that way? Well, you may say what you please. I say—telepathy. One shaft of my agony leaped across space and stabbed him from behind. So he turned and saw my need.

I was so wobbly and weak with relief, with thankfulness, that I even forgot how thirsty I was. I slumped down on a chunk of rock, and, when he jumped down before me, I could only grin up at him in an idiotic way.

Well, he didn't have to ask any questions. One glance at my cracked, bleeding lips was enough to tell all that any Westerner would want to know, and the next moment the muzzle of his canteen was hurriedly pressed to my lips.

Well, when I handed back that canteen to him, my eyes and my head had cleared a little, but still I wasn't myself by a long distance. I rolled a cigarette in one twist and lit it. I dragged down a great puff of smoke and, as I blew it out, I fanned it away from before me and now I found out I could see him sanely.

He looked like—I don't know what. Why, he looked like a girl's idea of what a man ought to be—and never is. He was designed after the original model of those spick-and-span young men who appear in the illustrations of love stories in the magazines. He looked as cool and as crisp and as flawless and as fresh as a collar advertisement. I knew, with one glance at him, that when he wore his Sunday clothes they would always look as if they had been pressed just ten minutes before.

There wasn't a line in his face. And his age might be twenty-five or thirty-five, or anything in between. But what a face that was! When I say that he looked like a picture, I mean that he looked like a *manly* picture. He was just pretty. He was the "winning halfback" type of hero, you see. He had a chin made broad and square-ended. He had lean cheeks and a tight chunk of muscle at the base of his jaw. He had a perfectly straight nose. He had deep brows with a pair of eyes as steady and cool and self-possessed as you please. He looked like the sort of a chap that could step up to any girl at a Saturday-night dance and make her cut her next dance with her best beau for the sake of having a whirl with him.

Take it by and large, you may have seen for yourself, by this time, that my rescuer was a jim-dandy. But I wasn't very much impressed—not even when I looked him over clear down to his feet and found that he was made in proportion. In proportion with the love-story illustration idea, I mean. He was exactly six feet tall, I suppose. And he must have weighed about a hundred and eighty pounds—or whatever the perfect weight for that height may be. He looked strong, and he looked agile, and he looked fast and he looked in good training. You couldn't imagine that young man sitting up late at night or drinking too much red-eye, or smoking cigarettes all day long. He looked so doggoned delicate and perfect, he must have used bay rum every day after shaving.

I'll tell you why he didn't impress me a lot. I've met up, here and there, with quite a flock of these young college heroes. And they don't amount to any great shucks when it comes to a fight, most of 'em. They may be pretty boxers and they may be game, but they aren't hard, and a man has to be hard before he can fight. I see the editors of the sporting pages wondering when a college boy will be a prize-ring champion. I can answer that question. At the same time that a college degree is given for rolling baled hay and piling Kansas wheat seven high, or for mucking coal on the three-thousand-foot level, or for swinging a sledge-hammer in a boiler factory. At the same time that college degrees are given for that sort of agony and when college graduates are toughened and hardened and tempered by the long hell of physical labor—at that time they will begin to turn out ring champions.

And the same thing holds with other kinds of fighting. A man who has labored will be apt to hold life cheap, after a while. When you put in sixteen hours a day riding range or feeding a hay press for $3 or $4 a day—or a lot less—you begin to see that life isn't such a sweet song, after all. You begin to see that the schoolteachers and the Sunday-school books only had one angle. They were written by the birds that have the monopoly on heaven in the life to come and the monopoly on the easy jobs and the high pay in the life that we have to wear every day. But what do they know about hell on earth? Nothing!

Well, I knew all about hell on earth. I learned it young. I

found out that a fellow might as well get ten minutes of happiness out of whiskey—if he can. No matter how hard he has to pay for it. Not even if he's robbed while he's stupid drunk. Not even if he's down and out for a month after his spree. That ten minutes of happiness is worthwhile. To see heaven for ten seconds, even—that's worth five thousand pay days when the money has to go into the savings account. At least, that was the way I looked at things then. And out of that attitude came the result that I didn't care a continental damn what happened in this life of mine. Neither did I care a great deal more for the lives of other people.

So I looked at my rescuer, and I sized him up pretty fast. He might have some poundage in advantage. He might be a lot more scientific in hitting. But when it came to standing punishment and when it came to hitting hard and fast and keeping it up—I knew, I thought, that I could beat him. He might be a good hand with a gun, too, but I would have sworn that he didn't belong in my class when it came to shooting at a human target.

You'll say that these were pretty mean, low thoughts for me to have concerning a benefactor like that chap. But I'm trying to show myself as I was. Not an ideal picture, but a dirty, sweaty, honest one. For that matter, the *face* of honesty is almost always so dirty that it disgusts polite society. And when I sat there looking up to that fine-looking, clean-looking man, I was saying to myself, all the while, that in some ways I could beat him.

He spoke just the way I knew that he'd speak—nice English. Terribly nice.

"You seem to be spent," he said. "And I can't imagine how you happened to get out here, without a horse."

"My wings gave out while I was flying over," I said. "And this was where I landed. Lemme see the insides of that canteen again, will you?"

He passed it to me without a word. Then he said: "I suppose that you'll come back to Amityville with me?"

"Amityville," I said. "Amityville! Do you mean to say that you hang out there?"

"Yes," he said. "I live there."

"You do? Young fellow," I said, "you'd melt and run away in that town. Don't tell me, because I've just been there. I've been through some hard-boiled towns, but in its own quiet way I think that Amityville ranks up with the toughest of the lot. What might *you* be doing in that burg?"

He looked down at me patiently—not smiling. He looked more like a picture man than ever. No, he certainly could not come from Amityville. I was determined to find out where the joke or the lie lay.

"I have a little business there," he said.

I thought that I understood. A good many prosperous ranchers would send their boys through an Eastern school and then bring them back home and have them practice—or at least hang out a shingle—in the little home town. I suppose that my new friend had that sort of a job.

"You're a lawyer, I guess," I said.

He smiled this time. "No," he answered. "Unfortunately I am not following my profession."

I shook my head. "Then I don't make you out," I confessed.

"Well," he said, "the sun is getting no cooler. Shall we start for Amityville?"

"Not for that town," I said. "Not unless I have a company of regular infantry alongside of me."

"Oh," he said, "if you've been in trouble there, I think that I may be able to take care of you."

"You do?" I yelled at him. "Now who in the devil might *you* be in the world?"

"My name is Peter Gresham," he said.

Chapter Five

It was a knockout drop for me. I looked at him again to make sure that I had heard right. And I listened again—to the mental echo, you might say—to make sure that I had the right words.

Gresham! The hotel, the saloon—the whole of that establishment that was the biggest thing in Amityville—the man who, it was said, kept the little town running and warded off from it the danger of I knew not what. Then the solution jumped into my mind.

"You're the son of the gent that runs Amityville. Is that it?" I asked him.

"I'm the only Gresham in Amityville," he said. "But I don't run the town. However, I think that I could take care of you if you want to go back. And if you don't go back, there isn't much for you except to die of thirst in the desert here. Isn't that the way it looks to you?"

Well, it completed the knockout drop. I didn't have enough strength left in me to put a dent in a tin can after he had finished saying that. There was no doubt about it. He was the man. And a man strong enough to keep up such a decent establishment as him in a town like Amityville—well, he was a good deal of a hero even if he had nothing but that to go on.

You have to admit that the quiet man has something in his favor. I'm not a quiet man, myself. When I'm surprised, I open my eyes and shout, and when I'm mad, my eyes open and shout again, but in a different key. If I have something on my mind, I speak it out. But though that makes an impression, sometimes, at the start, it doesn't always keep the impression going. But your quiet man, who you look on as a dub, scores a ten-strike if he scores at all. That was the way with Gresham. I had been putting him down as a magazine hero. Now that I saw there was something behind him, it made me score him as a real man, underlined.

I looked at him again. I *searched* him, you might say. And this time I say, by the little wrinkles at the corners of his eyes, that he was a good deal nearer to thirty-five than he was to twenty-five, and by the set of his jaw I saw that that square chin of his was not a mere decoration. Take it by and large, I saw that I had judged him like a fool. But, for that matter, I was rather used to making a fool of myself.

I said: "Partner, I had you wrong. If you say that I can go back to Amityville and find it lives up to its name, I'll believe you."

"Well," he said, smiling in a very good-natured way, "I don't mean that you can go back into town letting off a revolver at every other step. That might get you into trouble again. What was the first mess?"

I told him about it. I don't believe in hiding behind a false front. If people won't like me for what I am, they may damn me and be damned, for all I care. I tell the facts—good and bad. And I told the facts to Gresham, then. He listened without laughing and without frowning. There was only one change in his expression, and that did not come when I told how I had knocked Kenyon down. It was when I related how I had given Sambo the rough side of my tongue.

However, when I had finished he merely said: "I'm sorry about Kenyon. He's a good fellow. But just now he's a little nervous. I can tell you what they meant by the remark they made. Kenyon had the bad luck to capture one of Red Hawk's gang a little while ago, and, of course, he's waiting for bad luck to come to him, just the way that bad luck has come to everyone that ever had anything to do with the killing or the capture of one of Red Hawk's men. Kenyon is mighty nervous, and I suppose that the whole crowd was a little suspicious of you for the same reason. People in Amityville are a little on edge, and if you come to know them better, you won't wonder very much at it."

It was rather a mysterious speech, and I said so.

"I'll tell you about it as we go in," said Gresham. "Here, hop up on the horse and ride."

"And let you walk?" I asked.

"And why not?" he said. "I can see that you're pretty weak. For that matter, I've been out in the desert myself. And I know what it does to a man inside and outside. Get up into the saddle, man."

"Not me," I said.

"Then we'll both walk," said Gresham. And darned if he didn't start off beside me, with the reins over his arm and the horse behind. Of course that was too much for me. I swallowed my pride, admitted that I was fagged out, and took the saddle, and so that was the way that we went in toward Amityville—me in the saddle that belonged to Gresham and Gresham walking along beside me.

It would have peeved most men a good deal to be in that position. But not Gresham. He walked along as though he were out taking the air for the fun of the thing, and, as he walked, he broke off his story to point out everything that lay around us, that was of interest. But, for that matter, there was little that did not interest Peter Gresham. He was one of those fellows who can settle down in a cheap boarding house and make the place and the people seem so attractive that a millionaire would want to change places and come over to see those faces.

That was the way with Gresham. Even in that desert he knew

the right leads. He could tell you about the rock formations and dip into geology to make a story out of a boulder. And a mighty interesting story, at that. Or he could stir about and give a lot of information about various places that we passed that had a bit of historic interest. For it was a great Indian country, and where the Indians hadn't made a spot celebrated by scalping a few whites, they had made it celebrated by scalping one another.

The Apaches had made most of the noise when it came to raking up trouble with the whites, but the Comanches were the big thing in the inter-tribe wars. Those bow-legged Romans of the West could outfight their weight in wildcats. And it was out of the Comanche stories that Gresham worked up to his account of the troubles in Amityville.

I won't give the story in his own words—partly because it would take too long and partly because I can't reproduce everything that he said during that long journey back to Amityville. But the general effect was something like this.

About five years previous to this time Gresham and his brother Leicester had come out West and they had paused in Amityville in the middle of a hunting trip. The whole journey was just a sort of pleasure-exploring party for them. But while they were in the town, a gang of Apaches had made a raid and carried off a lot of horses from the place. A few whites made a hasty pursuit, and a couple of the leaders got close enough to the Indians to be shot at and killed.

So Amityville had sent out a punitive expedition in which everyone old enough to ride a horse and shoot a gun went along. They didn't overtake the Apaches until it was too late. Their work was done in another way. For while they beat up the rear of the Apaches, a war party of Comanches coming in the opposite direction hit those Indians and went through them like fire through dried grass. By the time the whites came up, the Comanches were dabbled with crimson, full of songs and victory, and doing scalp dances all over the mountainside.

The whites congratulated them, and the two parties very foolishly camped close together for the night. That night wasn't two hours old, of course, when the trouble started. It hadn't gone very far when the whites got together and delivered a charge, and in the midst of the charge one of the whites was knocked from his horse by a ball that grazed his head.

That charge started the Comanches on the run, but, as they ran, they carried along with them the man who had been knocked from his saddle by the rifle bullet. When they got the poor fellow safely away, they sat down one day to enjoy him bit by bit. That is to say, they tortured him to death with every species of devilishness that they could devise.

The point of that story lay in the fact that the captured man who had been done to death piecemeal was none other than poor Leicester Gresham.

When the news came in to Peter Gresham that his brother had died in this fashion, he made a vow on the spot that he would never leave the country until he had avenged the death of his brother by finding and killing the chief devil presiding at the ceremonies of the torture, and that chief devil was a tribal leader named Red Hawk.

To carry on the war, Peter Gresham settled down in Amityville, because the town was right on the road of the Comanche excursions toward Mexico, and because there were enough mines in the vicinity and enough of a growing cattle industry to make the town living and attractive as a goal to the Comanche marauders. Amityville—it had another name in those days—was the bait to catch the Indians. And Peter Gresham acted the part of the trap.

He had a good deal of luck, at the first. He led out several parties that ambushed and cleaned up a number of war parties in which the cream of the Comanches went down yelling to find the happy hunting grounds. After a while, Red Hawk found himself without such a powerful band of warriors at his back. And then he himself decided to start playing a new game.

He was a man of talent, this Red Hawk. If he had been a white man, he would probably have been a leading captain of industry. As it was, he decided that instead of plaguing the white men with an occasional onslaught, started from a distance, he would take up a permanent residence among the tangled hills near the town. Here he would maintain a gang of cut-throats, not large, but concentrated in vicious strength. He would not limit himself to his own tribesmen. There were other villains beside whom only the most talented Indian braves could stand for a moment in accomplished villainy. And even the best of the braves lacked the steadiness of purpose and the qualities of bulldog persistence that the members of the Red Hawk party had to possess.

So he enlisted, little by little, a handful of half-breed Mexicans from the badlands and the danger line just across the river, and he thickened the gruel with some white outcasts from the northern side of the river—experts in scoundrelism of all kinds, veteran gunfighters, thieves, and throat-cutters.

Now, when he had assembled men of this kind, another thought came to this talented Indian chief. He saw that he had in his band only a random few of his own kind, and that they were diminishing in number with the process of time. His band was composed of just the same sorts of people who walked and talked in the streets of Amityville. And so Red Hawk decided that in those crowds some of his own men might very well mix.

It was no sooner decided upon than it was done. Straightway a chosen few of his retainers began to filter through the town, and by what they learned there the chief and his band directed their robberies. If money moved in the mails, if gold was ready for shipment, if a gambler left Amityville with his wallet filled with money, the news of it was sure to be carried to the ear of Red Hawk, and that warrior, with his terrible face and his one eye—for the other had been knocked out on some foray—was sure to swoop down on a new victim, or at the least he would send his emissaries to do the work for him.

It started as a nuisance; it was ending by becoming a dreadful menace to the very existence of Amityville. And, worst of all, though all men knew that spies walked the streets and stirred in the houses of the town, no one could be sure of their identity. And, for that reason, there were suspicions, side glances, and continual dissension. Friendships did not continue long among men. And the name of the town covered a thousand or more cold enmities.

Such was the story that Peter Gresham told me as I rode in—interspersing his tale with all manner of side remarks about the country.

What I gathered from his tale, however, lay outside of his words. And that was not the duel between Amityville and the terrible Comanches, but the struggle between Red Hawk and quiet Peter Gresham, who had not as yet avenged his brother, but who would never rest until he had done so.

It filled me with a dim sort of wonder. I could not imagine the sort of perseverance that keeps men for five long years in one town, waiting, waiting, waiting for the big chance that will give them revenge. And, in the meantime, building up a whole business career out of the only elements that were at hand. I thought of the hotel and all that was in it. And I decided that no one could blame Gresham for starting a gaming house and a saloon. He had simply come to the town and done as others did in the West. The vices were the vices of the country—not of the man.

While I thought of this, we came in sight of Amityville.

Chapter Six

After we saw the town, you can be sure that I did not have so much time to pay attention to my new companion. I began to remember the straight way that those men in the saloon had looked at me, and the memory made me fairly sag in the knees. I told Peter Gresham about it because, as I've said before, I don't mind letting people know just what goes on inside of me. Peter Gresham listened and smiled, and then he shrugged his big shoulders.

"I don't think that you'll have any trouble," he declared. "Not so long as you have somebody to vouch for you."

I saw that he was right five minutes after we came inside the town. We were going down the street—both of us walking, now, and the horse led behind us—when a pair of men stopped on the wooden sidewalk and gave me a brace of looks that bit through me right to the heart. I kept my right hand near my gun and gave Peter Gresham a side glance.

He was in the act of waving his hand to the two, and that wave was the only thing that kept a couple of bullets from flying my way, because both of those fellows had been in the group at the saloon when I was ordered out of Amityville and told to stay out.

They came straight up—not to me, but to Gresham.

"Pete Gresham," said one of them, "you don't know this chap that you're walkin' with. I want to tell you. . . ."

"I know all about it," said Gresham, "and this man is my

friend. I want you to meet. . . ."

"We don't want to meet him!" they shouted in unison. "Did you hear that he came rarin' into the saloon and started . . . ?"

"I know the whole story," said Peter Gresham. "And I know how he walked over Sam and then got into trouble with some of you fellows and knocked Tom Kenyon down."

"Did he tell you all of that?" they asked him, and they looked at me with new eyes. I began to be glad for the hundredth time in my life that I had a habit of telling the truth and the whole truth. I could see that these fellows did not like me, at once, and they couldn't be blamed, but I could also see that they began to doubt their first judgment of me. And that was all I wanted.

"He told me all of that," said Gresham. "And when he said that he wanted to come back to Amityville and show the boys that there was another side to his nature, I told him that I knew Amityville would meet him more than halfway. Was I wrong?"

They looked silently, doubtfully at me. But they had heard too much from Gresham, and they seemed to respect him too much to wish to say anything insulting. This was all of two or three minutes after they had been ready to shoot me down in the street in cold blood. Well, I could see the influence of Gresham working smoothly and easily on them, and I decided that he was just a shade bigger and stronger in Amityville than even I had imagined him. He was picking those two fellows up in the palm of his hand, so to speak, and making them feel and think just as he pleased.

"Well," said one of them in another moment, "I'm glad to know any friend of yours, Pete. I'm glad to know him by the first name, too. Here's my hand on that."

"The devil!" said the other one. "I ain't so smart that I can't take a lesson from you, Gresham. Your friends are good enough for me, I guess."

And, in another moment, I had shaken hands with both of my bitter enemies. And now I listened to them as they promised Peter Gresham that they would do their best to keep the others who had been at the saloon from talking about me through Amityville. For, as we came into the place, I could not help saying to Gresham: "Partner, if you think the town could stand me, I could stand the town. I'd like to hang out here."

He turned, at that, and shook me gravely by the hand. "You're the sort of man that we need in Amityville," he said to me. "And we'll be mighty glad to have you." And that was one reason, I suppose, that he seemed eager for me to make my peace with everyone in the place. When he had converted these two and made them into allies of mine, he announced that we must go instantly to find Tom Kenyon and make my peace with him.

I did not like this so well. Because, as you can see for yourself, when one has knocked a man down and done it in a public place, there is nothing left for him to do except to return the compliment either in public or in private. And the Western custom—at least in those rough days—was always to repay with interest. I felt that going to the door of Kenyon's house and trying to shake hands with him would make him pretty sour on me, and I told Gresham what I thought. Well, sir, that fellow simply waved me and my idea away.

"Hard feelings have to be thrown away," he said, "if a fellow is to live comfortably in Amityville. I'll tell you what I've done since I came here, Sherburn, and that is to go without guns . . . just as you see me now . . . every day and all day, except for those times when I have to take the trail of that red devil, that murdering Indian . . . that. . . ."

Here his emotion was too much for him. And I looked at him in a new wonder. He had been so calm, even when he told how Red Hawk had killed his brother, that I could hardly believe my eyes. But I liked him a thousand times better for this bit of human nature. He was almost too perfect, before. And now that I saw him capable of hating one man—even an Indian—as sincerely as even I had ever hated in my life, I wanted to shake hands with him all over again. However, he had said one thing that was almost too much for me. I taxed him with it at once.

"Tell me what you mean by that. Gresham, do you mean that you never carry a gun?"

"I mean it, Sherburn. I mean it, of course."

"Do you mean to tell me," I pursued, "that you haven't a gun hanging under the pit of your arm? That you rode outside of Amityville with the country liable to blossom out with Indians at any moment, and not a sign of a weapon in your hands?"

"I have a hunting knife," he answered. "In case of a pinch, I can always fall back on that."

"A hunting knife!" I cried. "A hunting knife!"

"Well," he said, slipping the knife into the palm of his hand and weighing it there, "a knife isn't such a bad weapon at close quarters. I think that I'd much rather have a man throw a bullet at me with a gun than a knife with his bare hand . . . always supposing that he knows how to handle bare steel."

I did not have to ask him if *he* knew how to handle bare steel. His careless way of fingering that knife, with its razor edge, was my answer already prepared. He put it back into its sheath without giving it a look. He had plucked it out and put it back with as much careless surety as another man would handle a watch. My respect for Gresham, if possible, went up another notch.

Of course it was hard for me to imagine any man with his proper senses about him, living in such a community without powder and lead ready at all times. But I could say freely to Gresham: "I believe. Only tell me why you do it, and why you take your life in your hands every time you go into a crowd."

"Does it seem that to you?" asked Gresham, smiling. "Well, you're not the first that has wondered. But, frankly, it's not dangerous at all. It's the reverse. When a man carries a gun, he's prepared to find trouble anywhere. His eye goes hunting for it and everyone he meets can see in that eye that here's a man prepared to take nothing from anyone in the world. Well, when a man steps out in that fashion, all set for trouble and ready to back step for no one, he's pretty apt to find another person who's just like himself, and if he meets that man face to face, and neither of them will side-step, there's a crash and an explosion right away.

"A big noise, I tell you. But when I go into a crowd, I haven't a gun and I know it. Which is more than having other people know it. If there is danger coming my way, I simply side-step it. I let trouble pass on ahead, and I keep in the background and I'm always ready and willing to let the other fellow have the best of the argument. It doesn't ruin my self-respect to duck out of danger when bullets are about to fly. And the result is that I haven't a single scar from a street quarrel or a saloon fight . . . and yet I run a saloon, a hotel, and a gaming hall. So there you are. And I think it proves that a man gets what he's prepared for in this world . . . even in a hell hole like Amityville."

Well, I listened to what he had to say and I believed that, too. And I couldn't help breaking out: "Gresham, what's true for you maybe isn't true for other people. You're one man in ten thousand . . . you're one man in a million."

"Stuff," said Gresham. "Here's the house of Tom Kenyon."

When we tapped at the door, Kenyon himself came out. He gave one glance at Gresham, and then he turned the rest of his attention on me. I had hit him pretty hard. There was a blue, swollen place at the side of the point of his chin. And there was a bandage around his head—for I suppose that the scalp had been cut by the violence with which he had struck against the end of the bar when he fell.

He said: "Young fellow, I'm glad to see that you've made up your mind to come back to Amityville by breaking through the danger line. I want you to know that as soon as I can go inside and get a gun, I'll come hunting for. . . ."

"Half a minute, Tom," said Gresham. "I want you to listen to me, if you will. I want you to understand, first of all, that my friend Sherburn has not in the least. . . ."

"Good Lord, Gresham," said Kenyon, "is this fellow a friend of yours? Really?"

He looked at me as though he were looking at a species of snake, and Gresham had to grab me by the shoulder as I started for the man in the door.

"He's my friend, I'm glad to say," said Gresham. "And I want to make him *your* friend, too."

"I know," said Kenyon. "I know your way, Pete. But it won't do this time. I can't take it from any man . . . what I took from this Sherburn . . . if that's his name."

"He's come here to apologize," said Gresham.

You might not believe it, but when Gresham said it, it did seem possible for me to apologize. For the first time in my life it seemed possible.

"I'd as soon ask for an apology from a bulldog," said Kenyon. "No, Pete. I have to fight it out with this scoundrel. And I want to have the boys see the fight."

"Kenyon," said Gresham, "I don't think you're acting wisely."

That was all he said, but I give you my word that driven snow in front of a blizzard off the mountains is a warm zephyr compared with the coolness of Gresham's voice as he said that to Tom Kenyon. It seemed to me that Gresham had turned to steel. And Kenyon was hard hit, at once. He reached out and caught the shoulder of the saloonkeeper.

"I'll tell you, Pete," he said, "that we're not all saints, like you. This fellow has insulted me in front of the whole town. Everybody knows about it. And do you think that I can stand having fingers pointed. . . ."

"Why," said Gresham, "I tell you, man, that the fingers will be pointed at my poor friend Sherburn, when it's known that he has apologized to you."

"Do you mean," said Kenyon, "that he would really apologize?"

"I do," said the other.

I felt my blood turn into water.

"I don't mean here in private . . . but in public . . . right in the barroom where he . . . knocked me down?"

"You're asking a lot," said Gresham. "But he'll do even that."

Kenyon gaped at the pair of us. As for me, my brain was whirling. Every single atom of my heart revolted at the part that Gresham was planning for me.

"If he'll do that . . . ," said Kenyon, "well, it'll be worth the price, I suppose. Tonight at eight, I'll be around at the saloon. Maybe I'll see you there, Sherburn. But I don't want to see you here." And he turned on his heel and left us standing there.

You would have to go a long distance to find worse conduct and more insulting conduct than that of Kenyon on that day at his own front door.

But that was not what made me sick as we went down the street. It was the thought of what Gresham had planned for me for the evening. I could see that he was full of the same idea, and his face was black with it.

Chapter Seven

We did not speak for some time, as we went down the street. But then he said, very quietly: "I'm afraid that Kenyon is very much in the wrong." Somehow a judiciously spoken phrase like that had more weight than a complete damning would have had. I felt as though Tom Kenyon had been sentenced by a judge and jury. But then Gresham added: "How about it, Sherburn? Do you think that you want to go through with it?"

I made a wry face. But the thing had a sort of queer attraction for me. Because I had never been humiliated before a lot of men, the thought of standing up in front of a crowd and apologizing to another man tickled me. I said: "It's a great deal to do."

"It is," admitted Gresham. "It's more than any other man has ever done in this town, I suppose."

"The whole gang will think that I'm taking water," I said.

"They will," he said. "Perhaps they will."

Of course I didn't expect him to agree with me like that. "And what the devil good will it do me?" I went on.

"None at all," said Gresham. "It won't do you any good with other people. I suppose that Kenyon may be fool enough to even despise you, but it would do you a lot of good with yourself, maybe."

"What you mean by that?" I asked, very curious.

"It might make you respect yourself more," he said, "and that's always a gain, I suppose."

That was a new one to me. I said: "Well, I suppose that I was in the wrong in hitting him the way that I did . . . without warning. But to apologize before a whole crowd."

"Kenyon will be down there at eight o'clock," he said briskly. "You can make up your mind in the meantime."

Then I broke out at him: "Well, Gresham, I'll tell you the big reason that makes me want to do it. You think that it's the right thing, and just now that weighs a good deal with me because I don't mind saying that I write you down for the whitest gent that I've run into in my travels, and I'm going through with this dodge just to see what comes of it."

He looked me over in his quiet way, and then he nodded. "That's a big compliment," he said. "I think it's about the biggest compliment that was ever paid me. Sherburn, I hope that this affair doesn't turn out bad for you."

Well, he said it in such a way that it was the same as saying good bye. So I said so long to him and went off to sit by myself and mull things over in my head. There was no good mulling. I found myself cleaning up my gats. Because I had decided that if the job didn't come off—if anybody in the saloon as much as grinned when I stood up to apologize to Tom Kenyon—I'd pull my two guns and start spraying lead around in a more large and liberal way than even Amityville, in spite of its history, had probably seen. You'll say that that was not a very Christian spirit, but, in those days, I don't know that I was a great deal interested in what a good Christian would or would not do. I was interested in what was comfortable or uncomfortable for one Sherburn, alias Grip Sherburn, alias a lot of other names of which Bulldog was one of the lot.

You may have made out that I didn't have a very good reputation. I suppose I had been in three or four hundred towns of one kind or another, chiefly tough and Western. And out of a good percentage of these I had gone by invitation, usually pointed with a few leading remarks from the muzzles of guns.

Now, as I sat there that afternoon and turned these facts over and over in my mind, I decided that my thirty-two years of life hadn't been spent any too well. I had roved and I had roamed. My friends were just chance pick-ups that I had run across here and there. There wasn't a man, or a woman, or a child that I could really depend upon. And, when a fellow gets to thirty-two, there aren't so many years left for the formation of friendships. I had fought my way through the world. And I had made people respect the weight of my punch and the speed of my draw. But what else was there about me that they *did* respect? Not a great deal, I had to admit.

Altogether, it was a blue and gloomy afternoon that I spent with my guns, getting ready for the apology at the saloon of Gresham. I wanted a lot of time to turn things over in my head, but time ran on wings that day. It was dusk before I knew it. And then I had to get ready for my appearance.

It was almost exactly 8:00 P.M. when I went into the saloon, and then I saw that someone—it must have been Tom Kenyon—had let the town know beforehand what was to happen. I had thought that I could breeze into the place and walk up to Kenyon and say my piece without making more than two or three people hear me. But when I went in, I saw that Kenyon was banked about with a dozen men and the rest of the saloon was as full as it could hold of other people.

I suppose that half of the males in the town were there. And they were waiting for me. The instant that I came in sight, all eyes flashed across to me. It was mighty disagreeable, I can tell you. And I stood in the door for a moment and fingered the butts of my Colts. They were friends that would speak for me—the only ones in the world, I suppose. No, there was big Peter Gresham, standing at one end of the bar with a glass of beer in front of him, talking and laughing with a young Mexican. And though the eye of Gresham merely flashed across me without any recognition, I knew that he saw me and that he did recognize me.

I thought that I read his mind. He didn't want to give me any encouragement. If he stepped out and shook hands with me, it would give me all of his weight to help me through the time to come, and what he backed in Amityville was pretty sure to have an easy passage of it. I thought that I read his mind to that effect, and it rather pleased me to think that, if I passed the acid test, Gresham would be willing to call me his friend.

Well, there is nothing like taking bitter medicine at a swallow. I stepped toward Tom Kenyon, and, as I walked, I could see every eye fasten harder on me. And I could see scorn and disgust in the faces of every man there. They thought that I was taking water. Yes, I saw big, hard-looking half-breeds actually turn red for shame to think that any man could fall so low.

I went straight up to Kenyon. And there was a sort of fierce and hungry satisfaction in his face.

I intended to mumble out the words just large enough for him to hear, but when I opened my mouth, there was so much emotion that the sound came out loud enough for a regiment to overhear.

I said: "Kenyon, I knocked you down this afternoon. Well, I'm sorry for it. I should have given you a warning before I hit you. I've come in here this evening the way I promised that I'd do. D'you accept this here apology?"

Kenyon gaped at me as though he really couldn't believe what his ears had heard. And then for an answer he nodded and gasped.

I had said my piece, and I turned on my heel and started for the door again. It was the hardest thing that I ever did in my life, I'll promise you. I've never seen so much contempt as there was on the faces of the men in that barroom. You could have scraped it off by the bucketful. And disgust and a sort of sickness of shame that made me cold to see.

Well, I got to the door, some way, and just as I was about to step out under the stars—and mighty glad to see them—I heard a big voice call behind me: "Sherburn!"

I hesitated.

"Sherburn!" he called again.

I turned around, at that, and then I saw that it was big Gresham who had spoken to me. He was coming with long strides through the rest of them, and he came up and took my hand with a hard grip. "This is a fine thing, Sherburn," he said. "I've seen a lot of men die pretty well. But I've never seen one do a harder thing than this. I congratulate you. Will you have a drink with me?"

It was, really, just about what I had been expecting, and the word and the hand of a man like Gresham, I can tell you, was enough to make up for the contempt of a whole roomful of people like the rest of them. But what he had said seemed to make all the difference with the others. When I stepped for the bar at the side of Gresham, those hard-boiled frontiersmen drew back and made a path for me to get up to it. And there was nothing but wonder and chin scratching all around me.

I heard the big fellow saying: "Boys, drink up all around. I want you to meet a friend of mine. His name is John Sherburn, and here he stands. You've heard him apologize to Tom Kenyon for a wrong thing that he did today. Well, I want all of you to understand that Kenyon forced it on him. I want you to know that I took Sherburn to the house of Kenyon this afternoon and Sherburn offered to make amends very handsomely. But that wouldn't do for Tom. He had to make a show of it. He demanded that Sherburn come down to the saloon, here, and speak his piece . . . and you've heard him speak it. I'll tell you why he did it. It wasn't for fear of Tom Kenyon or any other man. Sherburn isn't that kind. If you want to know anything about him, in the line of fighting, get in touch with half a hundred towns in the West and they'll tell you plenty. But that isn't the kind of a reputation that Sherburn wants out here.

"Boys, he wants to throw in with me and with the rest of you that are trying to checkmate Red Hawk. And he wants to have the best men in the town for his friends. He's not here to show his hand as a gunfighter. He's here to show himself as a keeper of the peace. And I think that you'll agree that he has played a handful of aces this evening. What you'll think of Kenyon for forcing him to it, I don't know. That's a shoe of another kind. In the meantime, here's drinking to John Sherburn."

Well, the glasses went spinning up and down the bar and the bartenders filled them, thick and fast. And, pretty soon, they were sparkling in the air. There was a shout, and the drink went down, and the empty glasses flashed in the air and then clattered on the bar. After that, half a hundred men were crowding around me, telling me their names, and shaking me by the hand. That was what Gresham had done for me. That was what his strength amounted to in Amityville.

There was another way in which his strength showed to me. While the drinking went on, there was one man who did not reach for a glass but simply strode out from the room, head down. That man was Tom Kenyon. And I knew that if it had been any person in the world other than Gresham, he would have had to pay high to Kenyon for the sort of talk that had gone around the table that night. I knew, too, that if the evening had given me a town full of friends, it had given me an enemy, and that a hearty one.

CHAPTER EIGHT

At that time I had no care for the ideas of Tom Kenyon. He could love or hate me without any concern of mine. All that I wished to make sure of was that I was seated in the respect of the town, and there could be no doubt of that with such an introduction as Peter Gresham had given me. That big fellow ruled the town so absolutely that without a gun he could stand up in a crowd and put a man in his place as I had seen him put Tom Kenyon.

I asked a ruffian at the bar about it that same evening, when I had a chance. "How can Gresham," I said, "take the chances that he takes without a gun in his pocket?"

"It ain't so much of a chance now," he said. "It used to be a big gamble with him, I suppose. But now it's different. He's got his reputation, I suppose. And the crowd is with him. They're ready to fight his battles for him. I've seen two gents right here in this barroom try to make a name for themselves by shooting up Gresham. They both come out the underdog."

I was interested and I told him so.

He went on to explain. "The first time," he said, "the whole town heard about how a gent had blowed into the saloon in the middle of an afternoon when there was nobody there but the big fellow. He pulled his guns and started picking a fight. Sam, the bartender, come in and wanted to pull a gun, but Gresham made Sam stay out of it. The stranger got Gresham out on the floor, and then started the old gag of shooting at the floor and ordered Gresham to dance. Gresham danced, too. He did a real Irish jig, and simply laughed at the stranger instead of showing he was scared. Which, of course, there ain't no fear in Gresham.

"The stranger went out around town and blowed about what he'd done and swore that he'd wait in town until Gresham come gunning for him, and then he'd shoot it out fair and square. But Gresham never come to shoot it out. He stayed at his work and acted like nothing had happened. When some of the boys asked him about it, he simply laughed and said that he had done a little dancing to entertain a customer. That's the way with the big fellow. He takes things easy. I listened to that chatter and the rest of us waited to see what the stranger would do.

"He had a big name back in Kentucky as a first-class bad man. And, a couple of nights later, darned if he didn't show up in the saloon with his guns all greased up and ready for working. He stood right over yonder under that picture of Lecompte and sang out a couple of pretty rank remarks to the big fellow. Then he yanked out his gats." My informant paused and pointed to the upper part of the picture. "You see that hole?"

I crossed the room and made it out—a neat, little, round puncture.

"That's where one of the bullets went when the boys opened. They were watching mister man, and when he showed a gleam of steel outside of his holster, there was about twenty guns in action. He was not only dead before he hit the floor, he was nigh blowed to pieces."

"What was the other case?" I asked.

"A gent come down from Montana and said that he heard they had a real man in Amityville, but that he disbelieved that they growed real men in Texas. He come in and tried his lip on the big fellow, and collected nothing but smiles from Gresham. Pretty soon he began to cuss Gresham out. Then he fetched out his guns. Well, it was the same story over again. Only, he didn't die so soon. There was only three gents in the room, and though they all planted their lead in him, he lived long enough to put a slug through the bar and smash the big mirror. It cost the big fellow a pile of money to send East and get another mirror to take the place of that one. But he done it. And there it is, brand new and shiny. But the big fellow, he says that the high cost of mirrors is going to drive him out of the saloon business."

Here he stopped and began to laugh, and I moistened him with a big shot of red-eye. That made some more conversation grow on dry ground. And it was all about Gresham. There wasn't nothing else in Amityville that folks liked to talk about except Gresham. He was half the town and the biggest half and a sight the best half, everyone said. And they pointed out to me that he was enough to keep a town, all by himself. Because the news of him had got spread so far and wide that folks kept coming in to have a look at him. Gents from the South traveling north and from the North traveling south, or bound east or west, would all turn a good piece out of their way so's they could have a look at the big fellow. The name of him had gone all over the range.

There was always a pretty thick sprinkling of strangers in the town who were there just for the sake of registering their names in the hotel book of Gresham. Besides that, he had the best selection of drinks of anybody inside of a hundred miles either way from him. And when cowpunchers got paid off, they would always save up their thirst for a few extra hours till they got to his place where they had good beer or wines, if they didn't want to get poisoned quick on the sort of red-eye that most bars kept in those days.

Or, when some old sourdough got a belt loaded with dust, he would travel an extra week for the sake of blowing his stuff at Gresham's place. Partly because he knew that he wouldn't be robbed while he was asleep, and partly because, if he blew in his whole roll, he could get staked again by Gresham. It was a fact that when some of the old boys came in to drink themselves blind, Gresham used to rob them on purpose. He would have the bartender charge them double when they were blind with drink, and then, when they thought that they were all out of funds, he would pay them back from their own money.

That was one of the ways of Gresham that made men love him. And, at the same time, it was a pretty profitable thing. People felt that they could trust him, and so they went to any distance for the sake of doing business with him.

Above all, the gamblers hunted up Amityville, and in Amityville, of course, they had in mind only the place of Gresham. There was no room for any other saloon or hotel or gaming house in town. Other people had tried to open up, and they had all failed. No one could stand against the opposition that the big fellow could offer to them. But particularly the gamblers flocked in to try their luck.

Two things attracted them. One was, of course, that every roulette wheel and every other gambling device in the house was honest. And so was every dealer who sat behind the tables of the big fellow. The other thing was that the sky was always the limit.

I can tell you an incident that happened the very first night when I was in Amityville. It's just the sort of thing that gamesters love, and it shows you the sort of triple-tempered steel that the big fellow was made of. A Portuguese renegade, a swarthy-faced, black-eyed, thin-lipped devil who had probably raised trouble in half the ports of the world, was in the gaming room working away at the roulette wheel and losing steadily. Finally he got into a raging temper and came hunting for the big fellow. He swore that the wheel was crooked and demanded an honest game so that he could lose his last $50. Gresham didn't change color, and, when a husky murmur of anger came from the hard-handed cowpunchers standing around, he raised his arm and stopped them. There were at least two score of men who would have willingly torn that Portuguese limb from limb. But Gresham told the Portuguese calmly that they would cut for the first ace to settle the ownership of that last $50.

They cut, and the $50 was doubled. The Portuguese bet again. I myself stood by and saw them cut fourteen times and I saw the Portuguese, by some sort of a black magic, win every cut. The money mounted like the wind—$50, $100, $200, $400, $800, $1,600. . . .

It stood at $51,200. The Portuguese was a madman. He hung over the table with his mouth fairly slavering, a mighty disgusting sight to see. And every time he won, a sort of scream came from him. "Thee whole thing . . . another cut, *señor.*"

And he would push out into the center of the table every cent of his winnings. And it was a huge stack, at last. And, when it came to betting for the last time, Gresham laid out the contents of every till in the gaming room and sent into the bar. He stacked up $42,500.

"I will mortgage the whole establishment to you for the lacking sixty-two hundred," he stated.

"Curse all mortgages!" screamed the winner. "I cut for the whole place and all the money on the table!"

"Done," said Gresham, and leaned over the table with a smile.

"It is your turn," he said to the Portuguese.

"No, curse you!" yelled the madman. "It is yours! I cut last! I cut last!"

The cursing seemed to make no difference to the big fellow. He simply smiled and shook his head. "But whatever you wish," he said, and he cut the pack and turned up an ace.

All of that agony of the spirit, as you see, for the sake of a single $50 that had pyramided until the whole fortune of the big chap was hanging on one turn of the pack. But Gresham seemed to thrive on it.

The Portuguese dropped to the floor as though the sight of the card had been a bullet through his forehead. They had to carry him out into the air. And there they fanned him and threw water on him until he came to. And, the next day, they sent him out of town.

But Gresham, a moment after he had made the winning turn, was just as calm and as self-possessed as though he had been chatting to the Portuguese, not fighting for his entire fortune. However, that was Gresham's way, and that was why gamesters loved to come to Amityville to sit at the gaming tables there.

I have given all of this space in order to let you have some knowledge of the sort of a man that Gresham was. And also so that you will know how I felt when, at 2:00 A.M. when the big doors of the building were closed and the heavy bolts shot clanking home, I heard Gresham say: "Stay a while in here with me, partner. We must have a little chat."

He sat me down to a bottle of ripe old port. "Sherburn," he said, "I want you for a partner with me . . . in fact, I want you to handle this place while I hunt down the scoundrel, Red Hawk. What do think of the idea?"

Chapter Nine

If some Van Astorock had asked me to become his heir, I should have been less astonished. Because the very last person in the world that I could imagine in need of help of any kind was this same Peter Gresham. And, what made the thing more absurd, was that a man as calm and judicious as he should wish to put such a trust in a common gunfighter and rowdy—because I'm afraid that I was not much more, at that time. Above all, a man who he had not known for a single full day, even if we had seen a good deal of each other in that time. I told him these things as I stumbled through a few sentences to express my wonder and my thanks.

But he put all of these matters to the side by saying: "Of course, I'm gambling when I ask you to become my partner. But then, I'm used to gambling. It's my whole profession and business. You look like a good thing to me, and I'm willing to bet on you. If you were a *sure* thing, why, you wouldn't be out here in the sticks . . . you'd be back East handling some first-class business there. I get you cheap by taking a chance on you. On the other hand, if you tackle this job, here, you'll have about all that you can do. I want you to represent me. If somebody walks into the place and wants to gamble high, I trust that you'll do as I did . . . bet as high as he wants and put the entire value of the plant on the turn of a card, if he wants it that way.

"The rest of the time you'll have to go the rounds and watch the games and the men that are playing them . . . the drinking in the saloon, and the people who come to the hotel to register. Because we get bad ones of all kinds in this place and you have to watch their faces and their hands.

"If you do these things for me, you get a straight split of twenty-five percent of the profits, and that ought to be enough to give you a pretty fat income. I donate the establishment and the reputation. Also, I help out when I am able to get any free time. Does this idea sound good to you?"

I simply said: "Gresham, it scares me. I've never been trusted like this before. If I wanted to, I could gut all the tills and the safe and get away with a fortune."

"You won't do it," he said, "simply because you *are* trusted. I put my money on you, Sherburn. A man who has the nerve to stand up and go through what you went through with Kenyon tonight, has the nerve to stay straight when there's a big temptation. Sherburn, you may have gone wrong in little things. I don't think that you will in big ones."

I didn't answer him. I couldn't, because there wasn't breath in me to reply to him. But, just the same, I was swearing to myself that I would see myself hanged and quartered before I'd betray an item of his trust in me.

There was no more talk that night. He showed me where my quarters would be, right on the second floor, with a pair of rooms big enough to suit a prince, and I went to bed there feeling like a newly crowned king.

It was the middle of the morning when I opened my eyes, after being up so late. I smelled tobacco in the air, and, when I looked around, I saw between me and the window, with his heels cocked up on the sill, a thin-faced old chap of about sixty years, with eyebrows covered with hair as long and gray and stiff as the whiskers of a walrus.

I took another look around me at the height of those walls and the size of the room and the bigness of the windows. I had forgotten what had happened the night before.

"Is this the town jail?" I said. "And are you the keeper?"

"By a way of speakin'," he said, "I'm the keeper, but it ain't the jail."

I began to remember; everything that had happened jumped across my mind. "What is it, then?" I asked him.

"It's the death cell," he said.

It sent a shiver through me, it was said so simply. "It's what?" I said.

"The death cell," he said again.

"How does that come?"

"It gets its name by what happens to them that bunk down in this bed. I suppose that you're a new partner, ain't you?"

It was pretty staggering to have him so pat as that. "Suppose that I am?"

"If you wasn't, you wouldn't be in here."

"And the men that sleep here die young?"

"Two of 'em have," he said.

"The third man has the luck," I said.

He simply shrugged his skinny shoulders. "You don't look none too lucky to me," he said.

"You're wrong," I said. "I was born lucky."

"Well," he said, "you're in Amityville, ain't you? Is that luck?"

I sat up on the side of the bed and stared at him. "Look here, who might you be?"

"I'm Doc," he answered.

"I thought you was the undertaker," I said. "What's your job?"

"Makin' things easy for any of the friends of the boss. Particular for his partners."

"Do you start out with all of them the same way?" I said. "By telling them what's coming?"

"The first gent," said Doc, "come from New York. He was a

pretty bright and lively kind of a feller. About fifty. But he could ride a horse pretty good and shoot straight. He'd been in big business, and the big business got *too* big for him and just big enough for somebody else. So the other gent put the business in his pocket and left Carson to make a new start. He tried it down here. Well, he lasted about two months. Then he was shot right through that window there. A mighty neat shot, too. Right between the eyes."

Doc paused to get a chew, and this took time, for he had to work it off with his back teeth, his front ones being more for the show of gold ware than anything else. He stowed the quid in the center of his cheek and began to munch solemnly.

"Well," I said, "there was another one?"

"He come from Michigan. His name was Stillwell. He took pretty kindly to this here town and the town seemed to take kindly to him. But one day he got into an argument about a horse that a gent said that he wanted to sell. The result was a bullet through his back. And the funny part of the thing was that nobody had ever seen that horse trader before that day, and nobody has ever seen him as far as I know, after that day."

He stopped again. But by this time I was growing pretty thoroughly interested, you can believe.

"Look here," I said, "did you warn the second man?"

"Why for should I warn a Michigander?" he asked. "Up in them cold parts of the country they're supposed to have brains enough to learn how to take care of themselves, ain't they?"

"And what state do I come from?"

"Louisiana," he answered.

It startled me a little. "The boss told you," I suggested.

"He didn't."

"How did you guess?"

"Some is born with eyes," he said, "and some grows eyes later on, and some gets eyes by study. But speakin' personal, I was born with eyes. I growed better eyes later on, and then I made 'em better still by study."

"You tell Louisianans by sight, eh?"

"Yes, Mister Sherburn."

"You old liar," I said.

"Well, sir," he said, "it's partly by the hearin', too. You've been around the world quite a mite, but there's still a good deal of the old home state around your tongue. Yes, sir, it ain't so hard to tell where you come from. If I was to close my eyes like this and listen to you talk, I might be able to locate pretty close to what part of the state you come from."

"You old rascal." I grinned at him.

"Yes, sir, by the sound of your talk, I'd say that you come from somewhere near to . . . well . . . Rackam?"

I jumped to my feet. "You old rascal!" I shouted. "Who are you?"

"And how might your father and your mother be, Grip?" he asked.

It was my first nickname, and it gave me a thrill to hear it. "What's your whole name?" I asked him.

"I been called Doc so long," he said, "that I can't hardly remember no other name."

"You were in Rackam, then. Well, I think that I remember your ugly mug."

"I wore mustaches, then," said Doc, grinning. "But it ain't likely that you'd remember me, because them mustaches was dyed."

I couldn't help laughing at the old scoundrel. "Anyway," I said, "I'm mighty glad to see you, or anybody from the home town and. . . ."

"I was layin' here rememberin' a little thing," he said.

"What was that?"

"The day that you and the Porson boy had the fight in the

yard behind the school."

"Were you there?"

"D'you disremember how that there was some repairin' work goin' on in the roof of the schoolhouse?"

"I remember that. Yes."

"Well, there was about four of us that was up yonder, and, when the fight started, we laid off of work and watched the carryin's on. It was quite a sight. And when Porson knocked you down and grabbed up that stick. . . ."

"I remember," I said, and I laid a hand along my eye. For one of my many scars—and one of the biggest—had been made by that same stick in the hand of that same Porson boy.

"When he started whalin' into you with that stick, we thought that he'd brained you. And a pair of us started in to climb down and wring that kid's neck. And when we got part way down, we heard them that was left on the roof crowin' out . . . 'He's up ag'in! He's up ag'in!' I looked down, and there I seen you, sure enough, on your feet once more, with your face a big red smear. And sailin' into the other lad!"

"My face was such a sight," I recalled, "that it scared the wits out of Nick Porson. And that was what won the fight for me."

"Howsomever that might be," said Doc, "it was a terrible lambastin' that you give him when you got him into a corner, and there ain't no mistake about that. But, young feller, when one Amityville knocks you down, you ain't gonna have a chance to get up on your feet no more, because, when they hit, they don't hit with a stick."

He had finished off his bit of reminiscing in such a serious vein that I frowned at him. "You're giving me a real warning, then?" I said.

"I'm givin' you a real warnin'," he concurred.

"I haven't had a chance to make many enemies here," I told him.

"That may be. And the two that held the job before you didn't have time to make many enemies either, they thought. But I'll tell you what the trouble is. The job that you're steppin' into is too big for anybody in the world except one."

"Who might that be?"

"Why, nobody but your friend Gresham, I guess."

"You mean that this three-ringed circus he runs needs him in the center ring all the time?"

"That's what I mean. That's just exactly what I mean."

Here he fell silent, and then leaned out the window to watch something that was passing slowly in the street. I could tell that by the gradual turning of his head.

I went and stood beside him and I saw a girl going down the street, bareheaded in spite of the brightness of the sunshine and the heat of it, and swinging her hat by the strings. It was red hair—bright as fire. And she walked with her head up and her heels hitting like a man. And she swung her arms and her shoulders like a man, too. And those arms were as brown as the arms of any boy who spends most of a summer in a swimming pond or lying in the heat on its bank. Her dress was a faded blue calico with a string tied around the middle of it. But that was all she needed to set her off. In spite of the red hair, and the faded dress, and the brown arms, and the swing to her walk, I tell you that there was something as sassy and as fine and as fresh about that girl as any I ever saw.

I don't know where the secret was, because I couldn't see her face. It may have been just the back of her neck, or the smallness of the hand that swung the strings of the hat, or the roundness and the slimness of her body when the wind hit her clothes. Well, I don't know what it was about her, but it brought my heart up into my throat as quick as you could snap your fingers. I watched her around the corner.

"Hello!" sang out old Doc beside me. "Don't fall out the window."

I straightened up. I suppose that I was a little red, but I couldn't help it, and I didn't much care. I said: "Lord, Doc, isn't she a peach?"

"She is," said Doc.

"What's her name?" I asked.

"Jenny Langhorne."

"It's a good name," I said, turning it over on my tongue. "I might have known that she'd have just some such name as that."

"However," said Doc, "it's a pretty good idea for you to get that name and the girl that wears it right out of your head."

It made my fighting blood come up pretty quick. "Why?" I snapped out.

"Don't get sassy," he said. "There's a claim staked out and filed on that girl and there ain't a man north of the Río Grande with the nerve to jump his claim."

"Doc," I said, "I hate to call an old man a liar. But that's what you are. If she ain't married . . . tell me the name of that lucky fool of a prospector that found her?"

"Peter Gresham," said Doc, and sat back to enjoy the scene.

Chapter Ten

I've heard a good many men talk about love at first sight, and I suppose that there isn't much doubt that there is such a thing, but if a man were to say that he fell in love with the looks of the back of a girl's head—why, folks would simply put him down as a fool and a big one. So I won't say that I really fell in love with Jenny Langhorne at the first glimpse of her, but I could feel myself weakening very fast.

I said: "I hope that I never see the face of that red-headed girl."

"A good many have said the same thing," Doc said. "But tell me . . . are you one of these here soft-headed young gents?"

"I am," I said.

"Do you fall for 'em easy?" he asked.

"I do," I said.

"Then heaven help you," he said. "Do you mean it?"

"Mean it?" I said. "Why, I've been in love in every town that I was ever in . . . except this one. And I've been in all of the towns in this dog-goned West. I've had my heart broke so many times that I can't even count the scars."

"Well," said Doc, "you're such a nacheral young liar that I don't know whether to believe you or not. All that I'm hopin' is that you ain't the man that's gonna take Jenny's eye."

"Wait a minute," I said. "I thought you said that she was staked out by Gresham."

"I did say that."

"But now you aim to say that she's open ground?"

"Don't misunderstand me and get no foolish hopes inside of that head of yours, young feller," Doc explained. "What I aim to say is that the matter is all settled on the side of Gresham. And Jenny is willin' to marry him, she says. It's all taken for granted. But . . . she was engaged to him three years ago . . . and they ain't married yet."

"Three years! How old is she?"

"Twenty."

"Did he get engaged to her when she was seventeen? Is he a cradle robber?"

"If you think that she was a baby three years ago, you're all wrong, my lad. She was a handful for a giant. No, it ain't lack of years that's kept her from marryin'. But the point is that she says that she doesn't feel old enough."

"I never could understand women," I said. "And I never could pretend to. It's an easy thing to love a girl, but if it isn't a hard thing to know her."

Doc nodded. "I got to explain everything with footnotes, like a guidebook, to you," he said. "Don't you see by the color of her hair that if Jenny Langhorne really wanted to marry anybody, she'd laugh in the face of an archangel, if he tried to forbid the union? And that's why I say that her mind ain't really made up. She likes Gresham. She thinks that she loves him. But Peter is a fool if he don't force her hand before she asks for a new deal."

I thought this matter over little by little. Then I decided aloud: "I'll never meet that girl, and, if I do, I won't look in her face."

"Can you dodge a sawed-off shotgun loaded with bird shot?" asked Doc.

"What of that?"

"Just that you can't dodge Jenny. You're a new man, and she'll see you and look you over plenty . . . if she thinks that the first look makes another worthwhile. Also, young feller, you'll look back at her . . . you'll look her right in the face, and you'll keep right on lookin' as long as she wants you to. That's all that there is to it."

"Look here, Doc," I said, "I seem to be in a devil of a fix, between an irresistible gent and his irresistible girl. What am I to do?"

"I was comin' to that just now," he said. "If I was you, I'd saddle my horse and slide right out of town as fast as horseflesh fed on steel spurs would take me. This town ain't meant to bring you no good luck."

I half believed him. But of course I couldn't take that advice, no matter how good it may have sounded to me. Here I was in town with the biggest job a thousand times over that had ever come my way. And here I was to the windward of a girl who made my heart turn somersaults in my throat by a mere hint of what she was like. Of course, I couldn't pull out. But, just the same, I have to admit that I felt rather queer about the whole thing—rather weak and gone in the pit of the stomach. Just the way I felt for about a week after a mule handed me both heels in the same spot.

I said to Doc: "It appears to me that you're talking out of school quite a pile."

He said: "Son, I dunno what would happen to me if it was to be known just how much I had talked. I'll tell you this, though. What I've told you already ain't the half of what I could tell you afterward."

He got up and went to the door, leaving me pretty flabbergasted behind him. But, at the door, he stopped to stretch and he said to me through a yawn: "I'm supposed to be your handy man, run your errands, and put you wise to some of the traditions around this dive, and to some of the gents that ain't traditions around it but that would like to be. If you need a quick messenger, press a button and you'll find me at your elbow when you turn around. That's the Doc." He laughed in his lazy fashion, and then he walked away through the door.

Of course, after he had gone, I could easily sit down and figure out that the old rascal, having been sent to work for me and to act as a sort of general roustabout, had decided to feed me fat with a large bluff, and after that use his time to please himself. That was an easy solution of the way he had talked to me. But still something of what he had said stuck in my craw and made me want to know what else he might have in the back of his mind. I decided that I would at least keep my ears and my eyes open.

Before I left my room I stood still and shut my eyes and thought to myself: *Shall I do like Gresham and carry no guns?* I opened my eyes and said aloud: "No! If I try to do that, they'll laugh at me and then shoot me full of holes." So I buckled on my gun belt and I walked slowly down the stairs, thinking about as hard and about as fast as I had ever thought in my life.

You see, I could tell every minute that what old Doc had said had been about two-thirds true. This job that I was trying to step into was cut for a fellow of the size of big Pete Gresham. Two men already had been murdered because they attempted business that really belonged to him only. By the way, I wondered that a man as frank and aboveboard as Gresham had not pointed out to me all the dangers that I was facing. I wondered that he had not spoken to me about the two dead men who, in a way, lay before me in my path. It didn't seem like Gresham. It almost gave me my first doubt of him.

Well, two other men, who were supposed to have courage and experience and fighting skill and some brains, had failed in the work that I was going to undertake. Why had they failed?

I only had to take one thought about that place, and the smoothness and the quiet with which everything was handled inside of the premises of Pete Gresham. That quiet and all of that order wasn't natural. There should have been stampings and cursings and a gun let off every now and then, just to liven things up a bit. But Gresham made those roughs behave just like circus ponies. And, when a new ringmaster got in, the ponies turned into wild mustangs and kicked his head right off his shoulders. That was easily seen. But it was pretty hard if no one else in the world could handle things as the big fellow did. So, hoping that I would find a dull spot in the day to begin with, I stepped into the saloon.

I had no luck. I looked around me and I saw about twenty fellows—half of them just down from the mines. There was more trouble in their faces than there was dust on their shoulders. They looked like they were carved out of dynamite. And they had eyes that were like laid fuses—with the fire just about to touch. I never saw a dozen hotter characters. When they saw me, those big huskies weren't contented with smiling behind their hands. They began to guffaw right out loud.

Said one of them: "Look here! Here's the Sunday-school teacher. Big Gresham is tired of work, and this is what he brings in."

Said another of them: "He ain't serious givin' us this. He's just aimin' to keep us amused."

Well, that may sound a little funny. But it wasn't funny. It flipped the coin to me right then and there and I had to call heads or tails before she hit the ground. I've told you before that I liked fighting. I did, and I do like it. It's in my blood, and it's in my bones. But, just the same, I'm not too anxious to start bullets when I've got a twenty-five-percent interest in a $1,000 mirror behind the bar.

I walked across that room with my head sagging a little, because, I'll tell you, I was having thoughts so big and so fast that I simply couldn't handle them. At last I saw one clue to the reason that two men had failed and had died before me. It was because they had tried to imitate big Gresham, just as I had had it in mind to imitate him. And, of course, they couldn't do it, any more than I could do it. He was inimitable. But, for that matter, everybody has his own sort of strength. And I'm not a weakling myself. I decided that I would hit out for myself and in my own way.

I stepped up to the bar and I hollered in the roughest and the biggest voice that I could: "You knock-kneed suckers, you parboiled sapheads! You've been handled with gloves by Gresham. He was too good for the likes of you. Well, sir, I've come in here to treat you the way that you ought to be treated. I'm hard, friends, I'm hard. I've tried to pipe down and talk small, but I can't stand it no more. I've decided that I got to be myself. And myself is a lion, boys, that is fed on raw meat three times daily and exercised walking on the frames of low-down hounds like you-all for the rest of the day. Here's where I start runnin' this little shell game. Here and . . . *now!*"

And, with that, I fetched out my gun with a snap that made it jump up right over my shoulder and it came whirling down in front of my face. I had practiced a good many hours on that silly trick. I caught that gun by the muzzle and I slammed the butt against the bar so hard that every drink jumped in its glass. And there was a dent left that would have held two fingers of whiskey.

Chapter Eleven

You can believe that I reversed that gun, double-quick, and had it by the handle before you could wink, and I had my left hand on my other Colt at the same time, because I really expected that what I had done would draw one rattling volley of oaths first and a volley of hard bullets second.

But to my wonder and to my delight, they were staring at the big dent that I had struck into the surface of the bar. I suppose that there were a dozen men in that room who half wanted to fight with me then and there, and I suppose that there were three or four who would have licked me fair and square at that time.

I had no reputation—in that town. And reputation is half the battle. Why does a second-rater who becomes champion suddenly turn into a first-rater? Because he is his old self plus reputation. And that's a big difference. It makes him a little cooler. It puts a heavier wallop in each hand. And it starts the other man with a handicap. He *expects* to be licked because it's only the lucky fellow who beats the champion in anything.

Well, as I was saying, I had no reputation in Amityville, up to this point, and those big fellows were willing to eat me up, but when they saw that big dent in the bar, they seemed to pause. I didn't give them any chance to recover. I bellowed out to Sam: "Trot me out a little drink, will you?"

God inspired Sam at the right moment to do the right thing. He saw that I was reaching well over my head and trying to play a new part. So he came to my assistance nobly. As calmly as you please, Sam walked a great, big water tumbler down the bar and spun a bottle of Old Crow along beside it.

I gave the glass and the bottle a look and it made me feel a little faint, because I saw what Sam had in mind. I saw that he was right, and that I would have to go through with the thing, and yet I was badly frightened, I can tell you. Whiskey never did agree with me. I like my glass of beer as well as any man, but the dry days didn't hurt my feelings when they ruled out all the red-eye. And of all the whiskey I ever tried, Old Crow was the strongest. It carried a kick like an Army mule. It was one hundred percent what it claimed to be, and it claimed to be dynamite. That was why I was so badly frightened when I looked at that big black bottle. And I could see that everybody in the barroom was interested, too. They stared at me and they stared at the size of that glass and they stared at the bigness and the blackness of that bottle.

Well, I decided that I would carry the bluff through, fighting with both hands, so to speak. I grabbed that bottle by the neck and I scowled around the barroom. "Saps and kids and flatheads," I snarled at them. "No sense, no nerve, no nothing!"

I suppose that most of them would have fought at once, when addressed individually in such terms. But I was talking to the crowd and each man could shift some of the responsibility by looking a little sheepishly at his neighbor.

I turned the bottle right upside down over the glass and it let the liquor come rushing out. It filled the glass almost to the top, and when I upended the bottle again, some of the stuff splashed upon the bar.

"Here's poison and an early death to all tenderfeet who trot into Amityville looking for an easy thing. It ain't an easy town. It's hard. And I'm here to make an imitation of a bed of thorns. Gents, if any of you want trouble, come looking for me. If you find anybody anywhere that wants trouble, send him to me. I was raised fighting and I'll die fighting. And here's to the devil with the whole lot of you."

I tipped that infernally big glass of liquor to my lips. God be with the immortal Sam. It was tea! It was nothing but weak, weak tea put in that villainous-looking bottle. It was the very bottle out of which Sam poured his own drinks when the treats were too much for his head to stand the punishment. How I blessed that taste. How I blessed it. And, in front of that wide-eyed, gaping crowd, which watched every movement I made with a hungry interest, I swallowed that glassful of tea in big mouthfuls. I paused only once to smack my lips a little, and then I tossed off the rest of the bumper. It was the sort of a drink that would tear the lining out of the stomach of an ostrich—if it had only been what it pretended to be. Then I slammed down the glass and yelled at Sam—who was mopping up that spilled tea: "You black-faced son of night! You thieving scoundrel, you've *watered* the booze!" Then I turned on my heel, but slowly, so that every man there could see that the water had not started to my eyes at that tremendous potation and my face was not wrinkled with the effort of heavy drinking. And I walked slowly out of the room.

They waited, quite spellbound, as I got to the door. Then I saw the hand of a big man shoot out and grasp the arm of Sam as he put the bottle away under the bar again. "Wait a minute!" yelled the big man. "I want to have a look at that. It's faked stuff . . . and that's all. There ain't nobody in the world that can punish Old Crow in that style. Nobody in the world. I've seen the leather throats and the hard boys all over, and I've seen Scotchmen shifting their booze, but I never seen such a slick guy as this here Sherburn. I tell you, the stuff in that bottle is tea!"

I paused in the doorway, just barely beyond their sight. I

paused there not because I wanted to stay, but because all the starch had gone out of my legs and I was too weak to walk another step. When they found out that it was a faked-up drink, Amityville would be no place for me. It would be my clue to start on the run and to keep running, and to start running again all during my life whenever an Amityville man came in sight of me. I stood there, dazed, pretty sick at heart, feeling that I had ruined myself forever. And, at the bar, I could hear the voice of the big man as he made the most of his situation and tried to form himself into a hero.

He was saying: "Here's the same glass that Sherburn used, or one mighty near the same size. I'm gonna show you just how easy it is to put down a glass of whiskey like that and never bat an eye. I used to be able to handle beer pretty smooth. And . . . well, here goes, looking you all in the eye . . . and I guess that this glass is a bit fuller than the one that Sherburn drank."

"Go to it, boy!" half a dozen yelled at him.

And I knew by the stirring of feet that that crowd was getting on its tiptoes preparatory to making a lunge and a run at me, if the big man downed the glassful.

There was just a breath of silence. Then I heard a terrible gagging, a choking, a gasping. And, last of all, a faint stifled voice that groaned: "My Lord, boys, it was real."

I was saved! That grand black man—that Sam—had switched the bottles under their very noses and substituted a bottle of real Old Crow—old dynamite!—for the bottle of weak tea from which I had drunk.

Of course, I could tell well enough what had happened. Sam had saved my life, and I swore that I would do two things. First of all, the next time I was alone with Sam, I would apologize for the way I had spoken to him the first day I hit Amityville. Second, I would cherish that Negro the rest of his born days.

But he had set up a precedent that had to be followed. The

sight of a man putting away a whole tumbler full of whiskey was something that tickled the very spinal marrow of Amityville. They had seen gunfights and knife fights until they were sated with the spectacles. But there was one kind of battle that the old West did not tire of seeing and talking about. It was the booze fight, and the fellow who could shift his liquor the best was considered, in many ways, the top man of a crowd. In a way, it was a quality superior to physical courage.

Before the day was half an hour older, everyone was talking about me. Not about the brutal way in which I had swaggered into the barroom, but about the manner in which I had put away that Old Crow by the glassful.

I was pleased. And when I had a chance, in the middle of the afternoon, I sent for Sam and talked to him in my office—Gresham's office, that is to say.

He was grinning from ear to ear.

"Sam," I said, "you're a great man. You've got brains and you've got enough nerve, too. Do you know what would have happened to you if they had found out that you were switching the bottles on them?"

"Do I know?" Sam said, showing the whites of his eyes. "Why, sir, they would've peeled the skin offen Sam, inch by inch, and they would've pegged him down on his back and let him cook in the sun, nice and slow."

It was an idea that made me shudder, but, just the same, I felt that he hadn't overstated the probabilities very far. He went on to another idea that did not make me so cheerful.

"We got to encore that little act, Mister Sherburn."

"I'll be darned if I do," I said.

"It's makin' a great man out of you," said Sam. "It's makin' out of you a greater man than even Mister Gresham was."

I liked the way the scoundrel put his real master into the background to flatter his newest boss.

"Mister Gresham could shoot straight and hit hard and rule 'em by his talkin', sir, but he never could handle whiskey like that, sir." And Sam grinned wonderfully. "The boys are all talkin'. I've heard gents say that they'd give 'most fifty dollars to see you put away another jolt like that."

"Well, they never will," I said.

"Mister Sherburn, I just been tellin' them that it's sort of your habit to come in four times a day and take a swig like that."

"My Lord, Sam! Four times a day?"

"I been tellin' them that that's the way you get rid of one of the three quarts that you drink every day."

"Sam! Three quarts a day! They'll never believe that."

"Sir, seein' is believin', with them. They've seen you drink one tumbler. I'm gonna give you a bigger glass . . . three to the quart . . . when you come in for refreshments this afternoon."

I was quite staggered and feeling pretty sick.

But Sam followed up his idea with a rather convincing argument. "You just keep in the center of the stage, Mister Sherburn, and you ain't gonna have much trouble with these gents. Because why? Well, because they're just like so many kids. They got to have somebody that they can look up to or else they'll pretty soon fix him so's they and everybody else can be lookin' right down on him."

"You mean they get him ready for planting?"

"By a way of speakin', that's what I mean, sir."

I could see that there was a good deal of hard-headedness in Sam, and, though I hated to go through with that sham bottle four times a day, I appreciated the fact that I had to keep myself before the eyes of these ruffians.

"I got your bottle all set aside," said Sam. "I got a bottle of real Old Crow laid aside and I show it to the boys and let them see what you got to have three quarts of every day . . . to keep you feelin' fit."

"How do I drink it?" I asked him gloomily.

"A quart before breakfast, while you're lyin' in bed wakin' up, and then another quart at the bar, scatterin' through the day. And another quart after you go to bed at night. And that's the way that you always drink . . . to keep your stomach in shape."

"Thank heaven," I said, "that you have two of the quarts drunk off-stage."

"Yes, sir, I knew that'd please you. I thought some of havin' you drink two quarts in the saloon, but then I figgered that so much tea might spoil your digestion some."

You couldn't beat that Negro. In his own way, he was a genius. So, four times a day, I had to walk in and stand at that bar and cuss the weak-kneedness of the modern world, and wish that there were a few more real whiskey drinkers living, and then toss off a wretched glass of tea while the rest of the town stood by and wondered and gaped at me.

Chapter Twelve

You may wonder why I have given so much space to that tea drinking in the saloon at Amityville, but the reason that I've done so is because it is the true explanation of why I stayed above ground so long in that hot town. It gave me a reputation so hard-boiled that, inside of a week, I was famous, and my fame was traveling as far and as fast as cowpunchers could take it over the range when they returned to their ranches, and as prospectors could go when they started voyaging for no place in particular through the mountains.

It made a particular ten-strike with the Indians. It was before the days when the government herded the Indians onto reservations. Whether that was wise or not, I don't know. Anyway, I do know that they used to come into Amityville and that they made the worst part of our bargain there, a part of the time. They would walk around or sit around—they were always great sitters—wrapped up in their blankets and looking like Roman senators with painted faces. They were always very grave except when one of two things happened—either they got away where they thought no stranger was looking, and then I have seen a party of old braves whispering like schoolgirls—or else they lit into the red-eye, and then nobody knew when and where the lightning would strike.

Well, those red-skinned rascals—they were never anything else, so far as I could see—used to love nothing so well as to stand around and watch me at my potations. I suppose you all know that no Indian was ever born who could stand the effects of alcohol. The chief feature of the poison that the traders sold to the Indians and called whiskey was its weakness. Alcohol was too expensive to waste in the right proportions on redskins. I think a white man could drink quantities of the stuff without being hurt—except that the coloring matter would have ruined his stomach. However, the Indians would go happy on one drink—wild on two—and murdering mad on three! And when they saw a man stand up to the bar and put away a third of a bottle at a single swig—well, their admiration could not have been kept inside a ten-foot wall.

I've known celebrated braves to make a two-hundred-mile journey and then stand all day in the saloon, from early morning—stand all day in one corner, without moving—a feat that would have killed a white man with fatigue—for the sake of making sure with his own eyes that I had come in person to the bar on four separate occasions and drunk an enormous potation of whiskey. On each occasion he had advanced and demanded a taste from the same bottle, and always, beneath the shelter of the bar, my wily Sam had switched the bottles.

I began to be quite big medicine among those childish murderers. And they got me a brand-new name that was so odd that it began to catch, and finally ran through the town and over the range like magic. It's that way with a queer name. It spreads like bad news. You might say that I went to sleep one night by the name of Sherburn and woke up the next morning to find myself famous by the name of Fire Brain. That name in itself would have been worth a good deal to a saloonkeeper. It was the sort of a name that needed a little explaining. And the explanation in this case was always interesting.

Of course, the great feature about my drinking was not the immense size of my potations alone. It was the fact that my head was never in the slightest degree turned by what I had taken. To establish a proper breath, I took a bit of sherry wine three times a day and then chewed a clove to make it appear that I was trying to kill my breath.

Oh, well, it was all a frightful sham, of course, but the thing that kept it from being simply disgusting was that there was so much danger attached. I never knew when some curious fellow—who might have traveled two or three hundred miles chiefly for the sake of watching my drinking feats—would reach across and get the wrong bottle from the quick hand of Sam. And then, of course, there would be the devil to pay. My tea-built reputation would tumble about my ears, and the whole world would learn that I was a faker. I had to pretend to grow angry when people asked to see the bottle and taste it. In this way I sustained myself.

You will wonder how I got on with the rest of the premises? I used to ramble casually through all the rooms of the saloon and gaming sections, and every day I sat out on the verandah of the hotel and took the air. I used to sit in the same chair, in the same place, and at the same hour until, one day, a young chap at the appointed time slipped into my chair by mistake and got a bullet through the chest. Of course, that bullet had been meant for me, and, although the youngster did not die, I stopped being so regular in my appearances. I had no set times for anything. But, just as the humor moved me, I walked into a room and out of it again.

Oh, I could not have lasted a single week if it had not been for Doc. He knew when to do everything, and he generally tipped me off. He could whisper so that I could hear him and nobody else could. That old rascal had a wonderful memory for names, and so he used to walk behind me and keep repeating them all the day to me, and then I would call each man by the right name.

It's funny how much difference a name makes. The poet says

that a rose by any other name would smell as sweet. But men are not roses, and if you call Smith by the name of Jones, you'll probably have a fight on your hands. Everybody was very much pleased by the fact that I knew their names, particularly because I wore such a mask as a bad man and a gunfighter and a booze-hound. I went around scowling, but, every now and then, I would relax and smile and call somebody by his name. I did that when old Doc gave me the tip, because he knew just which were the most important men, which were the dangerous fighters, and which I ought to have on my side.

Well, sir, in a short time I could feel that I was beginning to be popular. Really popular. And my popularity was built up on the memory of a useless old hanger-on, and the sleight of hand and low cunning of a Negro bartender. For that matter, I know of a political boss who built up a great power because, although he was blind, he had a great ability to remember names and voices. He would rarely go wrong on a voice, even if he heard it ten years after a single meeting. And people were so tickled to be remembered by a blind man that they couldn't do enough for him. Partly they admired him and partly they admired themselves. He made everybody feel important, and that's the secret of political success, I suppose. He could have run for any office in his state and been elected. But there was more money in it for him if he put other people into good jobs, and then pulled the right strings.

But in telling you how I rambled around through the establishment of Gresham, and how I built up his business, and how the dollars flooded in even more than when Gresham himself was there—while I have been doing all this, it looks as though I have forgotten the main history of what happened in Amityville—the story that begins with what the old prospector said to me when I first turned the shoulder of the mountain and looked down into the great valley with the flush of the rare spring flowers in pastel shades everywhere.

But I haven't forgotten. All of this may seem to move blindly, but it has to be recorded before you can see how the strands of Gresham and Doc and Sam and Tom Kenyon and Red Hawk and Jenny Langhorne and Fire Brain all weave in together and make the strange happenings that came after a while. But, as you will see, a great deal of it could never have happened if it had not been that my first days in Amityville had equipped me with such a reputation—a peculiar one, but just the kind to impress the imagination of a Western crowd.

Going back a ways, you come to the prisoner who Tom Kenyon had brought into Amityville. The name of this man was Dan Juniper. Dan had been tried and found guilty, and he was now waiting for a means of safe transport before being shipped to the prison where he would be duly put in the death cell, and then duly hanged by the neck until he was dead.

Well, my story suddenly hooks up with the person of this same Dan Juniper. For one morning the jail guard sent a yell over half the town and brought a crowd to which he pointed out that a great section of the jail wall had been broken down—from the outside. And in another five minutes there would have been a hole large enough to admit of the escape of Dan.

It was decided to redouble the guard over Dan Juniper until the hour of his transport to the prison arrived. And, to make that guard doubly safe, they looked around them for a good, dependable, and sound fighting man. Gresham was away, and so their choice fell upon Gresham's own substitute—namely upon me.

A committee of three waited upon me and begged me to undertake, personally, the guarding of this desperate man. For much was hoped for from him. It was felt that he had much to confess that might involve other members of the gang of Red Hawk, but that he would not confess until the very moment of execution, so certain was he that Red Hawk would contrive his deliverance from the death penalty. I was to guard him and keep him safe for the law. Of course, I could only aver my perfect willingness to undertake the task.

Chapter Thirteen

I saw Juniper for the first time in the jail. He was a long, lean, sallow-faced boy of nineteen or twenty. He had a drape of shiny black hair that, when his head was lowered as during my first glimpse of him, showered forward in front of his face. He had bright, black eyes, with yellowed pupils. And his face was handsome, but narrow across the temples, narrow across the jaw. There was a weak mouth, always somewhere between a smile and a sneer. Altogether he had a weak, handsome, evil, useless face.

He wore a blue silk shirt set off with a small crimson stripe. That is all I remember about his costume—a blue silk shirt that was frayed at the wrist bands and at the elbows. The collar was very soiled. He had on, too, a red tie, wrinkled to a string by many knottings and re-knottings in different places.

He looked like a boy, but like a boy who knew too much. An unclean body and an unclean mind. There was a thick cloud of cigarette smoke in the room, and the smell of it was choking—stale smoke as well as fresh, if you know what I mean by that. A smoky atmosphere that has been breathed and re-breathed. There was a window, but Dan did not care to have it opened too wide.

"I ain't got too strong a throat," said Dan. "Ma always used to say that my lungs and my throat was my weak place. Drafts and colds, they're mighty hard on me, you see."

Can you picture Dan Juniper, now? Weak, vicious, much

mothered, spoiled, vain of his good looks, a hero with the ladies. In addition, there was the possibility of mischief in him. He had long-fingered, active hands—made well for speed and strength. He looked as if he could have learned to handle well a sketching pencil—or a gun.

But I wondered, most of all, how the terrible Indian chief, the plague of Amityville, the bane of the life of the hero, Gresham, could have made so gross a mistake as to accept this scamp into his employ. Instantly my belief in the intelligence of the redskin sank fifty percent.

When I came in, Juniper drew deeply on his cigarette and then let the cloud issue slowly from his loose lips. He did not look up. "If you've come to ask questions," he said, "I ain't gonna answer any of them. Not me. I ain't feeling like talk today."

I looked at him in silence for another moment until his lazy, impertinent gaze was lifted curiously toward me. Then I saw clearly the face that I have described to you. I did not speak to him, then, at any length. I merely said: "I don't want to ask you any questions, now. I just want you to know that I'm your new guard."

He yawned in my face. "Interesting," he said, "but it ain't important."

"My beauty," I said to Juniper. "When I do come to ask you questions, you can make up your mind that I'll have all the answers that I want."

At this his eyes widened a little. "What'll you do to me?" he asked.

I only smiled at him. Then I withdrew and spoke to Tom Kenyon in person, who was on duty that day. I drew Kenyon apart and turned loose on him.

"You and me have had some rough times together," I said to him. "But there's no reason why the pair of us can't get along smooth in this here Juniper job."

He didn't like me, and he showed it. It stuck out all over his face. He was as stiff as a poker as he answered: "I don't see what good the pair of us can do . . . except to keep him safe until hanging day comes for him."

"Look here," I said, "you're scared that before long somebody is going to sink a knife between your shoulder blades clean up to the hilt, aren't you . . . because you got one of the chief's men?"

He shuddered, and unbent a little.

"Well," I went on, "if we can get a confession out of this young rat, and out of the confession we find the trail of Red Hawk, won't it take the danger of death off of you?"

I saw half a dozen years drop away from his face at the mere naming of such a chance.

"Heaven knows," he said. "If you can do that, I'm with you to the finish. If you can make him talk . . . but you can't do it."

"What's been tried on him?" I asked.

"Everybody in town has had a whirl at it. They've stuck guns under his nose and threatened him in every way that they could, without actually breaking the law outright and manhandling him."

"Well," I said, "between you and me, I think that I know just how to handle that young feller. But, first, I'd like to know how you got him?"

He told me a mighty interesting story. He was riding down one of the ravines one night when the moon was half out and shining as hard as half a moon can. Where the cañon narrowed down, he heard the trampling of horses ahead of him and, just for luck, thinking of Red Hawk, he drew his horse back into a clump of boulders that sprouted out of the floor of the ravine. He hadn't more than stowed himself there when the cavalcade came wheeling right in view around the angle of the ravine wall.

And in front of the procession, as clear as a picture and painted to the life of all the stories that were told, he saw the great chief, Red Hawk.

He was a man of gigantic size, just as tradition painted him. He rode upon a huge horse—a thoroughbred, if Tom Kenyon had ever seen one, he said, and he was a man who had known fine horses all of his life. Red Hawk was naked, except for light moccasins upon his feet and a loincloth. He was a dark-copper color, glistening as if rubbed afresh with oil. And that, too, was said to be a peculiarity of Red Hawk. He liked to take the war path anointed in this fashion.

His face, according to Tom Kenyon, who said that he had a perfect view of it in the broad moon shine, was not as ugly as tradition painted it, however; there was only a broad, black patch across one eye, secured at the back of his head by a pair of leather thongs, and knotted there. He wore his hair long. And it was as coarse as horsehair and as plentiful as the hair of a woman. It was braided behind his shoulders and stuck full of feathers, after Red Hawk's fashion.

After this destroyer went past him, Kenyon said that he looked over the followers with equal care, but they were all masked to the eyes, and therefore he could make nothing of their faces. But they seemed to be men of all kinds—Mexicans, whites, and Indians, according to their clothes.

They had only one attribute in common—they were wonderfully well mounted. Their horses, each of them, seemed to rival the mount of the chief in sheerest beauty, and they danced and pranced against the rein. Perhaps a dozen of the rascals swept by, behind the chief. And Tom Kenyon swore that not a word had been spoken, not a sound had been made.

They passed around another corner of the ravine wall, and Kenyon waited for the sound of them to die away, because, as he freely and very manfully admitted, he was almost frightened to death. He finally heard the noise of the horses' hoofs sink to a murmur and he was about to leave his hidden nest when a belated member of the gang shot past. He was masked like the others, and he was just as well mounted. Whatever had made him fall behind, he rode briskly, sweeping his horse along at a fine gallop. And yet he rode with an easy confidence, like one who knows that his goal is not far away.

Kenyon was ready for action instantly. He was frightened when there were a dozen in front of him, naturally. But when he saw only one, he was ready for anything, in spite of the rumor that said that one of the followers of Red Hawk was more dangerous than a dozen ordinary men.

He could not risk a revolver shot, because the cavalcade that rode with the famous chief was not far ahead. He had a second weapon that might prove even better, in this pinch. That weapon was his lariat, and, as the cavalier shot by on his fine horse, the rope of Tom Kenyon slid through the air, took him about the throat, and snaked him neatly out of the saddle.

Luckily the horse was so gentle that it did not run on ahead and give the alarm in this fashion to Red Hawk. It stood in the near distance and began to sniff at some dead moss on the face of a rock, while Tom Kenyon got to his victim and loosed his neck from the grip of the rope just before he stifled. Then he tied his man, made him mount his own horse, gagged and silenced him, and made the lead rope of the beautiful horse fast to the pommel of his own saddle.

When that was done, he started softly down the gulch, trembling for fear, lest some sound he made might come to the ears of Red Hawk, which were said to be more acute than the ears of a listening rabbit. Then he remembered that the chief might miss his belated follower and turn back. This made Kenyon start on at a strong gallop. There were eight miles to go to Amityville, and he rode at such a speed that, as he came over the last grade in sight of the town, his own horse staggered and then fell dead beneath him. At the same time, he saw a dozen sweeping shadows fly across the hollow behind him and up the slope in pursuit—the men of Red Hawk—and Red Hawk himself riding in the lead.

Tom Kenyon, like a man in a nightmare, could hardly move he was so benumbed with ghostly terror. Then he scrambled on the back of the gallant horse that already carried the prisoner. He had a good mind to cut the prisoner free and throw him from the saddle, and he certainly would have done so, had it not been that there was no time for delay, no matter how small.

He had to shoot the big horse down the slope toward Amityville. And nothing but the stoutest pair of legs could have stood the pounding to which Kenyon subjected the gelding. They went crashing down to the bottom of the slope, with Kenyon shrieking at the top of his voice for help.

But what difference did it make to Amityville? That town was used to drunken voices pitched at any point on the human scale. Amityville merely smiled and took another drink as Tom Kenyon fled toward it, yelling for protcction.

He reached the streets of the town just as bullets began to whistle behind him. Bullets that sang perilously near his head. But nevertheless he felt secure at that point. For certainly he could not dream that even a daredevil like Red Hawk would dare to pursue a quarry into the streets of a crowded town.

The more fool he for dreaming that there was any limit to the insolence of that chieftain. For here came Red Hawk like a sweeping wind, with all his men behind him, and gaining like a storm on poor Tom Kenyon. The latter saw only one hope for himself, and, yelling the name of Red Hawk, he started for the first building. Luckily it was one with a tall door. With a revolver shot, he shattered the lock of that front door. Horse, prisoner, captor and all, he rode through to the interior. Two men, in answer to his maddened entreaties, leaped out to guard the door, and they were just in time to sink before a volley from the guns of Red Hawk's men as that wild warrior fled down the street with his gang behind him, and rattled away into the night.

And not a single gun was fired by Amityville at the invader, and not a rider issued forth in pursuit. No wonder that the chieftain had come to despise the white men. He had robbed and persecuted them with impunity for so long.

I heard this story with a real marvel. I had considered Red Hawk with a good deal of respect before. But now I began to have a touch of the same horror with which the rest of the community regarded him. And I was more eager than ever to try my new scheme with young Danny Juniper, for I really felt that I had in my hand the possible solution of the entire trouble.

I asked Kenyon if it could be arranged for me to have the key to the room of the boy and be allowed to confer with him in absolute privacy. He asked me what I had in mind, and I would only admit that I hoped to draw a complete confession from the young rascal. That was all that I would say, and Kenyon, much mystified, went to confer with the other guards.

Finally it was decided that I could do as I chose to do. The room would be turned over to me, and I could be alone with my man.

I advanced to what some of you may consider a very brutal experience. Well, I have to admit that I went to it with a relish. And I think that any one of you would feel the same relish if you could have seen the narrow, yellow face of young Juniper and the smile on it as he sneered at me when I entered the room.

Chapter Fourteen

People may say what they want about the value of laughter and the strength of ridicule and the power of scorn, but it is my belief that there is nothing in the human world that has so much edge as a little curling of the upper lip. And, when I saw this young scoundrel sneer at me, I saw red.

Perhaps you are a little amused when I speak of a scoundrel, after admitting that a good many things in my own rough life have been the acts of a scoundrel in the extreme. But you must remember that there is a possibility of actions that are wrong but not maliciously wrong. And I don't think that there was ordinarily much malice in me. Whereas that young toad, Danny Juniper, simply exuded it like a poison.

I took off my gun belt and dropped it in the corner of the room. It was a big room, and there was a big window at each side of it. And, through the window, we could look out at a line of half a dozen horses tethered at a hitching rack. Between our Danny Juniper and the back of one of those horses there was nothing save the closed window and the irons that fettered his legs. That is, there was nothing else except me, and I suppose it was the first time during the day that he had been left with but a single guard in the room. His quick, ratty eyes took in these facts.

But I didn't speak to him. I simply crossed the room and with the keys that had been given me, I unlocked the fetters. Then I went to the window toward the horse rack and raised it.

The fresh air came seething in and made the cigarette smoke, with which the chamber was filled, boil. It was a good thing to take a deep breath of that fresher air. But I could only snatch the breath because one would not ordinarily keep one's back turned to such a fellow as Danny Juniper when his hands and feet were free.

I looked back at him quickly and found him just in the act of standing up and trying his new freedom with a single half step. He threw back the long, dangling hair from his face with a jerk of his head, and he whispered: "Red Hawk?" As though he suggested that I must be in the league of those ill-doers.

I said: "Juniper, you're a fighting man. I'm going to give you a grand chance which any fighting man ought to be glad to have. I'm going to let you get to that window and through it, if you can only knock me out of your way. There's a string of horses yonder. That gray, the second from this end of the line, looks like a goer and a stayer. Once through this window, nothing could keep you from getting to that horse, because none of the guards are on that side of the jail. And, once in the saddle, you're a good deal of a fool if you can't get out of the town. Does it look like a worthwhile chance to you?"

Well, he threw up his head and for a moment those bright eyes of his became almost beautiful, and his narrow face became beautiful, too. For he saw freedom; he tasted it far off—and it was more than wine to him. He dragged down a great breath, and then he turned on me with the fire still in his eyes.

"Now, what's your deal?" he said. "How much do you want out of this? Because all you got to do is to name your price and you'll have it. The chief pays anything for a job like you're trying to do for me."

I looked him over quietly. Standing there, I saw that he was a good deal more of a man than I had suspected. He weighed a good twenty pounds more than I had thought. He was slender, but he was thick and round. He was taller, and there was more muscle in his shoulders. He had weight on his side and he had speed, perhaps—there could be no doubt of the speed of a man who stood as he stood, with his weight on his toes. Besides that, I thought I saw the danger coming up into his face.

"I'll tell you," I said. "You're going to have your chance to go through that window and get to that horse . . . that fine gray, yonder. But, first, you have to make a bargain with me."

"What's that?"

"In the first place, you've got to admit that Red Hawk has taken a long time about getting you free."

His face fell a little. "I know it," he said.

"So far as you know, that old gag of digging through the jail wall may be his last try to turn you loose. Well, kid, if you are beaten by me and can't get through that window, then you've got to give me your promise to turn state's evidence on the rest of the gang, including Red Hawk."

He grinned in a lop-sided fashion at me. He was anxious to make the try, but he was afraid. "It's no go," he said.

"You fool," I said. "We almost have Red Hawk already. A little more information, and then I'll be able to grab the red thief."

"Do you mean that?" muttered the youngster.

I lied: "Yes."

"Then . . . I'll give you my promise. And you'll keep away from that gun on the floor?"

"Yes."

"I promise," he said. "But get that gun away from you."

I kicked it to the other side of the room, and then he started for the window—and me.

The moment I saw him move, I began to feel that I might have been a fool in letting him have this chance, because he glided across that floor like a panther. Fast as a streak, and smooth as silk. And, as he came, he twisted a hand at his neck and that hand came away with a strip of bright light in his fingers—a needle-flash of steel no bigger than a hat pin—and just as dangerous if it were planted in the right spot.

That was his notion of fair play, of course. Well, there was only one way in which I could meet that move. I could try a flying football tackle and take a chance that I should move so fast that he couldn't plant that deadly little weapon in my body when I went in at him. Oh, yes, I had played football. Not the college game, but the sand-lot, harum-scarum variety. Everybody for himself and the devil take the other team.

That sort of football was a fine training for waterfront rough-and-tumble fighting. And I had been thoroughly trained. I made one half step at that scooting young demon, and then I threw myself into the air and twitched my body sideways. I struck him just knee-high. He made a pass at me with that hat-pin dirk in his hand, but he missed everything but a button on my trousers. It cracked the button, but the point didn't go through.

The next instant he was down with a crash. As he came up, I had him by the wrist and gave it a turn that ground the flesh against the bone. The dirk dropped from his fingers. But he dashed his other fist into my face—a clean punch that rocked me back on my heels. He gave me his other hand in the stomach, doubling me up like a jackknife. And if he had stayed there to finish the job that he began so well, he might have been done with me and off again. However, he saw me stalled for the moment and the open window was before him. The temptation was too great, and, before I could stop him, he dived for it.

I managed to reach him in time to grab one leg and drag him back by that. He whirled on me like a wildcat and came storming in with a flying storm of punches. Well, I was barely able to stave him off until I could get him to half-arm distance. By that time my head was ringing like a bell. He had clipped me twenty times from either side, but, when I got a bit of distance, I began to rip into him.

He melted like a snowman under a warm rain. Half a dozen tearing punches to the body wilted him. Then I looked up and tapped him in the right place. One little punch to the side of the jaw about an inch back of the point—and that puts your strong man to sleep and lets him rest a long time.

Juniper dropped into my arms and I lowered him to the floor just as a dozen strong hands began to beat at the door. They wanted to come in and they wanted to come in quick. They had heard enough noise to make up a cavalry parade on a boardwalk.

I was panting, of course, but I sang out to them that there was no trouble, that I had only been having a little game with my man. And, after a time, Tom Kenyon pacified the others, and they went back a little.

About that time young Juniper opened his eyes and sat up, holding his head. He gave one look at the open window, and that was enough.

"But I'll see you damned before I'll open my trap to you, you skunk," said Juniper.

I had the dirk and was examining it carefully. The hilt was a little metal cross just big enough to steady between thumb and forefinger. The blade was narrow enough to find a man's death through any crevice. It was made for taking a peek at the heart of a sleeping man and killing him before he could open his eyes a crack. I decided that I would keep that little dirk as a souvenir.

"Son," I said, "I only wanted to have a good excuse to make you talk, and, if you go back on your word to me, I'll show you a little trick that I used to know when I was a boy."

"Try your trick," he said. "But if you start torturing me, I'll yell for help, and. . . ."

I slipped out of my coat, and, before he finished talking, I had that coat in a bag over his head. A minute later he lay flat on his face and with two sharp knuckles I was prying between a couple of his vertebrae. Suddenly I got to what I wanted—that net of nerves around the spinal marrow. I felt his body go limp. I felt the quivering scream that was choked by the coat. Then I took the coat away and jerked him into a sitting position. He was as limp as a sack half filled with grain.

"Will you talk, kid?" I said.

"Oh, my Lord!" gasped Juniper. "I thought I was dead."

"A minute more and you would have been," I declared. "And I'd think nothing of killing you with my bare hands, you rat."

I talked a little more roughly than I felt, but one needed everything to make him toe the mark.

"I'll talk. I'll tell you everything," said Juniper.

"Good," I said.

"But . . . gimme a chance to pull myself together, will you?"

There was some reason in that. I had given him a pretty severe dose of that home-made article of torture, and the boy was badly shaken. So I told him that I was busy, but that I'd see him that evening and hear his story, with witnesses.

He said: "Only one thing . . . for heaven's sake don't let nobody know that I'm gonna spill the beans. Because you can't get much mouse catching out of a dead cat, can you?"

I nodded. But I hardly heard what he said. I wish to heaven that I had.

Chapter Fifteen

I left the jail in pretty high spirits. If anyone of the band of Red Hawk gave all the news they could about the chief and his men and their methods, the end of the reign of terror was pretty close at hand. Altogether, I was in pretty high spirits, and, when I went down the street, I told myself that I would be famous in the town before the next morning dawned, and the thought of being popular in any place makes it look a lot better. So, as I passed along the street, it seemed to me that Amityville was about as fine a town as anyone could wish to be in, and I decided that there was no good reason why I should not live the rest of my life right there. I would have been glad to meet the prospector who had said that the place was too hot for him. I wanted to laugh at him and tell him that all the town needed was a few people who understood how to handle it.

Oh, if I could have looked around the corner at tomorrow.

Well, while I was ambling along toward the Gresham Hotel, and the rest of that establishment where I was boss, who should come sashaying around a corner but a girl with flaming red hair and her hat swinging in her hand. It was *the* girl, of course. It was Gresham's own Jenny Langhorne. When she saw me coming, she went straight up to me.

I saw, then, that Doc had made no exaggeration. She wasn't beautiful. I suppose that her mouth was too big and her nose wasn't what they call classic—whatever that means. But she was made right. The finest horse in the world isn't always the most beautiful. But if he has the strength and the reach and something in his heart that shines through him, you will know his greatness even when he goes dancing to the post before he has run a stroke. It was that way with Jenny. You can't define and put your finger on these things. But there was something about the way her head was put on her neck and her neck on her shoulders. There was something about the way she walked. And there was what a thoroughbred horse has—a light shining from the inside. You knew that she would go till she dropped dead. You knew that she would never say die. You knew that she had a soul that would have filled the breast of the biggest man that ever stepped.

Well, she comes sashaying up to me.

"You're Sherburn?" she said.

"That's my name," I replied.

"I'm Jenny Langhorne," she said.

We shook hands.

"I've been wanting to see you," said Jenny, "because the boys have been making such a fuss about you. And I suppose that you've heard about me."

She started to laugh. It wasn't a free, breezy laughter such as you'd expect, but low and soft and easy. It surprised you a lot. It made you see that she was a rare one all the way through. She chattered along about nothing in particular for a minute. I was sort of giddy and hearing only every other word.

Until she said: "Are you trying to get famous quick, and then to die young?"

"A while ago," I said, "maybe something like that was in my head. But I'm changing my mind. I see that I have to last quite a while."

"To keep Amityville quiet?" she asked me, and grinned.

She had the laugh of a lady and the grin of a mischievous kid. I never saw the beat of her.

"No," I said, "I want to last a long time to keep Amityville amused."

"You'll need a brass lining for that stomach," she said, "if you keep it up."

"Oh," I said, "I've only been doing a little casual drinking since I hit this town. I've been keeping sober. But someday I'll stage a real party."

She grinned again. "You bluff it out pretty well," she said. "But if the boys tumble, they'll take you apart and see where that nerve is stowed in you."

How could *she* have found out about my fake drinking? "You've been talking with Sam," I said.

"I've been talking with Big Boy," she said. That was her nickname for Gresham, of course.

"He's back!" I cried.

"Sure," she said.

"With any luck?" I asked, because I could hardly imagine Gresham going on any trail without some results.

"He caught what they all catch," she said. "He caught a big breath of dust, and that's all. They'll never land Red Hawk until they stop riding so hard after him."

"D'you expect them to *walk* after that Indian?" I asked her.

"Sure," said Jenny. "They wouldn't have far to go, if they only knew."

She called—"So long!"—to me, and went off down the street with that light, swinging step of hers—like the step of a boy athlete, but somehow different.

And I went on up the street, wondering what the deuce she could have meant by that last remark, and wondering, most of all, how such a girl had ever been made, and how so much breath and fire could be put into one person. I was still a little giddy when I headed into the hotel. And there I found Tom Kenyon among the first. He had gone back from the jail to the hotel. As I found out afterward, he had gone there when he had heard that Gresham was back. He had gone there to complain about the rough-house that I raised with the prisoner that I was supposed to be guarding. But, when he saw me, he pulled me to one side.

"You really think that you are going to do something with the kid?" he asked.

I forgot all about the way that Danny Juniper had begged me not to let people know that he was expected to talk that night. When a man looked at Kenyon, you see, and watched the working of his face and the nervousness in his eyes and twitching in his mouth, and when you saw the way that he lived like a man with poison already working in him—well, it was too much. I had to give him what comfort I could.

I said: "I've already given my word. And I tell you that tonight is the time when he's due to talk. We'll know all that we want to know about Red Hawk before the morning."

That was all I said. Because, that moment, I remembered that the boy had begged me not to let anyone else know about what he intended to do. And I remembered what he said, then, of the fact that a dead cat cannot catch mice. So I told Kenyon that everything might be spoiled if a word were to slip out, and I made him swear not to tell a soul about the fact that the boy was due to confess—by promise—that evening.

He said that he wouldn't open his lips about it. He swore it and he grabbed my hand and told me that I was the finest fellow in the world, and he thanked heaven for the day that had sent me to Amityville. Because, of course, the end of Red Hawk meant the end of his fear of Red Hawk.

Then I went to see Gresham. He was in his own office, talking with Doc, and old Doc was sitting up by the window with his arms wrapped around his knees. I could hear his hard, drawling old voice when I came to the door. He was telling Gresham how I had tamed the boys and made them eat out of my hand. I was glad to break in and stop that foolish talk.

Gresham seemed glad to see me. He looked browner and thinner than when he had left the town, and I could see the strain of hard work and big anxieties in his eyes. He shook hands with me most cordially and sat me down. Then he began to fire a long stream of questions at me.

I simply said: "Doc has been filling you full of bunk about me. The fact is, that I've been bluffing the boys until I have them backed into corners. I don't know how long the bluff will keep going. In the meantime, it's fun and I like the game. Now tell me about your own trip."

He brushed that thought of himself away, as though what he did wasn't of any interest to the world,

"I want to hear about you," he said. "I want to hear a lot about it. To tell you the truth, Sherburn, I thought you'd never be able to stand the gaff very long. Other men have tried to become my partners. And they've died, old-timer, and I felt like a cur when I asked you to take the chance. But I had to have help. I couldn't keep the place going and hunt down Red Hawk."

"Don't apologize," I said. "You made me a fair proposition, and I took it. If there was danger, I might have known that I would have to take care of myself. Everybody knows that Amityville isn't a children's playground."

"Do you buck up under it pretty well?" he said.

I told him that I never had felt better.

"Well," he said, "if they *do* call you, they'll find something behind the bluff."

I grinned at him without much heart. "I practice for two hours every day," I told him. "I shoot away more pounds of ammunition than you could shake a stick at."

"Where?"

"Oh, back in the hills, where the sound won't carry into the town."

He fell into a muse. "I think that you're going to work the thing out permanently," he said. "What do *you* think, Doc?"

Doc nodded at once. "What Amityville has needed all along," he said, "was a *young* Louisiana man. And Sherburn, here, he just about fills the bill from top to bottom. I'd lay down my last dollar that within a month he has Red Hawk dead or behind the bars."

I tried to protest. Such flattery was too much.

But big Gresham merely smiled in a good-natured way. "Heaven knows that I hope so," he said. "And still, that's a job that I'd like to handle all by myself."

He told me, then, that he might only be in town for a day or so, because he had a clue that he was following hard. It was bad news for me, because I had hoped that he would be back for some time, to handle the place. He sent Doc out of the room and went on to tell me how delighted he was at my success.

I fired the first idea that was troubling him. "What does Jenny Langhorne mean," I asked, "by saying that Red Hawk won't be far to find . . . if we only have the sense to know where to look?"

At this he picked up his head and stared at me. "Has she been telling you that?" he said.

He seemed oddly moved, and I asked him why it was strange that she should talk to me.

"Nothing," he said, "except that I thought she would keep that idiotic idea to herself. Jenny has been spoiled. People have listened to her so much that she begins to take herself seriously."

"And what is the idea?" I asked.

"A mighty foolish one."

"But I'd like to know."

"Why . . . it will save you from hearing it from herself. The silly girl believes that the reason Red Hawk has escaped capture so long is simply because he is not an Indian at all, but a white man."

"What?"

"Who lives in Amityville and mixes around with the rest of us. Isn't that a crazy idea and a half?"

"And a horrible one, too," I said. "What put it into her head, anyway?"

"Sherburn," said my big friend, and he wagged his head and sighed, "if you can find out what puts ideas into her head, you're a better man than I am."

"Does she think that Red Hawk is a myth?" I asked him.

"She thinks that Red Hawk may have been killed years ago, and that the man who killed him happened to look like him and saw the chance of fixing himself up with that patch over the eye and stain, I suppose, on his body. And there you are. Nothing can get it out of her head."

"But what's her reason?"

"Because she says that no Indian in the world would stay five years in one place."

Well, when you come to think of it, there is a good deal in that idea, because, as everyone knows, Indians are a pretty restless lot. And the thought of one of those chiefs remaining quietly for a stretch of five years, picking his chances to slash in among the whites with his mischief was almost too much for me. And, after all, Red Hawk did not strike often. Perhaps not more than three times a year. But, when he did strike, he raised a dust, I can tell you. No petty prizes interested him. He wanted money and lots of it . . . money in heaps, or nothing at all. And that put a financial aspect on the thing that was totally unIndian, also. Because a redskin wants to raise the devil not just now and then, but all the time, and because your brave Indian doesn't want to go on the warpath for the mere sake of taking loot or even scalps, but for the sake of the warpath itself. He wants a certain regularly distributed amount of mischief just as your white man wants a certain regularly distributed amount of bread and meat.

But here was the copper-skinned Napoleon who had defied the efforts of the whites for so long, remaining like a cunning thief, hidden and silent for months at a time.

"By the heavens," I broke out at big Gresham, "I'm inclined to think that the girl has struck on the solution."

He smiled at me in a weary way. "Well," he said, "she convinces a new convert every now and then. They keep converted until they've looked around the town and tried to decide who Red Hawk might be."

The girl still seemed to have some reason on her side, but the faint amusement of Gresham made me stop talking about that point. I changed the subject as quickly as I could, and then asked him if he would be willing to come over to the jail that night and help the select few who were to help guard young Juniper.

He gave me his promise without so much as asking me what I had in mind.

As a matter of fact, what was stirring in my thoughts, every moment, was that last warning from the lips of Danny Juniper—that he would be a dead cat unless I kept quiet about the confession that he was to make, and I decided that I would stay at the jail every second of the remainder of the day and the night, until I had the mind of Danny reduced to black and white.

CHAPTER SIXTEEN

The first thing I did was to locate two or three more able fighters, with Rabbit Tucker at the head of them. I told them simply that I wanted an extra cordon thrown around the jail and that I was going to trust them to help me out. I told them that there was to be no drinking that night, and that I hoped for silence, too. Rabbit said that he was glad to be my man that day, and he suggested half a dozen other good men who I could have if I wanted them. But the new recruits, together with the fellows I had already sworn in for the work of the day, plus the gigantic force of the great Gresham himself, made enough men, I decided, to carry out my scheme.

Then I went to Tom Kenyon. I found him at his house, hastily finishing his lunch and getting ready to return in all speed to the jail itself. Because the man practically lived at the jail, overcome with dread lest the prisoner should escape—and also, I think, always glad to be in the company of armed men. The same people who kept young Danny Juniper from escape would serve to guard poor Tom from the long arm of Red Hawk.

I asked him at once if he had kept his promise and said nothing of what I had told him about the coming confession. He swore that he had not told a soul except his wife.

"A woman," I groaned. "Then it's as good as over the whole town. Darn it, Tom, you deserve anything that comes to you, now."

He was white with anxiety at once. He dragged me into the

dining room where his wife was clearing away the lunch dishes. And there he made her swear solemnly that she had not and would not whisper a word of the news he had given to her. Not if her life depended upon it. And, when Tom had finished speaking, and when she had already given her oath to me, I went on to tell her, solemnly, that, if she did break her word, it might very possibly cost her husband his life, very directly.

Then we left with the very sick and frightened face of Mrs. Kenyon behind us, and went together toward the jail.

On the way Tom paused suddenly and struck his hands together. "Sherburn," he said, "we shouldn't have been so violent about it. We shouldn't have made it so very important."

"Why not?" I asked him.

"Because," he said, "by making it so big, it'll be almost too much for her. It's like Bluebeard and the one room, you know. She'll almost have to tell the story to just one person."

"Nonsense," I insisted. "Your wife strikes me as a very sensible woman, and she won't be such a fool as to break her word after we made it so solemn a case."

"You're young, Sherburn," he said. "Take a married man's word for it. You're young when it comes to women."

It irritated me a little at the moment. A bachelor always feels that a married man is a good deal of a fool for pretending to know so much about the entire sex simply because one woman is his wife. But afterward I was to think back to Tom and what he had said. However, I don't know what else I could have done to make the evening safe for Kenyon, Juniper, and the town.

I want you to understand the position of the jail, in the first place. Amityville was laid out, like a good many Western towns, by haphazard. Perhaps wandering wolves and foxes, and fleeing rabbits, and other random beasts had first found a way across the hollow among the mountains, and that way was then good enough and worn enough to attract the cattle, and the cattle, passing back and forth toward water, had worn the trail into a course visible even to the dull eyes of men, and then, when men came, they rode their horses across the valley on that trail. And when wagons were used, wagons, took the same course and beat the brush flat and wore away the surface stones, and so made what had some semblance of a road.

Along that winding road the village had first been laid out, each little shack erected close to the face of the road, as though in a painful desire for some sort of company. And whenever I walked down that street, I used to wonder if the corner where the Grier house now stood had not marked the spot where the first wolf, trotting down the slope, caught a dangerous scent out of the wind and leaped sidewise out of his course. And so for each one of the bends and the sharp windings.

Every corner, I felt, had been made by suspicion and fear in some animal's mind, and, above all, at the jagged, sharp turn where the jail stood—what had the first wolf smelled there? Something, one would say, that remained in the minds of men, like a suspicion breathed out of the air, and made them select this very position for the site of their jail.

The building was built as a blunt-nosed triangle with the street curving around the nose—not following the outline of the wall closely, but leaving a considerable area of untenanted ground. Behind the jail and adjoining it on that side, there was an empty lot where one of Gresham's rival saloons had originally stood until bad times and Gresham's keen competition had starved out the owner. He decamped, and afterward, perhaps by the fire of some tramp, the building was burned down. There were only a few fire-charred timbers remaining above the surface of the ground, which was otherwise covered with a sun-dried tangle of weeds, never cut down from year to year.

On one side of the building there was the house of Tom

Matthews. But even this was not immediately flush against the wall of the jail. There was room for a fence between the two buildings, a tall, solid board fence about six feet high, and on either side of the fence there was a footpath leading around the buildings.

Altogether this made an empty lane about fifteen feet in width between the walls of the two buildings. And I reasonably felt that this was a sufficient distance to prevent communication between the two on this night. There was thus, as you see, empty space entirely surrounding the jail, and I proceeded to guard that empty space in the following manner.

At each of the four corners of the jail I stationed two men. One man was to sit down exactly at the corner and exercise as much care as he could to keep awake. But, if he did fall asleep, he would not be allowed to slumber long. For the second man, in the meantime, would be walking back and forth, touching the next man at each corner, and then wheeling about. I insisted upon that touching of man and man as a necessity, because I did not wish to have any gaps in the rounds that they made, and, when I explained this very seriously to the men, they all swore to me, gravely, that they would do exactly as they were told.

I had their separate words for this, and I was willing to trust to them. Eight men, therefore, were detailed to guard the outside of the building. As for the inside, that was a different and more complicated matter. I kept the chosen men for that work. First of all I had picked out four good men, and famous fighters. With these I went through the jail from top to bottom.

There is always a lot of junk in the attic and in the cellar of every old building—I don't know why. And the jail was like the rest. But we shifted every stick of the junk. And we tapped the walls and we tapped the floors, and then we examined every closet and every room and the walls of the cellar and finally my care went so absurdly far that I took a pick and, with the aid of a couple of my companions, we tore up the packed earth floor of the jail and tried to see if there were any possible hidden means of communication.

The boys were inclined to smile, at first, and nudge one another. But when they saw that I paid not a bit of attention to their smiling but remained grave and sort of desperate, they became just as serious as I was. And finally they began to talk to one another and wonder what was going to happen.

But by the common agreement of those twelve hard-fighting, clear-eyed men, there was not the possibility of an enemy being in the jail. And there were eight men on the outside to keep any enemy from entering. And there were four specially chosen warriors to receive the enemy if he *did* enter. Two were placed in the actual room of young Juniper, to listen to his confession, and two had a sort of roving commission, to watch all the entrances to the little building, passing them all in turn.

Besides, there was Tom Kenyon and there was Gresham, who could do what they liked.

How could these precautions have been surpassed? And yet two men were to be murdered in the jail that night!

Chapter Seventeen

Tom Kenyon chose to be with me in the room when the examination of young Juniper took place, and I was glad enough to have him. Tom was so nervous that, if he were roaming around promiscuously, he was apt to sound foolish alarms on account of some whisper of the wind.

Peter Gresham decided that he, also, would roam the house. I invited him, particularly, to come with me, telling him just what I hoped to gain from Danny Juniper, but Gresham, after a moment of thought, refused. I pressed him, saying that I might need his authority to back me up, and that he knew the history of Red Hawk so well that he would be able to tell, probably, if the youngster began to lie to us.

But Gresham had made up his mind. He said seriously: "There is more reputation in this thing than you expect, Sherburn. And if you really get on the trail of Red Hawk, whether you capture him or not, you'll be a great man around Amityville. But if I'm present in the room when you make the inquisition . . . just because I'm better known in the town . . . people will transfer most of the credit to me."

It was a pretty decent way to put the thing. But it was just the sort of delicate thinking and feeling that one could expect from Gresham. In spite of his bulk and his manliness, in many ways he had all of the delicate sensibilities of a girl.

I did not insist, after that, because Gresham was not the sort of a man who has to say a thing twice before one takes him seriously. I let him go his own way, and I hurried in to that examination of Danny Juniper, so brief, and so famous as it was afterward to become.

I had with me Harry Wells and Steve Barchet. And there was Kenyon, who sat guarding the locked door with a naked revolver in his hand. Juniper was in irons again, of course. But I had the irons unlocked. It seemed to me that this little taste of liberty—like a promise of the freedom that his state's evidence would give him—might loosen the tongue of Danny and make him talk somewhat nearer to the truth. In fact, I think that it actually had that effect.

But no sooner had we settled down in our chairs—me with a pad of paper on my knee to scrawl down the important statements—than I happened to glance up and saw a trap door in the ceiling just above the chair in which our prisoner was sitting.

It startled me, simply because in our careful search of that day we had not noticed the place. And, having made such a mistake, I had a confused feeling that we might have overlooked a great many other important points in the same way. I couldn't go on with the examination. I had to have a look at that trap door.

So we sent for a stepladder and I myself climbed up to have a look. It looked as sound as could be. I could even see the heads of big nails that seemed to fasten it to the main body of the ceiling, but, when I pressed heavily up against the door, it gave way with a sudden lurch that nearly dropped me off the ladder. The nails were there, but they had been broken off in the wood long, long before. The edges were all covered with rust. It frightened me pretty badly for an instant. Then I straightened and, very much to my surprise, found my head just above the level of the attic floor.

That attic looked darkly mysterious for a time, filled with

massed shadows, and all that, but in another moment the starlight through the skylight in the roof showed me familiar details. We had gone over that mass of junk with a fine-toothed comb that day. So I climbed back down the ladder and sat down in my chair again.

I found that everyone was smiling covertly, looking down at the floor. They did not want to offend me by laughing in my face, but they apparently thought that I was making a good deal of a fool of myself. And I grew hot with that idea. So hot that I had not the courage to climb that ladder again and cover the yawning hole of darkness in the ceiling that I had left by failing to replace the door. That hole bothered me. It watched me like a great empty eye all during the short examination. I didn't like it. But to climb that ladder and cover the hole would have been a silly thing to do, I felt.

But every ten seconds I had to glance up at that gaping hole. I could see the great bright stars that looked through the wind-scoured skylight. They looked tiny and dim enough, but I was aware of them always and they kept in my mind the outer night—in which Red Hawk roved and waited and framed his machinations. Altogether, you can see that I was in a pretty nervous and upset frame of mind.

Well, I began briskly on Juniper, because I didn't want him to feel that we took him *too* seriously. I said: "Now open up, kid, and hop for cover."

"I've thought it all over," said Juniper quietly. "I've been thinking all day. And the first thing that you got right is that Red Hawk can't bust me loose from this joint. There ain't any way." He said it with a profound conviction. "But I'm scared, just the same," he added.

"Look around you," I said. "Here we are . . . four of us . . . and every man as ready to protect you as he is to protect himself. And every man more than average handy with a gun."

He looked at us, one by one, letting his eye hang a trifle as he noted that shaky figure of poor Tom Kenyon at the door, gun in hand, twitching and stirring on his chair.

"All right," he said, "and I don't doubt that you want to keep me safe . . . till I get the story told. And I don't see how Red Hawk could get at me, anyway. Just the same, you dunno what that devil might be able to do. First place, I want to know what's gonna happen right after I've finished telling my story."

I explained that he would have to be kept under guard until Red Hawk had been located. And until he had been tried for his crimes, in case he were captured alive, which was not likely. Juniper did not like the idea of any delay, but he said that if he were put in the biggest and strongest prison in the country and allowed to wait there, he would be very happy. But he wanted protection—stone feet and steel bars of it!

He went on to tell what he wished to have guaranteed to him after his testifying was ended. He wanted to be promised a railroad ticket to New Orleans, and then enough money to take him to a far country. It was Australia that he had in mind. Or China would do. The farther off and the stranger it was the better he would be suited. He wanted to have at least two good fighting men to guard him to New Orleans and see him safely on board the steamer.

I undertook to guarantee all of these things, and the other boys in the room swore that they would testify that promises had certainly been made to that effect.

When all of this was ended, there was a change in young Juniper. Up to that point he had been white and nervous. And once he said that he would see us all in purgatory before he spoke a word—except that I had threatened to torture him. That made the other boys look rather queerly at me, but I kept a stiff upper lip. Well, when Juniper finally got all of his provisions off his chest, he settled back in his chair and seemed to steady down a lot. His color came back to normal. He lit a cigarette and smoked it as if he enjoyed the taste of the tobacco. And then he was ready to make his statement.

He said: "Where do you want me to begin this yarn?"

I said: "Wherever you want to start."

He thought it over for a moment and inhaled two or three drags on the cigarette. Then he said: "Start in with the fact that there ain't an Indian in the whole crowd and that there never was." He stopped and smiled down at the floor, the way a smart, self-satisfied young man will do when he expects to shock others with strange news. And this word shocked us, I can tell you.

I let it soak in for a while, and then I couldn't help giving him the satisfaction of repeating what he had said: "There never *was* an Indian in the crowd?"

"There never was."

"What about Red Hawk himself?"

"Red Hawk?" said the boy, and then he laughed.

My eyes lifted to the dark square of the opened trap door and I noticed, vaguely, that I could not make out the glint of the stars there any longer. It took me a stupidly long instant to understand what that little thing could mean, and, before I acted, the tragedy had happened.

Young Juniper started to say: "Red Hawk is no more an Indian than he is a. . . ."

And then there was a spurt of fire from the blackness of that opened door and Juniper crumpled in his chair, shot neatly through the head. A second finger of darting red fire and Tom Kenyon got the thing for which he had been waiting in so much dread. I heard him fall as I opened fire. And the two others were doing the same thing. We pumped a dozen bullets at that square of darkness, and then I lurched for the ladder.

I ran up it, with the two hurrying behind me. Outside the building there were shouts. Guns exploded somewhere. I hardly heard them. My brain was whirling. I told myself that my stupidity had cost the lives of two men that night.

I hardly cared what danger I ran into. I plunged into the blackness of that attic and fired a shot. The spurt of flame lighted the room for a hundredth of a second, and I seemed to see everything clearly. The man was not there, but just over my head the skylight was opened. I furled my hands over the edge of the sill and heaved myself up onto the roof.

Someone was there before me. In my madness I nearly pumped a bullet into the back of that big form, and then I saw that he was shooting, in turn, away from the roof of the house and into the back yard of the adjoining building. An instant later I saw that it was Gresham.

As I joined him, he hurled down his gun with an oath. "By the heavens," he cried in a sort of agony, "I think that I've missed him four times running!"

"Who?" I shouted.

"Red Hawk . . . I suppose. He jumped from this roof onto the next. I was in time to see that. And then he swung himself down over the eaves, back there. I got in two shots at him as he crossed the back yard. He went out of sight behind the woodshed. Raise the town. We've got some hard riding to do tonight."

There was no need to raise the town. That fusillade of bullets had made enough noise, and Amityville was easily raised.

By the time that we got down to the street, men were shooting into view in every direction, ready to ride hard and far, but asking for a guide to show them what to do. Gresham was instantly in command and giving directions. I was shoved into the background.

Chapter Eighteen

I did ride in a wild, blind way, with a group of a dozen others, half a dozen miles into the night. But we found nothing. And we returned to Amityville. Other groups had been plowing through the night in the same manner and with the same results. They were back, now, or soon coming. And they filled the streets of the town with noise and heavy cursing.

I went straight to find the victims of the shootings. Of course, young Danny Juniper was dead, and I suppose that there were few in the world who would say that he had not deserved his death. But it was my great tragedy that he had died just as he was about to redeem some of his evil work by one great service to the world. That sickened me at once. But it was nothing to what waited for me at the bedside of poor Tom Kenyon. He had been shot through the body, and, when I arrived, he was dying fast. But I found him a changed man. He knew what lay before him and his courage was superb. He asked for nothing; he regretted nothing. All the terror and the nervousness that had possessed him so long as he was confronted by an unknown fate were ended as soon as he knew that he was helpless.

As for me, who had indirectly brought his death upon him, he took my hand with a weak grip and smiled his forgiveness up to me. It was a hard moment, and I went away feeling that I had done more harm in the world than I could ever make up to it. I wondered what the town would think of me and my horrible blundering. And I was not long left in doubt.

Amityville, to my utter astonishment, seemed to think that I had not been at fault at all. And there was simply a more general agreement than ever that Red Hawk was a fiendishly clever fellow who would never be apprehended except by the sheerest chance.

I never examined the jail and the neighboring building from which the murderer was said to have got to the roof of the jail. But others did make such an examination, and they reported that they had found distinct marks on the old, time-rotted shingles of the house where a man had poised himself well up on the roof and run at a high speed down to the edge of the eaves. From these he had jumped so that, although the edge of the roof gave way a little beneath him, yet he cleared the long, fifteen-foot gap between the two roofs and so got safely to the top of the jail.

After that it was easy to see what he had done. He had simply raised the top of the skylight and lowered himself to the attic beneath. There he found that the trap door had been thoughtfully removed for him by my own hands. And the way was cleared for the double killing that, at a stroke, removed the man whose testimony threatened to be dangerous to him as well as that other man whose daring had ventured to capture a member of Red Hawk's band.

The moment he fired the two shots, he had jerked himself back through the skylight and, running down the roof, must have leaped back to the roof of the next house, although exactly where he had landed there could not be seen on the shingles. However, there was the testimony of Gresham, who had gone up to the roof by accident to guard the last place of access to the jail, that he had seen the scoundrel disappearing over the edge of the roof and down the side of the building.

According to Peter Gresham, it was a big man, with wide, strong shoulders. It was a man who moved with such speed of foot and of hand that it was impossible to credit him with being much more than a youth. And that seemed to speak against the possibility of it being Red Hawk in person. For that Indian was supposed to be well advanced into middle age, though still a formidable warrior. Furthermore, the man was dressed in a full suit of clothes, whereas it seemed more likely that Red Hawk, in a case like this, must have arrayed himself half naked for the warpath.

But it was another proof, if any were needed, that Red Hawk had sure spies in the town. Only two people knew what I intended to do in the jail. One was Kenyon and the other was his wife. As for Gresham, I had only told him at the last moment. Besides, it was inconceivable that he should gabble. Kenyon had been with me. Mrs. Kenyon was the only gap through which the news could have leaked out. I went to her and accused her, but she denied it tearfully.

I decided that there was no use in persecuting her. She had had her share of trouble that day and her bitter punishment, heaven knows. So I went back to the hotel and slept heavily the short remnant of the night, and awakened in the morning to find old Louisiana Doc, as before, in the room. He was chewing his everlasting cud of tobacco, and, as usual, he offered his plug of natural leaf to me.

I propped myself up in bed and shook my head. "What's the news?" I asked.

"The big feller is gone again," he said.

It was mighty unwelcome news. I wanted Gresham in town to run the place and face the people for a few days while I tried to recover my nerve, but I supposed that he could not resist the temptation to hunt for the trail while the sign was fresh. I had my confirmation in a note that Doc handed to me. It ran:

Dear Sherburn:

I am off again. I can't sleep and I can't rest until I've done something to get at that Indian devil. Or is he an Indian? Can Jenny Langhorne be right?

They say that before poor Juniper was murdered, he started to say that Red Hawk was not an Indian, after all. Perhaps they are right and perhaps I am wrong. But I am in a mystery. If Red Hawk is not an Indian, then I am no longer on the trail of the man who murdered my brother so cruelly five years before.

I am making a last desperate effort to find out something. And I think that I may be on my way to success!

That was all.

"I suppose that Gresham didn't sleep much," I commented.

"Nary a wink," declared the Doc.

"And he told you to be here?"

"He told me that you might need a little comfort. I told him that gents from Louisiana didn't need no help from nobody, least of all in the way of words. And then he slid out and left me. He seemed to be sort of in a hurry."

"Doc, what do the boys say around the town?"

"About you?"

"Yes."

"They say that you must have done some kind of magic to oil up the tongue of Juniper."

"Is that all?"

"That's all."

I pondered that for a while. It seemed strange. I expected that I would be surrounded by contempt and disgust for my bungling. But I had left out of my calculations the pretty important fact that human life meant about as little in Amityville as it means to other people during a time of war.

When I went downstairs, Doc went with me. He said: "The main thing is to let the boys figger that you ain't finished with the Red Hawk business. That you got somethin' up your sleeve still."

I understood him, and it made me wince. I had bluffed enough in my day, but, after what had happened to Juniper and Tom Kenyon, I didn't want to pretend to take the lead in this Red Hawk affair. However, I saw that he was right. According to the attitude that I had adopted since I began to run the hotel and saloon for Gresham, I could not let the boys think that I had been beaten.

There was no one in the barroom that morning—no one except Sam, polishing up some glasses behind the bar.

When he heard my step, he turned around and spread his hands out on the bar, which is the time-honored position of bartenders when they ask a man what he'll have to drink. I looked around to make sure that there was nobody near the windows. Then I whispered to him to give me a bottle of ginger ale. He poured a bottle into a tall glass, and he kept it out of sight until the bubbles were gone. When he gave it to me, it looked pretty much like a highball. So I leaned on the bar and sipped that cold drink and thanked heaven that I didn't have to go through with the silly sham of the tea drinking that day.

"Things are a mess, Sam," I said.

He was a wise fellow, that Negro. He nodded at me gravely. "When a gent gets into a pinch," he said, "there ain't more'n one thing that he can do."

"And what's that?"

"His best."

I saw that Sam understood. I was down-hearted—frightfully down-hearted.

"It's true," I said. "And heaven knows that I'll do my best. Sam, I would pay an arm or a leg for the sake of a fair shot at that murdering devil."

"Mister Sherburn," Sam said, "I believe you."

He winked at me, and just in time. Footsteps turned into the door of the saloon and I poured the rest of that ginger ale down my throat. I reveled in that act, while Sam was seen replacing on a shelf a tall, half-emptied bottle of Old Crow.

There was a roar of disappointment.

"One more, Sherburn," they begged me. "We been telling Ike, here, about the way you shift the red-eye, and he don't half believe us. Meet Colorado Ike. This is Fire Brain, Ike."

I shook hands with Ike. He looked as tough as tanned leather—and about that color. He was sun-dried and wrinkled of neck, and he had three days of red-tinted whiskers on his face.

"Fill up, Sherburn," he said. "I come a hundred and twenty-five miles out of my way to tell the boys that I seen red-eye downed like water, and what's more. . . ."

I was about to make some smiling apology, but smiling was not my supposed talent. I was supposed to be a bully and a brute and I had to live up to that part or be broken in about ten seconds, so far as Amityville was concerned. So I beat my fist on the bar.

"Go back to Colorado!" I bellowed at him. "Go back and tell your pals that down here in Amityville, where they raise real men, there ain't any place for baby faces like you and your gang. And why in the devil should I stage a show for your sake? I drink when I'm thirsty, and it don't raise a thirst in me to hear you talk."

I turned my back on him and strode away. If I had remained for another instant that withered little fellow would have had his gun out and dragged an apology out of me and died trying to get it. But when I turned, it gave him another chance to think.

Even then, he was game to the core, and, as I turned through the door, I heard him snarling: "I got to get at him. Damned if I'll take that sort of language out of nobody. I don't have to, and I ain't gonna do it."

They did their best to soothe him. "Look here, Ike," they

said. "He don't mean nothin' by it. It's just his way."

"A damned poor way!" growled Ike.

"Good-natured gent," they said, "and has a good heart, but hard as the devil. That's the way that he always is. Don't take him to heart. The next time you see him, he'll be settin' up the drinks for the crowd. Besides, if you tackle him, he's plain poison, they say. Even Gresham handles him with gloves, and that's why he's a partner here."

I listened to those voices trickling away small and vague behind me. And then I got out of the building by a side door. The strain was telling on me fast. I wanted to be alone. And yet just as I stepped into the open, three cowpunchers came right on top of me.

"Well, Fire Brain, what's gonna happen to Red Hawk now? We hear tell that he showed four of a kind on you last night." And they laughed.

"That crook had the cards stacked," I said. "But the next time I'm going to deal."

"Have you got a game framed?" they asked eagerly.

I winked wisely at them. "I'll talk when the job is finished," I said. And I went on down the street.

Chapter Nineteen

Well, a bluff is always hard work. Even the greatest actor that ever lived will have to admit that his business is a tough one. But on the boards all that an actor has to expect is a few catcalls and maybe one or two spoiled eggs and antique tomatoes in the sticks. But out there in Amityville, when the ladies and gentlemen decided that they didn't like my act, they would encore me with .45-caliber slugs of lead—all well placed.

Of course I knew this, and, when I went on down the street, you can lay your money that I felt sort of sick inside. It had been bad enough for me to bluff at being a great tank and a hard nut, but it was a lot worse when I mixed into the Red Hawk business, because that was holy ground, so far as Amityville was concerned. Men made or lost their reputations on that ground pretty quickly.

Well, I got more desperate with every step as I walked along. I had passed the boys the wink, as much as to say: "This little business about Red Hawk, which has been bothering your best talent for the past few years . . . allow me to remove that problem."

If I didn't stir up some dust in the direction of the Indian chief now, I would be a laughingstock. And, as I said before, they would punctuate their laughter by throwing stones, or little chunks of lead. The difference between a thrown stone and a fired bullet is usually not so much in damage done as in direction. The thrown stone usually heaves past the target by a dozen feet and breaks the expensive mirror on the wall. The bullet breaks your head.

I decided that I should have to go for help. Where could I turn? To Doc, of course—that doddering old inept. Or to big Gresham—no, for Gresham was out of the town. There was Sam, the bartender—hardly apt to be of much use in this sort of an emergency. And finally I came down to a surprising person—no other than pretty Jenny Langhorne.

Not that I really knew her; I had seen her only a brace of times, and really talked to her only once. But I had thought of her enough to make up for that, and I knew that she must have heard a good deal about me. With that in mind, I decided that I would go on to talk to her. Not that I could really expect any concrete help from her, but probably because I simply felt that I had a good excuse for opening a conversation. Down in my heart, that was what I wanted—just to see her again and chat with her.

I went to her house. It stood out on the edge of Amityville. And it looked like what it was—the home of a rancher who had come in from the country but who couldn't make up his mind to get any closer even to a small town than the outer edge of it. I don't like to describe that house, because a description of it seems to be a reflection on Jenny. There were half a dozen mulberry trees in front of the house, big, wide-spreading trees. White mulberry, I think they are called. In the summer you'll always see chickens under those trees, eating the fallen berries. A mighty pretty tree to look at from a distance, but a darned disagreeable tree to be under, with the berries falling down your neck or, if you sat down, squashing on the seat of your trousers.

There were chickens already on hand, too. Not eating the berries, because the berries hadn't grown yet—but cruising around here and there, jerking their heads back and forth as they walked along, and wearing that fierce and foolish look that all chickens are born with. Sometimes they knotted themselves in a group and combined their efforts in the good cause of rooting up some flowering plant that grew there. Sometimes they sailed about separately and ate the buds off of the flower bushes. What is there that can spoil things like a chicken can? One good-size hen can keep six gardeners busy covering up her trail.

There were the mulberry trees and the chickens, which don't go together very well. Then there was the ranch house. It was put together sort of fast and careless. There was an old adobe house that was the core of it. Out from that adobe house the rest of the place rambled—like a starfish that has had its legs smashed off. Some of the legs were long and some of them were short. If the wings of that house could have come to life, the place could have stood up and walked like a spider, except that it would have limped terribly. You could see that whoever planned that building never did any planning more than one day ahead. When he was crowded and heard that company was coming, he must have said: "Boys, let's whack up a couple of more rooms onto the end of that wing, yonder."

That was the way the house looked. It had a sort of scrambled-eggs effect. A man would have known that he could have been comfortable in that house, and a woman would have known that she'd go crazy there trying to bring order out of madness.

Well, all the rest of the place was planned just the same. Or *not* planned—whichever you want to call it. Mr. Langhorne, when he left his ranch, might have washed his hands of the whole business. But he wasn't that way. He couldn't stay on his ranch and he couldn't give it up. He floated in between like a fish half out of water. He quit the ranch, but he brought in about half of the livestock and the rolling stock. There were enough horses in that corral to have kept a crew working while a hundred thousand head of cattle were rounded up. And everything else was just the same. There were barns and stables, and haystacks and straw stacks, and sheds and what-not. And there were men loafing about here and there. They *looked* like they were working, but they weren't. The only work they were doing was to pretend that they were busy. And that is the hardest job in the world.

But there were a lot of people around that place, making a mess for one another to clean up. And there had to be food for them. And Mr. Langhorne had pigs and cattle and sheep, together with vegetable gardens, and he even raised wheat and had his own little mill worked by water power on the creek. He had nearly everything there.

I was sitting in the saddle, lop-sided and smoking a cigarette and wondering how the devil Jenny could live in such a wild place, when along comes a buckboard rattling down the street. Here were Jenny and her father pulling up beside me. He was an oldish man with a pair of fierce-looking mustaches, but very happy blue eyes. His face was thin. He was mighty nervous. He couldn't leave his horses alone, for instance. He had a pair of mighty fine bays on the end of his reins, but, when they stopped prancing, he yapped at them because they weren't standing with their heads up, keeping a pressure on the bits, and when they were dancing and keeping the reins nice and tight, he was yapping at them to keep them quiet. He could hardly talk, he was so mighty busy with his work on that team. He tried to talk to me, but most of the words were for the horses.

"Hello!" sang out Jenny. "Have you come to see the menagerie? This is Sherburn, Dad."

"How are you, Sherburn," said the rancher. "Will you . . . darn you, Si, will you keep up into that collar or do I have to bust your fool head? Sherburn, will you . . . steady, boys. Steady! Get down and rest yourself, Sherburn, and . . . *whoa!*"

Well, it was like that all the time, with Jenny laughing and making her father madder all the time.

"Get out, will you?" yelled Langhorne at last.

Jenny jumped over the wheel and down to the ground as spry as you please, and there she was beside me, laughing at her father.

"Hey, Bill! Hey, Bill!" shouted Langhorne. "Darn it, ain't you got ears? Will you come and put this team up!"

A man who had been going through the motions of sawing wood stopped his motions and looked up. He took off his hat and mopped his forehead with a big bandanna—as if he had been overheated with his work. And then he put the bandanna away and gave his trousers a hitch—all of this before he so much as gave the old rancher an answer.

Langhorne was fairly foaming before Bill came up. He started to dress Bill down. "Have I hired you to be a wooden Indian, standing around here decorating up the landscape? Did I ask you out here because you look pretty, you old rascal!" yelled Langhorne.

Bill fetched a plug of natural leaf out of his hip pocket and took the horses by the reins. "Are you comin' along," he said, "or am I just goin' to put up the horses?"

Langhorne jumped down to the ground, shouting: "Look out for that! That horse has got the devil in him today. Never give me a peaceful minute all the way into town and back again, and. . . ."

Bill turned his back on the team and on Langhorne. "Come along, ponies," he said. And the ponies stopped dancing, stopped fretting, stopped foaming. They walked along placidly behind Bill, cocking their ears toward the smell of the hay from the barns, and stretching their necks and jiggling the bits in their mouths.

"Look," said Major Langhorne. "Wouldn't you know it? Wouldn't you know it? Those horses are just nacherally mean.

Been raising the devil all day. Not because they wanted to raise the devil, but just because they wanted to plague me. I never seen such a pair. I'm gonna sell 'em. No, I'll give 'em away, if I can find anybody I hate bad enough to want him to have 'em."

"Bill, yonder, looks like he might want them," said Jenny.

"That good-for-nothing . . . ," said the major. "Well, Sherburn, I've been hearing a lot about you. The boys have been telling me how hard you are, and Jenny's been telling me what a fine-looking. . . ."

"Major Langhorne!" Jenny cried out.

"Well, we're glad to have you for dinner," said the major.

"He'll have to have lunch first," said Jenny.

"Darn it, I don't care what he has first, so long as he eats. That reminds me of a story about Colonel Henry Mortimer of Louisville. Did you ever . . . ? Hello! Who in the devil ever put that ladder up against that fresh paint? Wait till I get the born fool that did that. Charlie! Hey, Charlie!" He ran off, waving a hand at a distant man, and a moment later he was lost around the corner of the house.

Jenny and I were suddenly alone, drenched in silence.

"He's kept it up for fifty years, too," Jenny said, and smiled at the disappearing heels of her father. Then she said to me: "Do you want to look over the place with me?"

I told her that I would. I would have been glad to do nearly anything with her, as a matter of fact.

"Because," she was explaining, as we started out, "everybody thinks that this place is so queer that they wonder how anybody with a sane mind can live in it, at all. But *I* enjoy it. Not that I understand it. Nobody but Dad could ever explain it. And even he has forgotten his reasons for most of the things he has done to the place."

Chapter Twenty

We sat on the top rail of the corral. One might have guessed that Jenny would select a place as unromantic and as undignified as that for a conversation with a lover. Had I told Jenny that I was a lover? No, but she didn't need telling. She was so used to foolish affection from all the young men in the countryside that she would have been surprised if I had not fallen, I suppose. And she had become an expert in reading the signs, too.

The worst of it was that I *knew* that *she* knew—which made it as embarrassing as the deuce all the way around. Embarrassing for me, I mean. As for Jenny, she never took any notice of sentimentality. The poor girl had been surrounded by so much of it that she would have died if she *had* noticed it.

Looking sidewise at her, I wondered for the hundredth time what there was about her that opened the door to a man's heart so quickly. I was already two-thirds blind, and I was growing rapidly blinder.

Reason had told me that she was not beautiful. But reason was dying wretchedly in me now. She had become more than beautiful—she had become enchanting. And the more matter of fact and careless and good-natured and free and easy she was, the more I grew rickety with wonder and admiration.

She had finished pointing out a lot of things. I suppose that we had gone over the whole place pretty well, and it was even worse than the first glance at it suggested. There was nothing right or in proportion in that house. Not a thing. Everything was topsy-turvy and twisted and confused and unrelated to anything else. When we looked into the house, there was the queerest jumble of furniture that you ever saw.

"Your mother must have traveled a lot to get to like so many different things," I commented. You see, I was so afraid of Jenny that I wanted to praise everything that she was connected with. She didn't laugh in my face. She merely smiled. Oh, she understood everything. She was so darned universal, if you understand what I mean, that it wasn't so hard even if one *did* make a fool of oneself all the time.

"Mother never bought any of these things," said Jenny. "Dad bought them all."

"All this furniture?" I said

Somehow it went against the grain. I could hardly understand a man buying anything but kitchen chairs and tables, and things like that. But a full-grown man buying varnished furniture with a lot of screw-jiggers all over it—well, that was queer and sort of effeminate.

I said to Jenny in a sort of strained voice: "Well, Jenny, I suppose that all this here carving cost a terrible lot, didn't it?"

"Oh, that stuff," said Jenny. It relieved me no end to hear her say that, even if she was a little disrespectful to her old man in talking like that. "That stuff . . . ," Jenny reflected, "it's all machine carved. It's no good."

"Jiminy," I said, looking over a couple of acres of varnish in the living room and the dining room. "That doesn't seem possible.'

"Doesn't it?" said Jenny. "Well, Dad gets a mail-order catalogue for a library and every year or so he takes a liking to a new kind of furniture and he orders a lot of it whether there's any use for it or not. That's his way. We've got a whole shed full of stuff like this, besides what's crammed into the house, and the whole lot wouldn't sell second-hand for more than ten cents a hundred pounds."

That was the way with Jenny, and so we got out to the corral and sat there, looking at the horses.

"I always want to show people all over this funny house of ours," said Jenny, "because I like it, just this way." And she looked at me defiantly out of the side of her eye. It bothered me a good deal.

I was figuring that Jenny was about perfect by this time, and one likes to think that a perfect girl wants order, and all that. I thought it was a very good time to change the subject, if possible. I said: "Your father has got a lot of ground planted out here in vegetables and things and grain, hasn't he? I mean a lot of ground for a man that's retired from ranching."

"Sure," said Jenny. "Dad has stopped ranching for himself and started ranching for his hired men." That was like Jenny. She always put an unexpected twist on things.

Then I remembered the first reason that had brought me out to the house. Though one didn't seem to have to have a reason for calling on the Langhornes, they were so careless and hospitable and good-natured. But I said: "You've heard about what young Danny Juniper said when he started to make his confession?"

"Yes," she said. "He agreed with me, I hear . . . about Red Hawk being a white man."

"Yes," I said, "that was it. And what I want to know is if you have any sort of suspicions about who . . . ?"

"Not one," she cut in. "All I know is that when Red Hawk is spotted, it will be the last man that people have ever suspected. It'll be a white man with a lot of brains. Are *you* on the trail of Red Hawk now?"

"It's up to me," I said. "I was to guard Danny, and I failed. So I have to get the man who killed Danny and Tom Kenyon."

She said in a queer, sharp way: "I thought that you had a bargain with Peter Gresham that he was to hunt for the chief while you ran the hotel?"

"I ought to do both," I said.

She turned a little and stared, hard, at me. But she didn't say a thing. And I wondered what she was thinking.

In another minute she called: "Hello! There's Oliver Clement come to see us."

I turned and saw a young chap on a fine horse riding up. He was dressed up pretty slick and he had the look of a fellow who knew what he wanted and had come to get it. It wasn't hard to guess that what he wanted was Jenny Langhorne.

I said: "Well, it's about time for me to mosey along."

"Not at all," said Jenny. "I want you to meet Oliver. He's come all the way from Salt Plains. He's got a ranch down there."

Oliver was up to us by that time and out of the saddle. When he finished shaking hands with Jenny, she introduced us and he gave me a pretty hard look and a pretty cold smile. He was a fine-looking fellow—very young, and made clean and neat like a thoroughbred race horse.

"I've heard a good deal about you," he said, very cool.

It angered me a little, his way of saying that. "Am I to thank you for that?" I asked.

He shrugged his shoulders. "Perhaps you are," he said. "I'm sure I don't know."

Jenny slid off the top rail of the corral. "What's the matter with the pair of you?" she said.

I was glaring at him like a dog at a bone. I was mad all the way through.

"There's nothing the matter, I suppose," said Oliver Clement.

"Hmmm," said Jenny. "I suppose not, but let's talk about something cheerful. Who's gone up Cricket Valley lately?"

Cricket Valley was pretty famous in the town by this time.

There was a saying that when anyone wanted to join up with Red Hawk and his crew of murderers, he only had to ride up Cricket Valley by himself in the cool of the evening and wait to see what might happen. If he was the sort of material that Red Hawk wanted, he could be pretty sure that someone would be in view of him, looking him over.

Nobody could be sure about this legend, because if a man once joined the gang, he never got free from them. Not until he died—usually with a bullet giving him his last sickness. But the story about Cricket Valley persisted and I've no doubt that the only reason that Red Hawk's gang didn't grow was because a lot of the young fellows who rode up the valley weren't considered the proper material.

"I'm in a good frame of mind for riding up Cricket Valley myself," said Oliver Clement.

"And why?" asked Jenny.

"The old man and me have had trouble," said Oliver, "and I'm on my way to find a job."

"A job with Red Hawk?"

"Why not?" he answered. "And be a good citizen just the same."

Which goes to show you how the opinion had flourished that the thugs were apparently respectable men during the day, and, at night, robbers and cut-throats.

I said—"So long."—and started for my horse. "I got work to do," I explained.

"I'll see you again, maybe," said young Clement.

"Whenever you please," I said. "You'll find that the latch-string is hanging right outside and waiting for you."

"Thanks," he said.

"Don't mention it," I said.

I caught Jenny looking at me with her head bent and a frown on her forehead, as though she understood too well just what was in the minds of the pair of us. We hadn't said anything that looks particularly bad as I write it down. But sometimes the tone is a lot more important than the words that are spoken. We had used the sort of tone that has to have an after-result. And Jenny knew it as well as we did.

I was ashamed of myself on the way into town again. It was bad enough to let trouble grow out of nothing with any person. But particularly to start fighting in front of a girl—and a girl like Jenny—well, there was nothing bad enough to be said about it. I hated myself pretty thoroughly, I can tell you.

I went to the hotel and got to my room. I found that old Doc was already there. He was sitting in his chair by the window, as usual, playing on a fool mouth organ that made a noise like a swarm of wasps. I could have broken his head for his racket. And I told him so. He stopped playing, but he kept the mouth organ handy.

"My old man used to say . . . ," began Doc.

"To the devil with your old man!"

"That there was no excuse for bad nerves, except, possibly, in a drinkin' man."

I reached for a book and hurled it at him, but he ducked his head and the book sailed on harmlessly through the window and arched out of sight with a great whir of fluttering leaves.

Chapter Twenty-One

What should I say to young Oliver Clement when he arrived? Well, he was there soon enough, but not before someone else was with me in spirit. I heard a tap outside my door. I shouted—"Doc, you old fool, is that you?"—because he had fled from the room when my book missed him.

His voice answered: "I ain't here no more than as a sort of an announcer."

"What the devil have you to announce?"

"There is a messenger here for you."

"What? Who from?"

"He ain't sayin'."

"Confound you, find out who it's from."

"There ain't no way. I tried to make him tell me and he ran away and shied stones at me."

"Come in here."

The door opened and Doc leaned against the door post and yawned, to show me that he was at ease and without fear of me. But his eyes, all the time, were young and alert in his old face.

"Who is it?" I asked him.

"Toby McGuire."

"Who is he?"

"A boy."

The idea of a boy being a messenger appealed to me. "Show him in," I said.

"Go on in, you young devil," said the old man.

Toby stepped lightly through the doorway. He was a tow-headed imp of perdition. There was more deviltry in the flare of his eyes than in the look of any Puck of romance; the very twist and outthrust of his unmanageable white hair showed his nature.

"Who sent you?" I said, scowling at him.

"I dunno," said Toby.

"You dunno!" I shouted in rage.

"I dunno nothin' while this old goat is a-blattin' beside me."

There was a swift reaching of the long arm of my friend from Louisiana, but the boy dodged with the speed of light and danced away in safety.

"Get out," I said to Doc, and he vanished, with a baleful last glance at Toby that betokened ill for that youth.

"Now let me have it," I said, "and talk soft, because Doc is waiting outside the door with his ear against the keyhole."

"You lie!" shouted the outraged Doc from beyond the door. And then I heard his retreating footsteps.

The boy grinned in acknowledgment of the skill of this battle maneuver. For he was at an age when nothing matters in this world except the shock tactics of actual strife.

"It ain't in talk. It's in writing," Toby said, and he gave me a letter.

"Where do you belong?" I asked.

"I'm out on the Langhorne Ranch," he said.

That was enough for me. I was so confused and shaky that I could hardly get the letter out of the envelope. And it was from Jenny, right enough. She didn't fence around. She started right in with what she had to say. It opened with: *Dear John.* I was glad of that, because we had come to call each other by our front monikers without much delay.

Dear John:

I am trying to cool off Oliver Clement, and it is a hard job. He thinks that his honor has been offended. And he is coming to see you. Now, I know what that means. I've lived among men who wear guns long enough for that.

Two things pop up in my head, now that Dad is entertaining Oliver and I have a chance to send this word to you. One is that you're the older man, really, even if you did act like the younger boy today. And, being the older man, you may listen to reason and not fight, at all. The other is that, if you do fight with Oliver, you will use something other than guns. I mean your fists. You two have each a good hard pair of them. Aren't they what men should fight with?

I looked down from the letter at my own hands. A few of the metacarpal bones on the back of my left hand had been broken by not knowing how to hold my hand in the days when I was a fighting pup. But my fists were in pretty good shape. Yes, and I had no doubt that they might be good enough to do for young Mr. Clement.

The letter went on:

I'm sending this note to you to beg you to do something gentle and considerate. Other people have told me that you are a rough man. But rough, brave men ought to be gentle, too. I hope that you'll be willing to think things over and try to do what is right for yourself and for Oliver, too. I'll never forgive myself if this turns into anything serious, because it started out here on the ranch.

Jenny Langhorne

That was all, and that was enough. I wrote on the back of that letter:

I give you my word that I'll do what I can to ease out of this mess without doing any harm. I'm sorry that I acted like a two-year-old today.

Then I sealed that letter in a fresh envelope and gave it to Toby with a half dollar. He was startled by the coin and almost blurted out a confession, but I said: "It's all right, Toby. If you're paid at both ends of the line, it's because you're worth it."

He gave me his broad, wrinkled grin. Then he was gone.

When I looked out of the window a moment later, I saw Doc making a futile effort to put hands on him, like an old war horse trying to play tag with a racing colt. The boy scooted out of the way and around the next jagged corner of the street just as a cloud of dust dissolved and showed in its midst the galloping form of Oliver Clement. Even by the way he tossed himself out of the saddle and threw his reins I knew that he was bent on business, no matter what the girl had said to him. He left his own dust cloud boiling behind him and settling in gray sheets on the sweating horse, and then he disappeared into the hotel.

After a moment there was another knock on my door and Doc said that Oliver Clement was there. I had him brought in at once. And I sent Doc out. Clement stood for a moment near the door, rubbing dust off his trousers and looking me in the eye. I saw that I was going to have a hard time keeping my promise to the girl.

"Well?" said Oliver Clement.

"Well?" I echoed, and I advanced and held out my hand with a smile. It was about as much as anyone could have asked of me. I selfishly wished with all my heart that pretty Jenny Langhorne could have looked in and seen me try to be knightly and gentle for her sake. But there was no Jenny there. Her wise and understanding bright eyes were far away, and just before me there was a faint, contemptuous smile on the lips of Oliver Clement. I dropped my hand. And I was so mad that I nearly raised it again and arched it at his jaw.

"I've got a little talking to do to you," he said.

"Sit down," I said.

"I ain't sitting," he said. "I'm standing till I know where I am."

"Blaze away, young feller."

"Out there today. . . ." He choked.

"Go on," I coaxed as gently as I could.

"At the Langhorne place, it seemed to me that you was trying to make me seem pretty cheap in front of Jenny."

"Well?"

"I've come in to ask you what you meant by it."

I was so hot that I could hardly hold myself. I couldn't be easy-going and friendly any more. I had to let go in some way, and the next best thing to getting into a rage was to laugh at him. And so I laughed and watched him turn crimson.

"I seem to sort of amuse you," he said.

"You do, kid," I said. "It ain't every day that a four-flusher like you turns up around here."

"Am I a four-flusher?"

"Why, you young fool," I said, "you ain't hardly dry behind the ears, and you try to handle talk like a man. You've come down here hungry to get a reputation out of me. But I say . . . go get a reputation by yourself, and then come back to me, if you want trouble."

He bit his lip and then he shook his head. "It ain't gonna do," he said. "I ain't that kind. You can't laugh me out of it. Sherburn, you tried to shame me."

"I wish I may be damned," I said, "but I never seen such a one-legged thinker as you are. Why should I wish to shame you? Do I go around the countryside slapping the faces of the babies in the cradles? No, kid, I try my hand with the grown-up men that have done something besides *talk* big."

You'll say that was stinging enough to have brought a rise out of him, and it did just that. He didn't wait to get his gun out of its holster. He just threw his fist in the shortest way toward the point of my jaw.

It was a good, honest, healthy punch, with plenty of muscle behind it and all the weight of his body. But, to an old-timer like me, it was a pretty easy punch to see telegraphed. I simply pulled my chin out of the way and that fist went by like a baseball headed for the plate.

Young Oliver Clement came lurching in with his punch, and, as his arm flew over my shoulder, I did the thing that was easiest and quickest to do. I brought up a right uppercut with all my strength behind it. I lifted that punch as though I were tearing out a new board from the floor. I was coming onto my toes when that fist spatted fairly under the chin of Oliver.

It did what it was supposed to do, of course. It snapped his head back so hard and so fast and so far that I thought for a minute that I had knocked his head right off his shoulders. It lifted the whole weight of his body for a good bit. And then he turned into a wet rag and started for the floor. I reached for him, but he was so limp that he went through my arms like water through a sieve. Well, I stood back and looked him over. I had hit that young fellow so hard that my wrist ached. And I knew it would be a long time before he came to.

I had a cigarette lit before he opened his eyes. That cigarette was half smoked before he sat up and stared at me.

Chapter Twenty-Two

Perhaps you will think that it was a pretty calloused thing to do—to sit by like that and watch a poor fellow get his wits back. But I was in rather a callous frame of mind. It was almost the only time in my life that I had attempted to avoid a fight, and this young hothead had forced my hand.

What I was thinking of as I sat there was not young Clement, but Jenny Langhorne. What Clement thought was a very small matter to me, indeed. But what she thought meant nearly everything in the world. And she would feel that I had paid no attention at all to her letter, when she heard about this affair. I had no doubt that she would hear about it. It is only boys who believe that secrets can be kept. But grown men understand that the truth will out in the end. So I sat in my chair and hated young Oliver Clement with all my heart and really wished only that the blow that had knocked him down had broken his neck as well.

But his neck was not broken. He sat up and rubbed the back of his head, where it had struck the floor such a resounding thump. And he blinked his eyes until the light and the life slowly flooded back in them. When he could recognize me, he seemed to come back to full consciousness with a snap, and struggled to his feet. Still he was far from himself, for he stood there swaying, and staggering—completely out of his balance. And yet he had enough sense—or lack of sense—to sneer loosely at me.

"Why . . . why don't you finish the job . . . you . . . you crook

. . . Sherburn?" he said to me.

I wanted to break him into a thousand bits; I wanted to knock his head against the wall so hard that it would crack like a nut under my heel. But there is no fun in beating a man you know you can lick. I simply set my teeth a little harder and glared at him and said nothing. Besides, I was surprised. Because I could see that there was a lot of fight left in this fellow—and there would be still more fight after his head cleared. Perhaps he would even want to come at me with his hands again. But that wasn't very likely. However, I was curious. And so I rolled another cigarette and watched him in silence.

Presently he braced his back against the wall and looked at me, steadily, and for a long time. Before he got through staring at me, I could see that he was sound again—the weakness was out of his knees and the ringing was out of his ears. His nerves were strung strong again. In short, he was ready to go at me, and I knew by his look that he intended to have it out again. In what way? Well, he didn't leave me much room to doubt. He gave his eyes a last rub, and then he stood up, lightly, and on his toes.

"You knocked me cold," said Clement.

"Yes," I said. "You were pretty well out. I couldn't talk sense into your head. I had to try to knock some sense into you." That wasn't a very diplomatic speech to make. But then I could never pretend that I am a diplomat.

"Fists," he said, "are only one way of fighting."

"A good enough way, I guess," I said.

"For you, maybe," said Oliver Clement. "But speaking personal, I don't wear a gun for a decoration."

It was hard to believe that he meant it. Not after lying flat on his back only the moment before.

"You wear a gun to put spice in life, maybe?" I asked him.

"Salt and pepper," said Clement, as cool and as calm as you

please. "I use it on yeggs and gunmen . . . like you, Sherburn. You understand?"

I understood. That young devil had a natural talent for making me mad. If there had been any audience, I should have had to unlimber my own gat then and there. But there was no audience and I was thinking of the girl harder than I had ever thought of any other thing. I was thinking of her and swearing that nothing should make me go any further in this quarrel.

"I understand one thing," I said, because I decided that I should have to try the effect of one last bluff. "I understand that I have to finish up what I started, young fellow, unless you slide out of this room."

He only smiled at me, and I saw that my bluff was not worth a cent with him. He smiled, and he grew positively white with hate and the wish to fight. "Stand up," he said. "They say that you're a fast man with a gun, Sherburn. Well, I'm fast myself. And I want you to have every chance. I'm going to give you an even break before I turn you into dog meat."

"That's a fine, peaceful way to carry on," I said. "But why should I pull a gun on you, Clement? What does it mean to me?" He stared. "If I drop you, I spoil the rug on the floor and get all the folks to thinking that I prey on children."

Then he seemed to understand. "Oh, you'll fight," he said. "You'll fight, well enough, or else go down and plaster your name all over the town as a yellow-livered bluffer."

"They'd laugh at you," I said. But just the same, his point went home, and he knew that it had. "Besides," I argued with him," "is there any good reason why you should want to commit suicide this way? Just because your old man give you the run, why should you come around and get me to pay your funeral expenses?"

"You talk slick enough to be in politics," said the boy. "But it don't go down with me. I want action, old son. And I'm gonna have action and plenty of it. If you want a good cause for fighting, I'll give you one."

He had sauntered forward as he spoke, and now he reached across and slapped my face. It was just a flick from the tips of his fingers, but it was enough. That had never happened to me before. The people I had fought with were the kind that slapped with five hard knuckles and not with five soft fingertips. The boy seemed to know, because, just as he struck me, he was leaping back and there he stood crouched, with his right hand glued to the butt of his revolver.

I knew then that he wasn't any ordinary fighter, because he was so sure of himself that he didn't make a false draw, and wouldn't pull his gun until he had seen my hand go back for mine. But my hand didn't stir. I was fighting the big battle of my life, and this was one of my winning spots. It took all the nerve in my body to keep me out of what I told myself would be a murder. Because, no matter how practiced that boy might be, there wasn't much likelihood that he had my training behind him. So I didn't stir a hand. I merely stood up from my chair, feeling that, unless I did something desperate, I would *have* to fight, after all. And knowing, too, that if I killed this youngster, Jenny Langhorne would be through with me.

Yet, he wasn't a bad kid. He was as game as they come, and the real fighting stuff was in him. I hope I was something like him, at that age—but never with his looks, of course. I could understand him and sympathize with him. He had me angry a little while before. But now I had cooled off. I didn't want to fight for all of these reasons. But I began to see that I had to fight. And then I thought of two things. The first was that I *would* shoot this youngster down, but I'd trim him through a leg—and he'd be on his feet again in three weeks. The second thing I thought of was a cause for the fight that would make it worthwhile.

I said: "Clement, you want to finish your job with me right now, I suppose?"

"I've slapped your face," he said. "Do you want me to step on your toes, too?"

"That'll never be enough to suit me. But I'll tell you what I'll do. We'll make a bargain for what the loser in this scrap shall do."

"He'll take a short cut for hell," said the boy.

I smiled at him. "No, kid," I said. "I'm not going to put the bullet through your head. I'm going to drop you where it's soft. And after I'm done with you, you'll be able to ride out on the little job that I have in mind."

"You ain't a bit satisfied with yourself, I see," said Oliver Clement. "But I tell you, old war horse, that what I aim to do is to slide a chunk of lead between your ribs, so's to get myself remembered on your tombstone. Shoot straight, I advise you, if you get a chance to shoot at all."

"Will you listen to my dicker?" I asked.

"I'll listen," he said.

"No one bullet could ever tag the life out of me. I'm too tough for that, kid. If I was sprawled against the wall with my arms spread out, you couldn't finish me off with one bullet. But if you knock me down with your slug, or put me out of the game, then I'm the loser, and the loser has a job to do. As soon as he's able to ride, he sashays up Cricket Valley and he waits for one of those buzzards up yonder to speak to him from the cliff. And then he joins the Red Hawk gang, if he can. And when he has joined up with them, he learns what he can about the things that they do and the way that they do them, and, if he has a chance, he plans how he can put Red Hawk's head inside the noose. You savvy?"

Clement turned a shade pinker. There was no doubt that he was seeing at a glance all of the terrible possibilities of that bit of work. It even made *me* shiver, when I thought of how the boy would have to live among thugs and crooks and play his one chance in a thousand of nailing Red Hawk. I was sorry for Clement, just then. I was mighty sorry for him. But, just the same, I felt that I had to go through with the deal. And, after all, no matter what happened, it would be better for him to have my bullet through his leg than through his head.

"I'll take that bet," said he at last. "Will you shake on it?"

"Yes."

We shook hands, and then it was easy for me to grip his gun hand so that he could not budge it, and catch his left wrist tightly.

"Now," I snarled, close to his face, as he tried to writhe away from me, "I could bust you in two, you soft, young fool. If I play square with you and let you have a fighting chance for your life, will you keep the bargain you've made with me?"

"Yes," breathed Clement, and I let him go.

Chapter Twenty-Three

Someone in the street was singing *"La Paloma"*. Do you know *"La Paloma"?* Everybody in the Southwest does, of course. Perhaps some people only hear the tune drumming through their ears when they think of the name. But it means a good deal more to me. I can see serapes and smell Mexican cigarettes as though they were fuming in the same room with me. So when someone in the street started singing *"La Paloma"*, and when I heard the jangling of a mandolin, it meant a good deal. It put me south of the Río Grande and into an excellent frame of mind for fighting. Because I had seen a good deal of trouble in that country. And I *knew* that poor young Clement was in the hollow of my hand.

We stood on opposite sides of that room and eyed each other. I was smiling. I couldn't help it. He was pale and tight. I saw in his face that he was beaten already and that he was only praying that he could go down like a man. Yes, he was game.

"When he comes to the end of that song," I said, "we grab our guns, eh?"

He nodded, moistened his lips—and the wait began.

A pair of riders came down the street and the rush of their hoofs almost drowned the song for a moment. Then, as they stopped the horses suddenly, the song floated through the window—and a wisp of alkali dust from the street. A fine fragrance to me, because the desert is my country.

My fingertips were itching for the feel of my gun. I picked my target. The thigh of his left leg, where the big driving muscles bulged out. And I hoped that the bullet would not hit the bone. If I shot a fraction to the side of center, I would probably miss the bone, and I planned to shoot to the side. That was cutting it rather fine, you'll say. But I knew myself and I knew my gun, at that distance. And when a man practices two hours a day he ought to be able to try a trick now and again.

The song was dragging toward the close. I saw young Clement glance aside, nervously, toward the window through which the music was pouring, and by the look in his eyes I knew that his nerves were as rattling as the sound of the mandolin. I wondered who invented the mandolin, and then had the crust to call it a musical instrument? That thought had just popped into my mind when the last word of the song came and the hand of Clement flashed back for his gun. He was fast, very fast, but I was a fifth of a second faster. And split seconds are what kill in a gunfight if men know their weapons. In a sprinting race a fifth of a second means six feet between the winner and the second man. And it means a lot more in a gunfight, because the hand can travel three times as fast as a runner's feet.

Well, I flicked my fingertips under the butt of my gun and plucked it out of the holster. I mean that I caught it in the old flying grip that I had used ten thousand times in practice and in real fighting. And ten thousand times that gun had jumped out of the leather and buried its handles against the palm of my hand while I shot from the hip. But this ten thousand and first time something went wrong. I don't know what it was. But big Gresham always had said that he thought I wore a rather tight-fitting holster. At any rate, that Colt was jammed tightly in the leather, and, under the extra pressure, my flying fingers slipped from the butt of the gun and my hand jerked up into the air—empty!

There I stood, half bowed, looking bullets at young Clement, but firing none—and there was he with his own gun at the hip. As he saw what had happened, he jerked his arm out at full length and covered me through the sights of his Colt.

Through the sights! Yes, this boy was so green a hand that he had not filed the sights away as any old-timer in the gunfighting trade is sure to do. And yet mine was the gun that had stuck and his had come free! Other people can talk about luck, but, in view of all that was to happen, I call it fate.

But he did not pull the trigger. He merely gasped: "You're beat, Sherburn."

I didn't say a word. I still half expected him to fire. The men I had fought with in the past were never distinguished for generosity, and I could name a hundred who would send a chunk of lead through me tomorrow if they had a chance to catch me helpless. Yes, and do it with a smile. But not this boy. All at once I knew why Jenny thought so much of him. For he lowered that revolver and dropped it into the holster.

He stared for a minute. "We'll try over again," he said huskily. "Your . . . your hand slipped, I guess."

Can you come over that? No, I don't think that you can, because whatever he had thought when he came into the room, he knew by this time that I was a better hand with a Colt than he would ever be. And he was inviting sure death, I suppose. But he didn't flinch. By ten sizes, it was the biggest temptation that I ever looked in the face, but something came up in me, just then, and gave me the strength to play fair. And I shook my head at him.

"You're a square-shooter, Clement," I told him, and I meant it. "But you beat me, just as surely as though you drove a slug through me. You've won the game . . . and the prize that goes with it. *I* have to ride up Cricket Valley."

He seemed a little dazed. As a matter of fact, things had been happening a little fast between the two of us. He ground his knuckles across his forehead and then he said: "Sherburn, I think you could have blown my head off, if the luck hadn't been against you."

I would like to say that I made some courteous rejoinder to him, but my heart was a little too full for that, and I merely turned my back on him and looked out the window.

"You go to the devil with your fine talk," I said.

There was a moment's pause. I hoped, savagely, that he would take up that last insult, but in another minute I heard the door shut softly and I knew that he had gone. After all, he had done about all that anyone could ask in defense of his honor on this day. And I was left with the prospect of Cricket Valley in front of me.

I sat down to think the thing over, because it required a whole lot of thinking. I had to plan out a way in which I could break off my relations with Gresham. I had to plan a lot of other things.

What I first decided was that I would tell the truth to Gresham and to Jenny Langhorne. But the affair with poor dead Tom Kenyon taught me that it would be foolish to talk too much. The few words that had been spread by gossip in that case had brought the news to the ears of the omnipresent Red Hawk and that had brought death to Tom.

I could see, as I pondered this tangle from the beginning, that if I really wished to do any good work, the best way to go about it was to make myself into a deaf mute, so far as any other person was concerned. There was already one man who knew what I intended doing, and I decided on the spot that this was one person too many.

I sat down and wrote to Oliver Clement.

Dear Clement:

I've been thinking over what happened this afternoon, and I can see that the only way for me to do anything worthwhile with the job we arranged, is to take nobody into my confidence. I plan to break away as soon as I can see Gresham. You can't ask me to leave before I've done that.

When I leave, I'll tell nobody where I'm going or what I intend to do. I forgot to caution you not to breathe a syllable to anyone. Not to your best friend. This job that I have on hand is going to be bad enough, but, if the news leaks out, Red Hawk will have another party at my expense—the same as he had with Leicester Gresham. I suppose you know what I mean.

If I keep my mouth shut and if you don't talk, I may have one chance in ten to do something. But if a word is said, Red Hawk will hear. There's no doubt in my mind about that!

I sent the letter to Clement at once, and the next morning, while I was still asleep—because I had been up late that night watching the operations in the game rooms—the door opened and old Doc brought in a reply from Clement.

It was just the sort of a reply that you would want to write to a friend of yours. He said that the bargain had been my proposal, in the beginning—that he had never intended to insist on it—and that he would have spoken about the matter the day before, when he had left, except that I didn't seem in a mood very receptive to suggestions. All he wanted me to do was to forget that we had ever disagreed. And he would have come over himself to shake hands with me, if I were willing. But unfortunately he had turned his ankle, and he now had to sit still and cuss his luck.

It was pretty good letter, any way you looked at it. And it did just one thing for me. It showed me that I had made my bargain with a real white man and convinced me that I absolutely had to go through with it. It would not have been so bad to let the matter drop, if young Clement had turned out a small-time fellow. But he was so big that I had to play big, too. Nothing but four of a kind could beat a full house in this game that I was playing with Oliver Clement.

I folded the letter and then I reached for a match, and I had just touched the match to the letter when there was a quick, strong knock at the door, the knock of Gresham, and he entered before I had time to tell him to come in. It's a rather foolish position to be caught in—lying in bed and burning a letter over an ashtray. I was surprised into a blush. And though Gresham said nothing just then, he gave me a side glance that ripped through my armor and went straight to the quick.

He finally said: "How's things?"

I said: "Fair enough. What brought you back so soon?"

"Trouble . . . trouble with Red Hawk. He's raised so much of it this time that I suppose the United States troops will take a hand in it. And the job begins to look so big to me . . . so much like government work . . . that I've about decided to wash my hands of the whole thing and buckle down to my job here in Amityville. I've even almost decided to sell out the place and quit the West . . . if I can find a purchaser."

CHAPTER TWENTY-FOUR

That was exactly the style of Gresham. What he had his mind, he was apt to come out with in one big rush. I suppose that's a quality with men who don't care who sees the inside linings of their brains—or with men so big and bold that they don't care a rap for the opinions of others. But it takes a big man to do it; the sort of bigness that I can't pretend to.

I simply lay there, flabbergasted, and turned the business over and over in my head.

I began to repeat: "Leave Amityville . . . give up the trail of Red Hawk."

"I'll give up the trail of the red devil. It's as much use to chase the chief as it is to chase a lightning flash. I've fooled away my time for five years. I've worked all the time on that one thing. And what has it brought me?" He went on after that, pouring out a tide, I can tell you.

I began to see what life would mean when life had for a main object the chase of a criminal like that wild Indian—constant riding, constant hunting—constant dread of the knife that may be buried in the center of your back at any minute. When even big Gresham declared that he was through with the game, I could begin to believe him.

And still I lay there and babbled foolish questions at him until he interrupted me with: "Cut that out and ask me to tell you about what that red fiend has done this time. Or is Amityville full of the news and so used to it that it can afford to sleep through the news. Dead nerves . . . that's what this town has."

Dead nerves? I suppose that was the first time that any sane man ever thought of giving such a name to Amityville. But Gresham was a giant—a giant in body and in soul and in nerve, also. And when *his* strength began to crumple, I suppose he would think it queer if other people managed to keep pulled together.

I asked about the news of the latest escapade of that terrible Red Hawk. And he told me the whole story. He sat on the broad sill of the window and talked with his head fallen wearily back and his gaze turned out toward the heat waves that went shimmering up from the roofs of the buildings across the street.

He looked more than tired. He looked fagged out—and when a man like Peter Gresham was fagged out, it meant a good deal, I can tell you.

"A daylight job this time," said Gresham. "The chief and five men in masks swooped right down on Ludlow and swarmed into the Ludlow Bank."

"How did they get through the streets without being shot to bits?" I gasped.

For Ludlow, in those days, even, was a booming town with about twelve hundred people in it, and it was as tough and as rough as most of the Western towns that lived then on the border between law and outlawry. Everybody in that place, I suppose, carried a gun, and two thirds of them must have been good shots. A good gun and the skill to use it was a much bigger necessity than the ability to read and write. Even bankers and clerks in stores, for instance, used to go out in the back yard and practice at a mark with a big Colt.

Gresham answered my question with a groan. "I'll tell you how they got through the streets without being blown to bits. It was because men aren't around when there's trouble in the air.

If it had been a poor dog that had turned mad, then a hundred rifles would have been pumping lead at it. But so long as it was Red Hawk and five of his butchers, nobody was on deck except the women and the children. They saw the thugs go by in a whirl of dust and they ran to call their heroes. Of course, by the time the heroes showed up, the whirl of dust was gone by, and by the time the heroes got their horses saddled and started in pursuit, the job was over. There was only an old German keeping a fruit stand. He saw the mischief coming and picked two rusty old guns out of a drawer and began to throw lead at them. And by the heavens, he was the only man in town who did them any harm. He put a bullet through the head of a young half-breed Mexican who turned out to be Diego Calderón . . . you know that sleepy boy who lived at the west end of the town?"

"The one with the cock-eyed look?" I gasped.

"The same one," said Gresham. "Would you believe it?"

"Not I," was my answer. "There was that kid, young Juniper, too. Red Hawk must be a fool to trust to youngsters like those."

"Do you think so? I don't know. Perhaps he has sense enough to see that they're the only ones that he *can* trust. It's a rare thing to find a mature man who will put any faith in another mature man, after all, Sherburn. The older we grow, the more we trust in the children. But the grown people . . . well, they've been in the world long enough to be tainted by it . . . there's no doubt of that. Give me a boy to put through a hard job. The boys are the ones who fight the wars, while the grown men stand about and shake their heads and speak the pretty sentiments."

"Go on," I urged. "It was a boy, then, that the old chap killed? And what happened to him?"

"Oh, they salted him away with a bushel of lead slugs, of course. He went down nearly blown to pieces, and that crew went on and turned in at the bank. They tumbled off their horses and they slung through the doors of the bank and shoved guns under the noses of the men there."

"How many were in the bank?"

"Twenty men, nearly. There were a dozen men waiting for the cashier's window to open."

"A dozen men!"

"But what would they do? They had the picture of Red Hawk in front of them, and that was enough. That man has charmed the fancies of the people in this part of the world. When they see him, they're convinced that they're lost before he so much as makes a gesture at them. And when they had a glimpse of a few Colts swinging at them, they crowded into a corner and stuck their hands over their heads as high as they could shove them. The rest was easy. They simply made the cashier open the safe of the bank and they went through it in a few sweeps. What they got amounted to . . . no, it makes me sick to think of it."

"Go on," I said, breathless with interest by this time.

"Think of it, Sherburn. A quarter of a million went into the hands of a copper-skinned dog of an Indian."

"Good heavens, Gresham!" I cried. "A quarter of a million?"

Because money in those days was a different matter from money now. A dollar then could buy what three dollars now can buy. And a dollar was five times as rare as a dollar now. And a quarter of a million!

"Two hundred and sixty-five thousand dollars," said Gresham. "They could burn Amityville and rebuild it again for that amount of money. And in the hands of an Indian thief." He closed his eyes and groaned.

I could only repeat the sum total, dumbly: "Two hundred and sixty-five thousand dollars."

"There was a flat two hundred and fifty thousand in paper money. And then fifteen thousand in ten- and twenty-dollar gold pieces. They took the entire lot of swag and they dropped it into cheap gunny sacks and they galloped away out of town again."

"What? Untouched?"

"Certainly! Oh, there was plenty of shooting at them. But if men have a fever when they shoot at a deer, what do they have when they shoot at a man? Six of the boys came in last summer and said that they'd put at least a dozen bullets into a big yellow grizzly up there in the hills. Well, a week later old John Andrews killed that bear and found exactly one wound . . . where a bullet had grazed the skin of his back. But there were six men, all pretty level-headed, who swore that they had certainly put at least two shots apiece into a bear at pointblank range. Well, what happens when they have Red Hawk in their sights? They simply have shaking hands. They burned a hundred or two hundred rounds at the Indian this time, but he and all his men got away and left no blood on the trail. It sickened me, Sherburn. And that's why I'm back here," Gresham said.

"Have you given up the job?" I asked.

"I think so," he said. "I suppose the military will take the job in hand now. I'm tired to death of the game."

I told him frankly that I could hardly believe it. "And no one else will believe that you've admitted you're beaten, Gresham. No one else will admit that you've quit and turned back." Then I added: "Is that really all that has brought you back?"

"No," he said suddenly, "it isn't all." And he looked at me in such a queer way that I was filled with wonder.

"What do you mean, Gresham?"

"I mean you," he said, and he came and sat down on the side of the bed, looking me in the eyes all the while. And he had a hard eye to meet, as I think that I've said before. He looked straight through and through a man.

"All right," I said, and grinned at him. "Tell me what I've done to you."

"Shall I tell you?"

"Of course. Come out with it."

"Sherburn, we haven't known one another very long. But I have a feeling that we're pretty good friends."

"I hope so," I said, with a jump of the heart as he said it.

"And for a friend I'll do a good many things and let him take a lot of liberties."

"You're as open-minded as anyone I've ever known," I said in all honesty. Mind you, all the time he was watching me with that drilling look of his.

"Never mind all of that," he said. "Because I'm coming to an ugly thing now. I say I'm willing to take a good deal from a friend, but there's one subject on which I'll take nothing. There's one subject where I'm a blind bull . . . and perfectly unreasonable. Do you guess what I'm driving at?"

I blinked at him; I was really awed, because I could see that he was quivering with emotion.

"Come out with it," I begged him.

"It's the girl," he whispered. "It's Jenny Langhorne, Sherburn, that I'm talking about."

CHAPTER TWENTY-FIVE

The news of a $265,000 robbery was nothing compared with the shock of that last remark. I blinked at big Gresham and told myself that it could not be true. And then I hunted through my mind for an answer. There was no answer—only amazement that this glorious, handsome, strong man could fear any rival when it came to affairs of the heart. Above all, that he could be jealous of my ugly face simply made my brain numb, and I lay there in the bed, vaguely trying to right myself.

At last I said: "Gresham, you sound serious enough. Are you?"

"As serious as the very devil," he barked.

"Do you think," I asked him, "that I've been slandering you to the girl?"

He had bowed his head a moment before, thoughtfully, and now he lifted his eyes without raising his head and gave me through the shadows of his brows a piercing glance. There was a suggestion of cold malice in that look of his that unsettled me more than anything else during that strange visit of his. If it had been from any other man, I should have said that that look was filled with evil. But one could not very well associate big Gresham and actual evil, as you will have guessed.

He started up from the bed and began to walk back and forth across the room. "I don't accuse you of that at all," he said.

"And what do you accuse me of?"

"Of being in love with Jenny Langhorne," he said sullenly.

Yes, like a dogged schoolboy, knowing that he is wrong, but persisting stubbornly in his error. "Suppose that I am," I said. "How the devil can a man keep himself from loving or not loving a girl?"

"I'm not reasonable," said Gresham, flushing heavily. "And I know that I'm not reasonable."

"Why, man," I said, "the whole town and the whole country and nine out of every ten men who have seen Jenny have been in love with her. Isn't that true?"

He nodded.

"And did you talk to each of them as you're talking to me?"

He said after a thoughtful pause: "Since I was first in Amityville . . . and that's five years ago . . . I've had four out-and-out gunfights, aside from a few brawls in which I had to use a gun."

"Only four?"

"Only four. And they were all on account of one reason . . . Jenny! The first was when she was only sixteen years old. That made no difference. You might say that I was old enough to be her father. But that did not bother me. When I saw her the first time, I knew that this was the woman that I wanted to have for my wife. And I have never changed my mind. And all through these latter years, my friend, Sherburn, I've kept my eye on her. I tell you these things because I don't want to lose you. You understand? I open my heart to you and let you read what is inside it."

Certainly it was very frank talk. Only a strong man has the courage to let others see what he is made of in this manner. I nodded at him. I was listening with all my mind. I was trying to read and to digest this new Peter Gresham as fast as he was revealed to me.

"The first fellow," said Gresham, "was a flashy-looking boy of twenty-two or -three. He had made a name for himself. Down in Mexico he had sat down on a ledge of silver ore . . . sat down on it without knowing what it was, you see. He stood up again with a loose chunk of the ore in his hand, and, when he brought it into town, he found that he had a fortune. Well, he scooped in the fortune and started spending it. He got into so much trouble south of the border that he came north, shooting over his shoulder, as you might say. It was told about Amityville that that boy had dropped three men on the same evening that he swam his horse across the Río Grande. I tell you this to give you an idea about him. Well, he was a handsome blade of the supple sort . . . he talked well and smiled well and danced well. He could look fashionable and well-turned-out in a pair of overalls and a bandanna with an old felt hat to top him off. And he turned the head of Jenny . . . or, at least, I thought that he was turning her head.

"We met in the hollow outside of town and there we passed words back and forth. The next time I left Amityville, I carried a gun and I needed it. That young buckaroo . . . Duds Cochrane was his name . . . shot as straight as a string and as fast as a rattler striking for dinner. He put a bullet through the crown of my old felt hat just as I sank a bullet through his midriff. And we buried poor Duds that night.

"Jenny didn't grieve for him, so far as I could make out. But then, you never can tell about that girl. She's so open and so free and easy that you never know whether her frankness is pretense or real. She's deep . . . oh, very deep. Deep enough to drown horse and man, I tell you."

It was a bit too much for me, that very big description of a not very big girl. I was willing enough to call Jenny the finest person in the world, and all that, but I thought that big Gresham was piling it on a little. Not consciously piling it on, though; I could see that he was hypnotized. There was a quaver in his voice. There was a bit of wildness in his eye. And he had a longer, lighter, silent step as he ranged up and down through the room.

As I lay there, watching him and turning my eyes back and forth in pursuit of him, I decided that he was right. He would be dangerous as the very devil if he decided that I was encroaching too much on the time and the attention of Jenny Langhorne. I began to see the one flaw in the perfect man—the fly in the ointment, you might say—the crack in the mirror.

"The second fellow didn't come along for about a year and a half. Jenny was bothered by a regular whirl of young blades in the meantime, because, of course, at that age she was a flower full of fragrance and the scent of her filled this hollow and poured over the mountains and blew through all the wild gulches over yonder, and men came down to look at Jenny and wonder at her. But mostly it was a whirl of the boys . . . Bill and Jerry and Joe and John . . . they each danced with her in turn. And I kept my eye on them and saw that there was no harm in it.

"But presently there was a bird of another color in the field. Sam Darnley came to town. He was as stately as Duds was graceful. He was the strong, silent, older type . . . close to forty. Crooked as a snake, hypocritical as the devil. I followed his back trail and found out a lot about him. But Jenny took him seriously. There's a time like that that's apt to come in the life of a very young girl. She likes men older than her father. Well, it was that way with Jenny. She was upside down about this fellow.

"So I took old Samuel Darnley out and told him part of his history. He put up his right hand, swearing that what I had heard was not true, but, as he brought his right hand past his throat, he hooked the thumb under a little horsehair lariat that girdled his neck beneath the loose-fitting collar of his shirt. He whipped out a little Derringer and gave me a barrel of it before

I could more than move a hand. However, he fired so fast and with his hand so high that he didn't have very good direction. The bullet brought a drop of blood at the edge of my left ear. And then I planted a bullet in the pit of his stomach and watched him fold up like a dead frog.

"That was the end of Sam Darnley. And, after that, a little whisper went around that the fellows who paid a lot of attention to pretty young Jenny Langhorne died after a while. People even connected me with the killings.

"And Jenny wasn't bothered by much special attention for another ten or twelve months until the Montana gun buster and horsebreaker, Chet Ormond, came piling down here to make himself famous. He came into the saloon, here, and stated what he had come for. He intended to take the prettiest girl in the valley back under his arm, and he intended to lick the nearest thing to a man that he could find in Texas, where he had heard there were nothing but poor imitations of real men.

"I was in the barroom and listened to everything he said, but I let him go on his way while he looked over the girls and settled on Dolores Oñate, at first . . . but when he changed to Jenny, that was different."

"Would she have anything to do with a rough like that?" I asked him.

"She's willing to look at any man. She never makes up her mind on appearances. And what she likes most of all is strength . . . strength . . . strength. She still has a little regard for me because she knows that I *am* strong. And that was why she liked Ormond. Simply because his voice was so loud and his manners so rough. She thought that there might be some corresponding strength in the heart of that man. When I saw that things were coming to that pass, I took Ormond aside and told him that he hadn't yet found a man to his liking but that I would like to apply for the examination.

"He had a very high way about him, and he was a cruel devil, too. He told me how he was going to kill me and drag me by one leg back into Amityville. I listened to that for a time, and then slapped him. Book stuff, you know. It brought his gun out of his holster, but I was a little too hot to enjoy gunfighting. So I closed with Ormond and took his gun away from him . . . and . . . and I'm ashamed to tell you the rest of it."

"You didn't kill him while he was a disarmed man . . . not with his own gun?'

"Not with his own gun. No. I didn't kill him with any gun at all . . . or even with a knife, you see. And that was the horrible part of it."

I looked at his big hands and shuddered. I could understand, of course. There was strength enough in those fingers of his to have done Homeric things.

"The last one was Lewis Marcand," said big Gresham. "He was a Canadian, I think. He had a queer, pleasant dialect, and a laugh that was good to hear. He was well-educated. He spoke three other languages better than he did English. He had money behind him, too. That man was a good deal of a gentleman. He met Jenny . . . went mad about her, and then it seemed to me that she was not altogether level-headed about him.

"So I met up with poor Marcand. He understood at once. He told me that he was not familiar with guns. But he would be very happy to finish this argument with anything that had an edge. So we did our talking with knives. And I buried Marcand with my own hands among the rocks. And this, Sherburn, brings us down to you."

Chapter Twenty-Six

He was so excited that I almost expected him to take me by the throat and bash out my brains with a stroke of his other hand. Not noisily excited, but his eyes were burning in a way that made my flesh crawl.

"I've seen her twice, I think," I said. Yes, I was almost tempted to crawl out of the thing, if there was a loophole for me—that is how frightened I was.

"And after the second time she knew you well enough to write letters to you?" Gresham responded sneeringly.

How the devil could he have known that? But I tell you, I was not thinking of logic then—I was thinking of my life. Peter Gresham, so cool and debonair in other places—was really more than half unbalanced as he stopped his pacing and stood over me. And he fixed his eyes on the little pile of gray ashes on the saucer beside the bed, where I had burned the letter. I knew, then, what he meant by that glance. He connected the burning of the letter with the girl, and he was raging inside ever since he had come into the room—raging and burning with jealousy, though he had controlled himself all of this time. You can imagine that this did not make me any more at ease. But I knew that it was going to be a complete waste of time if I attempted to explain myself to him. I did not attempt an explanation.

"She wrote me a letter," I told him.

"And about what, if you please?" asked Gresham.

I could hardly believe my ears. Here was my fine gentleman

actually demanding of me what a girl had said in a letter to me. He saw the change in my expression.

"You don't like that, Sherburn. I see that you don't like that. And why not?"

I leaned back on the pillow and closed my eyes, trying to think. When I opened them, to my unspeakable horror, Gresham was leaning above me with a livid face and with his fingers mere inches from my throat.

"You lying dog . . . you sneaking dog," said Gresham.

I was in a pure panic, of course. Imagine your brother or your father going insane and threatening your life. No, it was worse than that, because my belief in Gresham was founded as deep as the roots of the mountains, upon living rock.

If I stirred a hand to escape, I was certain that his big hand would make my windpipe crackle like dead grass. I simply looked him in the eye with an effort that drained most of my strength and I said to him: "Gresham, you are talking like a coward and a cur."

You know how it is—fire to fight fire? Well, that was what I had tried on him, and as a matter of fact, when I snapped out that insult, it brought him back to himself like a dash of cold water in the face.

He stiffened and stood straight, and then he began to go back across the room with heavy steps—very much like the baffled villain in a melodrama. Frightened as I was, I remember being a little bit amused by that comparison.

He kept saying: "Curse it all, I've played the fool. I've slipped away again." He brought up back by the window presently. He said: "I've been giving you a rough time, Sherburn, old fellow."

They say that one should never antagonize a madman. And I certainly looked upon Gresham as temporarily insane, to say the least, but nevertheless, when he gave me a little clearance, I made one reach and brought up a Colt in each hand.

Gresham smiled in a sort of sick way at me. "There's no use doing that," he said. "I've recovered. The poison is out of my head, partner."

"Good," I said. "But the poison is still in mine. And if you try to get those big hands of yours as near me as that again . . . I'll let the light through you, Gresham. On my honor I shall."

Will you believe that in spite of two big guns looking him in the eye he could have the nerve to turn away and begin to pace up and down the room again with his swinging step? He was talking about her again. She obsessed him. I've never seen anything like it. It wasn't like mere love. It was rather an appetite sharpened by famine. He had dreamed about her for so long that the mere thought of her threw him into a mental fever. So I threw into his way an idea, as a sort of cake to Cerberus, as they say.

"Gresham, before you turn yourself into a complete fool, will you kindly look the facts in the face? In the first place, you're a madman on that subject. Otherwise, you would never have murdered four men on account of that girl."

His face was even more sad than excited now, as he turned back toward me. "Do you know the only reason that she really puts a value on me?" he said.

"I know," I said. "Because she sees a big, good-looking, husky fellow, with a clean reputation, a good income, and so forth. That's why she puts a value on you."

"You talk like a perfect child, poor Sherburn," he said. "Let me tell you that the only reason she values me is because she knows in her heart of hearts that I did kill those four lovers of hers. She knows it, and she likes me because I was strong enough to do that little thing."

"Peter, you *are* mad on this subject . . . completely mad."

"Do you think so?"

"Don't smile at me. It's not a smile that you need, but a doctor to listen to you rave."

"I don't know why I'm telling you the truth about her," he said, "but you may as well know. Why, man, do you think that I haven't dodged this truth about her? But the facts have been drifting in on me steadily, and I can't avoid them any longer. I know and you may as well know, also. What she worships is sheer power. And because I have power, she'll think fondly of me."

"In the first place," I came back at him, "she can't have known that you got rid of those four men."

"Ask the whole town. Everybody knows it. They were fair fights. Amityville knows all about the four fights."

"Man, she'd have nothing but horror for you."

"Does she seem to?" he asked me with a curious sharpness.

"We haven't talked about you," I told him truthfully.

And his brows lifted. No matter what I had to say, so long as that girl was the theme of it, he was bound to be suspicious still.

"Very well," said Gresham. "Very well."

But it was not very well. It was very bad. I wanted exceedingly to get out of that room or anywhere away from him. I was afraid. For the first time in my life I was afraid of a single man—even with a gun in my hand and with none in his.

"It's true," he began to mutter to himself, nodding. Then he added, as much to himself as to me: "It's because you're her own kind. That's the reason."

"Gresham," I said, "you're not only a little crazy, but you're mighty foolish. If I had any ideas about her, you're giving them the first encouragement that they've had."

"Have I put the ideas in your head for the first time?" he mocked me, smiling without mirth. "Oh, well, I think not."

"And as for me being the same kind that she is . . . have you really gone stone blind?"

"What are looks?" he said. "Nothing! The inside of you is a good deal the same and that's what counts most. She has no frills. Neither have you. She's rough and ready. So are you. She's honest. And I think that you're honest, too. And I? What am I?" He threw up his hands and looked at me in a sort of agony.

It was mighty unpleasant. It was almost worse than having him threaten me. He—Peter Gresham—the king of Amityville—the man who didn't need to wear a gun—not honest? It started me sweating, because I didn't dare think what he meant. And the grisly conclusion was forced on me that my first guess had been horribly right, after all. He *was* a little off in the brain on that day.

Then he paused in his pacing, and, glowering down at me, said: "Will you tell me the truth, Sherburn. Do you want her?"

"I'll tell you the truth," I said. "I'm not blind. I can see that she's worth having. Yes . . . I want her."

He blinked and then heaved a sigh. "Good," he said. "It's better for us to be out in the open. And I'm glad to know that I've been guessing right."

"Guessing?" I said with an ironical smile.

"You're right," he confessed with a queer frankness. "I had you watched, because I knew from the moment of our first meeting that you were worth watching."

"Was it Doc?" I asked savagely.

He shrugged his shoulders. "I won't answer that question, of course. If you have any suspicions, you'll have to work them out for yourself. But, man, did you think that I could leave a stranger in charge of the hotel without keeping some sort of a guard on him?"

It was a hard blow to me. Here I had gone along, telling myself that this hero of mine, this demigod, this big Peter Gresham, had had the sense to see that, in spite of all the evil in me, there was the core of an honest man to my soul. I had felt better toward the whole world, human nature, and myself included, because I had that idea of Gresham. And now it seemed that he had only *seemed* to leave me in freedom. In reality, his hand was on the rope all the time, and I was simply staked out, though I hadn't yet felt the end of my tether.

"I'm sorry to hear it," I confessed. "It makes me sort of sick, Gresham. And I think that we'd better call this a day's talk. I've had enough. Do you want me to pack my belongings and leave now?"

He turned his back on me and leaned at the window, and I saw that he was breathing hard. "She might think that I've sent you away," he said. "She might think that I've taken advantage of you."

"Man," I yelled at him, "you talk as if I were engaged to her!"

He merely shook his head. "Stay on here and work it out with me," he said. "I think that we may be able to come to the right conclusion without any real trouble. Will you stay on?"

I saw here, at least, that I had an excellent chance to break away from him with a good pretense—and excellent chance to leave him and ride to Cricket Valley—to Red Hawk, and to devil knows what else.

"I'll think it over today," I told him. "But I suppose that the best thing would be for me to get out and stay out."

"With her behind you?" said Gresham. "You'd never stay away."

Chapter Twenty-Seven

Well, I went out to think it over, at least. And there was so much to think over that I could have used a month as well as a day. I got a mean-mouthed pinto with a Roman nose, and a Roman-nosed desire to do everything except what I wanted. That gave me a chance to work out some of my meanness. By the time he had bucked through the town and back again and then raced away for the dead hills, I hardly knew in what direction I was riding, except that I was glad that I was away from Amityville.

When the dizziness that the long bucking had caused had cleared away a little, I was on the edge of a little valley—over the rim of the hill behind me, was Amityville, looking white and pretty in the hollow. So I dismounted and threw the reins—that mean-tempered fool had been well trained in that respect, at least—and I sat down in the shade of a tree and unlimbered a gun, for the lack of anything better to do.

Most people think better when they have their hands occupied. At least, I do. And there's nothing so satisfying in the fingers as the handles of a familiar old Colt, a little rubbed and thumb-worn. There was a black chunk of rock weighing ten pounds or so down the slope. I began to kick it down the slope with bullets, just shaving the top edge of the stone each time, and tipping it over like a bale of hay. And that went on until I had emptied both guns and then loaded them again. When I got through with that, I started in again with my new loadings.

However, that old stone had been getting a pretty good hammering, and my thirteenth shot, being aimed a little too low, caught the rock fairly in the stomach, as you might say, and made her fall apart in chunks.

I cussed a little under my breath. I was mighty glad that I hadn't cussed out loud, because just then a voice sang out behind me: "Thirteen is the lucky number for you, maybe."

I turned around and I saw that it was nobody in the whole wide world except the face that I wanted the most to see, and that was Jenny Langhorne, with her freckled nose wrinkling as she grinned down at me. She was a queer sort. She could grin like a man and she could smile like a woman. Mostly she grinned like a man.

I said: "I didn't aim to bust that rock."

"You did more than you aimed for, then," she said. "Is this where you practice up?"

"Ma'am," I said, "it's not. I'm up here trying to think."

"That's a bad habit," said Jenny Langhorne. "I've given up thinking a long time ago, John."

"Why?" I asked.

"Because it never works out," she said. "You always start thinking that you want to find out what's right. But you only end up with wanting harder than ever what's pleasant. So the first guess is about as good as the tenth, I suppose. They're all guesses, anyway." She sent her pony down the slope and then twisted around in the saddle and dropped her elbow on the pommel of the saddle and her chin in the palm of her hand. "You look glum," she said.

"I am glum," I answered.

"Have you been in a fight?" she said.

"No," I said.

"Not since yesterday?"

"I dunno what you mean."

"Oh, I've seen Oliver Clement."

I gasped.

"I went over to see how his foot was. But I found out that there was a sore spot under his chin."

"Well . . . ," I began, and stopped, having turned a brick red.

"But how," said Jenny, "do you make fellows like you after you've thrashed them?"

"I didn't thrash him," I said. "I . . . got in a lucky punch. . . ." Not that I was modest, but I wanted to turn the talk in another direction.

"He told me how lucky it was," Jenny said, and she grinned again.

"How much did he tell you?" I asked her in a good deal of alarm. And in my heart I was cursing that young fool with all my might. Why do men have to talk to women except in courtrooms?

"Only about how he fell . . . asleep," she said. And she added quickly: "How much else was there to tell?"

"Nothing," I said. "Of course, nothing else."

"Of course," she said, and still she grinned.

She went on: "I was sorry that you didn't think more of my advice. And that you didn't pay any attention to my letter."

I shrugged my shoulders. I felt that I was cornered. But I still remembered that old Frenchman's advice: *Never explain. Your friends don't need explanations and your enemies won't believe you, anyway.* Or at least, it went something like that. So I didn't try to explain this time.

I shrugged my shoulders, as I was saying, and I was hunting through my mind for something that would make pleasanter conversation, when Jenny Langhorne said quietly: "I know how you tried to dodge the trouble. And that's particularly why I wanted to see you and thank you. Oliver says that you tried with all your might to keep him from making a fool of himself and that you almost succeeded."

But had he told her about my proposed trip up Cricket Valley? That was the main thing, of course, and since he had chattered so much, it seemed quite likely that there was no place at which he had stopped. But she said nothing more about the interview I had had with Clement, and then I saw that he was a good deal more of a man than I had suspected. He had told her all that part of the scene that was to his disadvantage, but he had not said a word about how he had me helpless under the nose of his gun, or how he spared me then, and particularly he had not alarmed her with any story of Cricket Valley and the wild bargain that I had proposed to him—and then lost for my pains. All that he had talked about had been very complimentary to me, and particularly she said that he wanted to see me at once, or as soon as possible, so that he could dissuade me from a plan I had in mind.

"But he didn't tell me what the plan might be," said the girl.

She was a curious imp. There was no doubt that she was hinting that I might be a little more open in my talk, but I saw that here was an excellent opportunity for me to drive an entering wedge. If I went up Cricket Valley, there was probably small chance that I should come back.

I said: "Clement wants me to stay on in Amityville. That's what he wants to persuade me to change my mind about."

I could not help watching her closely as I said that, and I was rewarded mightily by seeing that her face had darkened when she heard me.

"You're going, too?" repeated Jenny Langhorne, and she looked gloomily straight before her, and over my head, and into the pale blueness of that Western sky where there are so rarely any clouds.

"I'm going," I said.

"Have you had trouble? Or are you simply tired of all the

fighting?" she went on.

What I said after that I've often regretted. But at the time I couldn't help it. "It's trouble with a friend of mine," I said. "I've seen too much of the girl he wants to marry." And there it was. I could have bitten my tongue out for saying that, the moment the words were in the air. But regrets are useless things, as you all know.

I suppose that almost any other girl would have passed over a remark like that. But Jenny Langhorne never allowed talk to be composed of hints and innuendos. She pinned words down and fastened them to facts. And though her color had heightened a little, she looked straight at me.

"You'd better not leave that up in the air," said Jenny. "Will you tell me what you mean?"

"I mean you," I said. "And my friend is Pete Gresham."

"I guessed that he was behind it," she answered me rather bitterly. "So he's driving you out?"

"I'm driving myself," I corrected her hastily. "I'm not afraid. But I have no right to make myself miserable for nothing."

"I don't understand," said Jenny. "Peter tells you that you mustn't see me . . . that you've seen too much of me already. . . ."

"No," I said. "I tell myself that I've seen too much of you." There, you see, the whole cat was out of the bag. I suppose that no one ever took such a clumsy, roundabout, stupid way of telling a girl that he loved her as I had taken with Jenny Langhorne. I hardly dared to look at her, I was so ashamed of my thick-fingered methods. And the color washed in a flame into her face. I couldn't tell whether it was scorn or some other emotion. I waited for lightning to strike.

Well, she straightened suddenly in the saddle, and I saw her spur sink wickedly deep in the flank of her horse. That stab of the steel points made the little mustang bolt to the top of the hill in a few leaps. There she brought him up on the curb with a strength that would have taxed the wrist of many a man. And sitting there against the sky, she turned a little toward me again.

"Has Peter Gresham the right to run my life . . . just because he *claims* to be the boss?" asked Jenny Langhorne. And with that, she was gone from my sight over the brow of the hill.

I was into my saddle in an instant and over that same hill in pursuit of her. Already the rocks were rattling down the slope behind her, and she was cutting across the face of the hill leaving a twisting little trail of dust that soon melted out of the air. I gave that pinto his head in front and the full benefit of the spurs behind. He had bucked the bad temper out of himself that morning, and yet there was still enough devil in him to give him strength, and he ran as if he had eagle wings buoying him along.

Jenny Langhorne was jockeying her bay mare into a good stiff gait, leaning over the pommel to throw the weight forward, where a horse wants it when it is on the run, but the pinto was gaining in spite of my weight in the saddle. I thought better of the little mustang from that minute. For I had known, before, that he was tough, but I never had guessed that he had so much foot.

However, I saw as I came to the back of the next ridge that he had not foot enough. Jenny Langhorne was heading homeward, and the bridle path went toward her ranch with very few windings—only one sagging loop to avoid the cliff-like descent that was now just before me. That descent was the one thing that could get me to the girl now, however. And I decided that I must see her immediately. Something told me that, if I did not get to her now, I was throwing away such an opportunity as would not come to me again.

It was a wicked descent, that cliff. But I paid very little heed to that. I was so hot on the trail, so blind with the love of Jenny, so keen with the chase, that, when I saw my course before me, I gave the pinto the spurs again—I gave him the whole cruel benefit of them and the stabbing pain thrust him over the edge of the cliff with a squeal of agony and of fear.

I should not say cliff, of course. But it was mighty close to one. It was a slide pretty close to straight up and down, and it was faced with a hard sand and clay mixed—as fast to slide down as though it were greased. Here and there was a stretch of slate-type rock that roughed up the surface, however, and I depended upon those rougher places to ease up the velocity with which I skidded along.

However, thc instant the pinto began to shoot down the face of that bluff, I saw what I was in for. I would have thrown myself out of the saddle, if I had had time. But I didn't have time to more than bat out one oath. We covered the first half of that drop with a whoop and a clatter, but, when we hit the streak of slate rock, I figured on the shod hoofs of the pinto really saving us. No, that confounded rock was no stronger than soap. It gave way at the first thrust of his hoofs, and, after a single wavering delay, we shot off again toward the bottom.

I knew what a bird felt like when it tumbled out of the head of the sky with a broken wing. There was a whir—a crash—the pinto turned on his side—and then I scooted into darkness, set around with shooting stars and sparks, and one flaming, flaring comet across the heavens. No, that was the sharp sound of a human voice—a woman's scream off there in that distance. I came to myself, and staggered around on loose knees that sagged at every step. I was saying: "Where's the poor pinto? Did I break his neck? Steady, boy."

Something rushed up to me. It looked like a whole troop of girls.

I said to the troop: "Get the pinto . . . where is he? What turned everything so dark?"

The troop said with a single voice: "You terrible idiot. Have you killed yourself?"

But the voice was that of Jenny, and the sound of it dissolved my stupor and let me see that the many girls made only one, after all. One Jenny, and a powerful comforting sight she was to me. She was as white as the back of the hand of a man that always wears gloves. And she had to make the motions two or three times before the words came.

"John," she said, "did your horse slip . . . at the top . . . of that frightful slide?"

"It was my only chance to get to you before you reached home," I explained, "and so, of course, I had to take the chance. Where's the pinto?"

Then I saw him. Dead? Not at all. There was the pinto as calmly as you please, cropping the dead bunch grass of the last year that grew on the north side of a big rock. And if his side was a good deal skinned and scratched, where he had caromed along the bosom of that mountain, it made no difference to the appetite of the pinto.

From the corner of his eye he watched me with a devilish interest and one flattened ear said to me: "Come and catch me if you can."

I didn't try. I knew that look before. I had seen it in too many of the distant cousins of the pinto.

"In the name of all good sense," said Jenny Langhorne sternly, "what brought you after me at all?"

"I don't know," I said. "But what made you run away?"

"Ridiculous," said Jenny with a delightful smile. "I didn't run away at all."

"Well," I said, "I'm too polite to call you a liar, but I hope that you can read my mind."

"You have a terrible black eye," said Jenny, "and your shoulder is bleeding. Come home with me this minute. Wait till I catch your horse for you . . . can you walk?"

"If you're going to catch the pinto," I said, "I'll wait for you."

She gave me a side glance that told me that she understood, but she sailed after the pinto, just the same. He let her come within a step and a half, and then he turned himself into a grasshopper and dropped out of the air forty feet away and stood there with his head high and his tail flaunting, and that happy look that a horse wears when it is making a fool out of a human.

"Your horse is an idiot!" cried Jenny.

"It's just his way," I said, delighted. "Try him again."

"I never heard of such a poorly trained horse," said Jenny with much point, and, with that, she marched straight up to that mustang, and, confound me, if he didn't stand and let her take it by the reins.

"But you see," gloated Jenny as she came back, "how quickly he responds to intelligent treatment."

I was too amazed to make any response. Besides, I was mighty glad to go out to the Langhorne Ranch again so soon.

But when we got to riding along, side-by-side, I began to watch Jenny. She was staring straight before her. And her face was a mask. I said suddenly: "I remember now why I had to try to catch you."

"It's of no importance," said Jenny coldly.

"I had to catch you before you got to the ranch because . . . I had to tell you something."

"Did you?" said Jenny without interest. "What might it be, if you please?"

"I don't know, exactly," I said, growing a little more abashed. "Perhaps it has been rattled out of my head."

"Oh," said Jenny.

But she lifted her head, and, as she rode on, I saw on her face a beautifully foolish expression of happiness. It sent an echo of the same emotion through me, of course. But I did not dare to say a word for fear I would break the charm of the spell under which we were riding.

I blessed the pinto, I blessed the steepness of that mountain-side, and I only wished that it had been twice as long. I felt that I had come tremendously near to Jenny's inner self. And it gave me a giddiness, like standing on the top of a mountain.

Chapter Twenty-Eight

When darkness closed upon that day, I had not accomplished much that could be reproduced in actual words. I had done nothing, you might say, that could be defined. But I felt that I had crossed a desert and climbed a mountain range and come within sight of a promised land. Yes, I had actually entered upon the borders of it.

Jenny said nothing, did nothing. But there was a change about her just as real as the change between the summer desert and the desert of the spring. Something like a delicate fragrance passed from her and made a sweetness in the air about her and kept my heart tumbling up and down like a boat at anchor in a heavy sea.

The scratch in my shoulder turned out to be deep enough to make Jenny say oh! and ah! in such a manner as she was dressing it, that I almost wished I had had an arm torn off in that most blessed fall. But afterward, as the day came toward its end, I saw that I should have to leave.

I climbed onto the back of the honest pinto and waved to Jenny Langhorne and rode back across the desert toward Amityville, swearing to myself that the mustang should never lack a home and a good one to the end of his days—because he had done a great and a good work for me. If he had kept on his hoofs and brought me actually in front of Jenny, she would probably have laughed in my face if I had grown sentimental.

And then, as I rode slowly along through the spring-colored

valleys, and through the faint perfume of the flowers that filled me with a faint sadness, like the thought of Jenny herself, I remembered the ugly things that Gresham had said about her, and about her liking for strength, her cruel and unfeminine love of power, whether in herself or in others.

It was a depressing thought, of course, for I could see that the reason my lady might have looked on me with a little more favor on this day was because I had managed that absurd and foolish affair of tumbling down the face of a bluff for the sake of getting close enough to speak to her. I suppose, in a way, it was a sufficient proof of devotion.

I paused under the edge of that descent on my way back to Amityville and in the dusk of the day the slope seemed indeed almost sheer, with a ragged black head pressed up against the sky, and I wondered with all my heart how I could ever have managed to come down that slope without breaking every bone in my body. Yes, it was little wonder that Jenny Langhorne was impressed, and only the wildest giddiness of heart could have made me attempt such a thing. So I continued my ride.

I was beginning to have a feeling something like homesickness in this part of the country. Everything seemed to be strange and wrong. The men were certainly different from any other men that I had ever known, and the Lord knew that this girl was not what other girls had been in my life.

I came back to Amityville in such a topsy-turvy state of mind that I struck in through a back street instead of the main highway. Then, as I passed Billy Marvin's eating house, I had a sudden horror of getting inside of the hotel again—a dread of having to continue the odd part that I had been playing there—and a greater dread of seeing Gresham again, whether it were to explain that I was going or staying.

So I stopped at Billy's and had my supper there, sat a long time over the table, and found that it was 10:00 P.M. before I was ready to start on. A boy had taken the pinto on, sometime before, and put him in the Gresham stable.

And all of these unusual things had happened one on top of the other; had they not come together, I should have never approached the hotel from the rear at that hour; I should, as usual, have gone to the front of the building and entered, and been in the gaming room three minutes after I arrived, wearing my usual lugubrious look and acting the part of the hard-drinking bully. Instead, there I was standing at the rear wall of the hotel and fitting the key into the lock of the gate.

I have to explain, first, that when Gresham built the hotel, he had arranged for one private, cool, shadowy place for himself, and that was a space of ground at the rear of the building, which he surrounded with a thick ten-foot adobe wall, with a little red-tiled crest against the rains on top. He had a pair of big-limbed fig trees planted in that spot, and a patch of shaven lawn, and a little fountain that used to bubble defiance at the hot evenings. Altogether, it was the one cheerful place in Amityville in the heat of the summer.

When he gave the hotel into my management, in that odd partnership that we had arranged, he had given me, among all the other keys, the one to the inner and outer door of his garden, but for some reason I had never used either of them, and had left that private place of his still sacred to its owner. However, on this night I did not want to pass many faces in review. I wanted to be alone and entirely free from the inspections of other eyes. And so I remembered, suddenly, that rear passageway through which I could get to the back staircase of the hotel and so up to my room unseen by anyone.

A sandstorm had been looming throughout the last half of the day. The northern horizon had been covered with a muddy mist, the air was still and hot, and, as I left Bill's eating room, I felt a sudden stir in the air, and heard a queer hushing sound far away. As I stood in front of the garden door to Gresham's hotel, the storm struck Amityville like a clapped hand.

I heard shutters crackling to, and I heard doors slamming like cannon reports. That was in the distance down the street—and then the first hot gust of wind sluiced down that alleyway, turned the corner to my left, and poured roaring about me.

Not, however, with a great load of sand and of dust, as yet. That was drummed up in the heart of the storm, which would come later. There was only a level-driving silt that whipped down to the bottom of one's lung if one so much as drew a breath without turning one's head away from the air current.

I was forced away from the door, for a moment, by the river-like thrust of the air. But I fumbled back to it, fitted the key into the lock with difficulty, and opened the door. I stepped inside and closed the door behind me and was about to relock it, when I saw a shadow moving in the garden near me. I can tell you that, if I had seen that shadow when I first opened the door of the garden, I should have jumped back for the street and run for it. But there was no way to run with speed, now that the heavy door was closed behind me.

I stared again. There was no doubt about it. There was a big double window on the second floor that threw out a considerable glow even in spite of its drawn curtains—always drawn, because it was one of the gaming rooms. The rapidly darkening flight of sand had diminished the glow of those windows to a pale thing, indeed, but against that ghost of light I saw a form stirring in the gloom of the storm—the dimmest outline of the form of a man doing what looked like a slow scarecrow's dance, with long and lanky, flopping arms.

Of course, I was fascinated. Twice I gathered my voice and my courage to call out, and twice I decided that it was better to leave the possibility of unworldly things to themselves and content myself with the earth and things of the earth.

Presently the dance stopped. The figure seemed to fall into the earth. No, I could see it now huddled close to the ground, as though upon its knees. And after that, it stood up and moved toward the house. I wondered how a ghost would melt into a solid wall, but an instant later I saw, by a faint glow of light from the interior of the house, that the back door of the hotel had been opened—the little garden door to which no one in the world possessed the key except big Gresham and I.

That was a staggering blow, you may well believe. And most of all, you may believe that I was flabbergasted when I made out that against the faint light from the inside of the building I could decipher the bulky outlines of Gresham himself. I was astonished because Gresham was not the sort of a man to expose himself needlessly to dirt and inconvenience—such as was implied by remaining extra moments in the midst of a sweeping sandstorm—and performing, in the meantime, an odd, slow dance.

It was very baffling, of course. I waded forward through the heavy-handed pressure of the wind and stood on what I thought was about the spot where I had seen the silhouette—was it Gresham's?—dancing. And there I kneeled and felt about me. I found something at once. It was a patch of soft dirt about two feet across, thinly sifted over with wind-sieved dirt. The explanation of the slow floppings of the arms and the bendings of the body as though in a queer dance was obvious at once. Gresham—or someone else—had been out there simply digging in the garden—a most ordinary matter. Ordinary—yes. Except at night. And most of all, except at night during a sandstorm. Gresham above all who, in spite of his ability to withstand desert hardships, hated nothing in this world so much as small inconveniences such as sore eyes and dirt down the back. But here had been Gresham swiftly and patiently doing such manual labor in his little garden.

I guessed at once that it had been no ordinary task. I started digging, in my turn. The ground had been stamped down a little, but it gave readily to my fingers. I scooped out a narrow hole almost as deep as my arm was long, and then, thrusting my hand down as far as I could force it through the soft mold, the tips of my fingers touched upon a coarse cloth, or a canvas.

Perhaps the most honorable and patient man in the world would have set about inquiring, at that moment, who had planted that substance at that distance beneath the ground, and gone to such an expenditure of time and labor to accomplish the matter—but none of those delicate scruples troubled me. I worked busily widening that hole in the garden muck until my prying hand caught hold of the loosely knotted top of a bag. That I gripped and started to draw up, but it slipped from my hand. I freshened my grip on it and tried again, and this time it came up.

I brought it out with a heave and a grunt, then, and dropped it with a sigh of triumph upon the top of the ground—a sigh of triumph that died at once and gave place to a thrill that was almost terror. For, as the canvas bag touched the ground, I heard the most exciting and the most musical of all noises in the world—the light jingle of metal upon metal—many sliding, faintly chiming bits of metal, one against the other.

Of course that bag was open in an instant. I knew the feel of the coins at once. Gold!

Chapter Twenty-Nine

It made me a bit giddy, at first. Then I thrust down my hand again, but I found the bottom of the hole by the hardness of the undug ground. And there was no more sign of buried treasure. After that, I hesitated for an instant as to how I should get that money to a private place and count over the extent of the sum. And I am ashamed to say that, at first, it did not occur to me to call in the sheriff and make over to him my find. However, I suppose that is no more than to say that I was simply human.

There was an easy way up to my room, however. And that was through the same semiprivate door that I had just seen opened by the digger of the shallow pit in which that gold had been buried. And, at this hour of the night, there was very little chance that anyone would be abroad in the upper part of the building, and thus encounter me. Or, if I were encountered, I did not doubt that I could put off the questioner with some gruff answer that told nothing. To find any other remotely safe retreat seemed much beyond me. I thought of every other alternative, but in the end the best thing to me appeared to be to go straight up to my room with my precious burden and there examine it behind a locked door.

That, in fact, was what I did. I unlocked the little back door and through it carried my canvas sack up the stairs and then, as lightly and swiftly as I could, through the halls to my room.

I threw open the door, and then my heart turned over with alarm and with anger. For there was old Doc seated at his ease, turning the pages of an ancient newspaper, much frayed at the edges from repeated handling. For, in those days, newspapers were a luxury—I mean the big metropolitan dailies. And they rarely got into our hands in the West. I have known a prospector to pay 25¢ for the privilege of perusing a newspaper. However, I had no sympathy with Doc at that moment.

I shouted at him: "Is this my room or a public library? Get out of here and leave me in peace, will you?"

Doc rose with a world of dignity. He removed his glasses from his nose and thrust them into a breast pocket of his coat. "Young feller," he said, "I come up here and I been waitin' up here because I got some news for you that would've meant a lot for you, but now I dunno that I see my way clear to tellin' it." And he stalked slowly out of the door, which he closed with an offended slam behind him.

However, I was not inclined to worry about the state of mind of that old loafer on such a night as this. I was at work in a fever on the contents of that bag. I merely paused to glance out the window and make sure that the narrow little balcony that ran past—purely for ornament and not for use—had no one upon it. Then, with the door locked, I felt that I could take my time.

Presently little glistening, yellow piles began to grow upon the table, for it was new-minted gold, fresh from the milling machine, and every $20 gold piece had a face as clear as the man in the moon. It was a separate thrill of pleasure to stack each coin. When all of that money was arrayed, I began the counting. There were fifteen stacks and two coins over in that little golden host—a fortune! Not in these days of diluted prices, perhaps. But $15,000 in the days when prosperous office men were contented with $60 a month—$15,000 in those times meant a lot—four or five times as much as it does now.

I sat in a pleasant trance adding up delicious possibilities. I saw myself leading the life of a retired gentleman. I saw that host of gold pieces laboring silently and earnestly for me, day and night.

Then another thought jumped with electric eagerness into my mind, for I remembered the story that had been told to me by Gresham about the bank robbery. Aye, and I had heard many rumors about it since his telling, for the story was on the lips of everybody. It was the common theme in the eating house where I had dined that night. When the bank at Ludlow was robbed by Red Hawk, over $15,000 in gold coin had been taken from the bank.

All of my exultation at my find left me and was succeeded by a thrill of fear that worked on my skin and drew it like a blast of icy wind. Cold perspiration oozed out. I was clammy with it. For the man who was found with this coin would be identified at once as Red Hawk himself, or as one of his chief lieutenants. And, such was the state of feeling throughout the community, that there was no doubt that the people would not wait for the process of a legal trial. They would arrange a noose for me and hang me up to the nearest tree.

What first ran through my mind was to go down to the garden where I had found the bag and re-deposit it. Because, when it was in its place, there, I could have some opportunity of watching whoever might come to reëxamine that spot. Then I recalled the bigness of him who had put the bag in the ground, and I remembered again that big Peter Gresham alone—outside of myself—had the key to that door. And my heart sank in my boots, Peter Gresham—Red Hawk!

I suppose that I should have dismissed the terrible idea at once, but, as I have said before, Amityville had turned everything upside down for me and I no longer retained my old beliefs and trusts. And that thought still bored in upon me until I remembered the whole history of Peter and how for five years he had been distinguished for his war against the chief, carried on in vengeance for the death of his poor, tortured brother, Leicester Gresham. I thought of this, and my heart was easier again.

The very privacy of that garden was doubtless what had tempted the thief, whoever he might be, to secrete the money there—particularly since, in a garden, newly turned mold is not looked upon with suspicion.

These things were passing through my mind. And suddenly I rose from my chair with a swing to start walking up and down the room and to try to get some better sense into my head. I swung out of my chair suddenly, as I said, and at that instant something plucked me violently by the coat under the pit of the arm, and there was a sharp sound of shorn cloth. I looked down in amazement, and there was a heavy knife hanging from the torn cloth.

I did not stop to ask questions, I got to the window in the split part of a second, with a gun in each hand, and leaned out ready to pump lead. But there was nobody in sight. Not a soul was clambering down toward the street.

I swung myself out through the window and started to climb up to the roof to look for the knife thrower there. But I didn't go far. I thought of $15,000 in gold lying on the table in my room and shouting silently, all the time: *I come from the robbed bank at Ludlow! I am wet with the blood of men!*

Yes, the thought of that exposed money brought me back into my chamber on the double-quick. But, when I sat down, I faced that window and I kept my eyes upon it with a gun balanced on my knee. What was I to do with that infernal white elephant?

And then a heavy knock came at the door to my room.

"Who's there?" I asked in a rather faint voice, I suppose.

"Doc, Mister Sherburn."

"Damn your old hide, what do you want?"

"Gresham wants you . . . not me."

"Gresham? Tell him I'm busy."

Gresham of all people—the tall, honest, saintly Gresham to find me with this mess of rotten gold. And yet he was the only man in the town from whom I could expect mercy.

"Tell Gresham that?" echoed Doc.

"Yes, damn you!"

The footsteps of Doc withdrew. And I sat crouched and miserable, but feeling my mind drawn into a tight knot and knowing that there was no power in me to make that knot loosen. A man cannot force himself to be intelligent. That is the devil of mental work.

And then, slowly up the stairs and slowly along the hall, a calm, measured step, and a quiet rap at the door. It was Gresham—I knew.

I saw, then, that the burden of this money was too great for me. I would have to let Gresham take part of the worry from me. I threw my knife-rent coat over the heap of money. I unlocked the door, and big Peter stood before me.

He was not in a passion because I had refused to come at his message. He merely said: "I want to consult you about that new dealer, Gregory. Do you think that he's . . . ?"

"Damn Gregory!" I gasped as I closed and locked the door behind him. "I've been sitting in this room alone with a murderer on my hands!"

Chapter Thirty

You could say even such a thing as that to big Gresham and never unsettle his nerves. He should have been a doctor. He had the presence and the calm for it. And he merely put his hand on my shoulder and murmured: "Your head is a bit unsettled. I think that this job has been harder on you than you imagine. Now tell me what's troubling you."

It angered me a little. I felt fairly close to the end of my world—what with buried treasure mysteries, a trip to Red Hawk, knives thrown in the dark—I was in a muddle to be sure. And I wanted to unsettle Gresham a little, too—sort of in spite, you know. I snatched my coat from the piles of gold and pointed it out to him.

Will you believe that when he saw it, he merely laughed?

He said: "You *have* been playing in luck, eh? I congratulate you, Sherburn."

But I snarled back: "There's a shade over fifteen thousand dollars in that pile of money!"

He only whistled. "That *is* a haul, Sherburn."

"Confound you!" I shouted. "That's the sum of money that was stolen from the Ludlow Bank!"

Well, that man was a miracle. He merely smiled at me and shook his head. "I suppose you'll be telling me that you are the famous Red Hawk, in a little while?"

I was so irritated that I determined to corner him and shock him if it were possible.

I stabbed an aggressive finger at him and barked: "Gresham, do you know where I got that money?"

He smiled gently at me, as if I were a raving child. "If I had known," he said, "I should have gone to beat you to it, I suppose."

"I'll tell you."

"Thanks."

"In your own garden."

"What?" Gresham smiled. "Under my own fig trees, I suppose?"

"Exactly there!" I cried.

"Hush," said the big man. "You really mustn't talk such nonsense as this, Sherburn. And in such a loud voice. There are other people in the building and some of them have sharp ears."

"I tell you," I whispered, "that I came through the rear door of the garden for a short cut into the house, and, when I came through, the sandstorm was just beginning. And while I stood there, I saw a dim silhouette against a window of the game room in the second story. A silhouette of a man digging. And when he got through digging and went away, I got to the spot and pulled out that canvas bag. There was more than fifteen thousand dollars in it."

"It sounds like a pirate story," said Gresham. "The tail end of a pirate story, I mean. With the hero about to marry the heroine. Which is your heroine, Sherburn?"

He had swung suddenly onto the dangerous theme of thought that I wanted least of all to hear him talk about. And I went on with my story. "There's one more thing that you ought to know, Gresham. The man who buried that money got out of the garden through the only other door . . . the door into the house . . . and he opened it with a key. . . ."

"Impossible," murmured Gresham.

"Why impossible?"

"Because you and I are the only people in the world who have keys to those doors."

"That's it. That *is* the point."

He saw my hinted conclusion at once and he spoke it out with that wonderful, disarming frankness of his. "I understand, Sherburn. Then I am the man who buried all of that loot?"

I could not say that he was. But here I caught him by the arm and cried to him: "It's too much for me, old man! I can't stand it. I've stuck by one thing like a sort of needle of a compass pointing north . . . I've stuck to my idea of you being honest. But the outline of the man in that door . . . against the light inside the house . . . it was a big, burly outline, like yours, Gresham!"

He whistled, and, freeing himself from my hand, he walked up and down the room after his way when he was puzzled.

"A big man. A big man," he repeated again and again. "That upsets all of my ideas. Do you think he was really as tall as I am?"

"I was looking through a yard filled with a driving sandstorm," I confessed.

"That's it!" he cried. "And a sand mist is distorting. Everyone knows that. Still, it could hardly have been a small man?"

"Hardly."

"I had a suspicion, but you've upset it. Confoundedly upset it. As a matter of fact, Sherburn, I came back from the trail with a feeling that I had spotted the right man in Amityville."

"The devil," I gasped at him. "And you thought it was a small man?"

"Yes."

"But everyone agrees that Red Hawk is a big fellow."

"His size depends upon what he has done, I'm afraid. And he has done a good deal. People have had flashes of him, here and there. But that's all. Mostly they've seen him whirl by with his men at night. And have you not noticed that a leader always looks bigger than other men? He's like the bank president, who always stands in the front of the photograph and makes his staff look knee-high by the contrast."

Of course there was a good deal of truth in that. But here Gresham came back to the point at issue with a crash.

"Have you sent for the sheriff?" he asked.

"In order to have him take me to jail?" I asked.

"Bah!" snapped Gresham in disgust. "I hadn't thought of that. But it's true. The first thing he would do would be to land you behind the bars." He suggested almost at once the thought that had first come to me. "Bury it in the place where you found it, and then we'll wait for the thief."

But I shook my head. "Fifteen thousand dollars in one bag is too big a bait . . . the fish might swallow it and get away."

Of course, he saw the point to that, but he did not know of any other alternative and asked me to try to invent one.

I suggested his own safe, at last, and for the first time I had the pleasure of making the big fellow start and change color a little. "It's a great responsibility," I admitted to him. "But what else would be better . . . until we think of some way? Every minute, this fifteen thousand in gold is threatening to put a rope around somebody's neck . . . whoever is found with it."

"Therefore, in my safe . . . ," began big Gresham. Then he broke off with a careless smile: "Of course we'll put it there, if you wish. I'll take it down now, perhaps?"

"And be seen?"

I was horrified at that idea, but he laughed, and presently he had swept the gold into the sack, knotted the top, and picked the burden up. I followed along and grew faint with dread and with excitement when Gresham stopped calmly in the hall to talk for a moment with a pair of cowpunchers who had just come in from the cow range. One of them happened to touch the heavy bag that Gresham carried and there was a noisy, if not musical, jingling in response.

"Hello!" shouted the cowboy. "What's that?"

"Gold," said Gresham calmly, and shook the bag. A shower of golden music came forth. But the two cowpunchers willingly and thoughtlessly broke into laughter. Gresham was simply magnificent.

The man's nerve was as bottomless as a pit. There was no fathoming the extreme limits of his capacity to outface danger and crises of any kind. So much so that, when I had seen him swing back the heavy door of his safe and deposit the bag inside, I could not help saying gravely to him: "Gresham, there's only one thing that baffles me completely, and that's how any Indian that ever lived . . . Red Hawk among the rest . . . could have beaten you off for five years. It doesn't seem possible that you could have failed, if you had put your mind seriously to the work."

He had closed the door to the safe, and the lock had clicked before he straightened and put a hand upon my shoulder. "I wish you could know more about it, Sherburn," he said. "I wish you could know what an oily, slippery devil he is. And now tell me how your nerves are riding?"

I took him back to my room again and showed him the slash under the armpit and told him how it had only been my accidentally sudden movement from the chair that had kept me from receiving the long blade of that same knife between my shoulder blades.

Big Gresham shuddered. "Let me see that tear again," he said. He leaned over it for a long time. Then he put a thumb and forefinger through the cut. "Gad, Sherburn," he said, "that must have been a heavy knife and a strong hand that threw it. See how it tore the cloth as well as pulled it?"

"It almost knocked me off balance," I admitted.

"If the blade had struck your body, I think it would have gone up to the hilt . . . even through bone. Sherburn, I begin to think that you're pretty lucky."

"Lucky to be alive, maybe, but unlucky to be in Amityville."

"Where's the knife?"

"On that chair."

"What chair?" asked Gresham, stepping to the place and moving the chair I had pointed to, to see if the weapon lay in the shadow beneath it.

I ran over to him. Certainly I had put the knife on the chair, and certainly it was gone now.

"Gresham," I gasped at him, "the devil who tried to sink that knife in my back had the grit to come back and steal the knife out of the room."

I had the weird pleasure of seeing even the big man grow excited. So excited that he spoke only in a whisper as he said: "Then depend upon it that you've had a call from Red Hawk in person, because nobody else in the world would have had the courage to come back in here . . . for the sake of a knife. Has he come for that alone?"

"It's enough," I groaned. "Because that knife might have been our clue to his identity!"

Chapter Thirty-One

When I tell you, after this, that I was glad to leave Amityville, I suppose that you'll understand a little more clearly. There was Jenny Langhorne behind me and my heart was filled with her, of course. But on the one hand, there was the agreement that I had made with young Oliver Clement, and on the other hand there was that horror of the old town of Amityville that was growing upon me every day, because I could not tell one honest man in the entire crowd. I had only one rock of surety, and that was Gresham, of whose perfect good faith, of course, I was convinced. But his calm integrity seemed to throw off the honesty of all the others in a blacker shadow by the contrast. Yes, and there was Doc, too. I felt that my old friend from Louisiana was probably as honest as anyone could desire—except, perhaps, in certain small things. He might steal a chicken now and then, but I felt an air of integrity about the old man. Particularly, I suppose, because he came from my own state.

I sat up a little later, that night, filled with my resolution. And I wrote this note:

Dear Gresham:

This is to tell you what I didn't want to say to your face, because it might have led to an argument, and I know that you argue a lot better than I do.

I have to get away from Amityville. I am pretty sure I won't come back. Partly I'm tired of the town. And partly I'm tired of work. I want another sort of a life. I suppose you'll be disappointed in me, but I have to tell you, in the first place, that the only thing that has kept me straight so long as this has been your trust in me.

I wish you all sorts of luck in case you don't see me again. Which you probably won't. Think a notch or two higher of me than any reports you get along the road.

So long.

Sherburn

I sealed that letter in an envelope. It was a lucky hour when I wrote it. I don't want to anticipate the end of this history that I am writing, but I have to say right here that if it had not been for the fact that two constructions could be put upon that letter, I should not now be alive to report what afterward happened.

At any rate, I left that letter behind me, and I slipped out in the cool of the gray light that comes before the morning sun. I got back to the stables at the side of the hotel, and I saddled the pinto, even with his side still scratched up a bit. Because, after my ride of the day before, I began to think that cayuse was going to be a lucky horse for me.

After that, I jogged him out of Amityville, and on the side of the next hill I turned and looked back on the town, looking all peaceful and sleepy in the early light of the day. Yes, it was a mighty quiet town—in the early morning. But I knew what it was dreaming about, and that pretty picture gave me no pleasure. Somewhere, in one of those houses, I felt middling sure, was Red Hawk himself. And it wasn't a comforting thought.

I sent the pinto away, again, and, by the time the sun was edging up above the eastern heights, I was well into Cricket Valley. I stopped, then, by the edge of some brush and built a fire and camped for almost an hour, making a big smoke and boiling some coffee. I ate my breakfast there, sitting on my heels, and pretty glad to be out of a town and under the sky again. It was easier to breathe, a lot, and I didn't mind the heat of the sun—even though the desert sun begins to bite through your clothes and bake your skin the minute it gets out of bed. I made that smoke on purpose, of course. If there was anybody watching over Cricket Valley, according to the report, I wanted them to know that I was drifting up that way.

What I planned on was this. I thought that Red Hawk would feel that I had been finally scared out of the hostile camp by that throw of the knife the night before—that he would trust me simply because I had played such a strong hand against him that he would not feel I was trying to deceive him now. Having done what I had done, it was a fairly bold move to try to desert to his side of the war, and I expected my boldness to win for me.

I had gone about halfway down the second winding of that famous old gorge when my horse stopped. I listened just as the horse was listening. And I heard part of what he heard—a little chiming, metallic echo against the walls of a ravine that prolonged that sound delicately, as a mirror will prolong and remodel a ray of light.

I began to search the ravine on either side, ready to see a rider come out from some tributary gulch, but, though one came out almost immediately upon my right, it was like a magic stroke, and I could not make out any ravine behind him. Rather he seemed suddenly to grow out of the solid rock. First the head of a horse—then horse and rider had issued from the living rock and were coming slowly toward me.

It was an odd effect. But when I strained my eyes, I could see something that ran up the face of the distant valley wall like a long crack. It was no crack. It was the screened mouth of a narrow gorge out of which the other rider had just come. That, however, was not the chief wonder to me, because, an instant later, I could make out the face of Doc.

Old Doc in Cricket Valley? Doc here in the very throat, as you might say, of the monster? Doc in the midst of the pleasure ground of Red Hawk, chosen by him so skillfully because the tangle of inter-crossing gulches, highlands, and lowlands made this an impenetrable stronghold for the chief? Doc here of all places on earth. But that was not all. The chief wonder of all was his horse. I had seen the nag on which he jogged around the town of Amityville. It was a broken-down roan. It stood an inch or two under fifteen hands, so that the long legs of the old man seemed to be stirring up a cloud of dust on either side as he went along. He seemed to be playing horse, rather than riding a real one. The poor old pony could sometimes manage a trot with his hind legs, but he never could get his stiffened front legs out of the way any faster than a walk, and the result was that at full speed he made the most ridiculous picture in the world. He was so old that legend said his teeth were as long as a man's finger. And his temples were sunk far, far in his head.

This was the horse that we all were accustomed to seeing pass through the streets of Amityville when Doc was tired of ambling around on his own legs. I used to wonder why Doc did not get another horse, because I was certain that Gresham would give him a new pony at any time rather than see his old hanger-on in such a condition.

Doc himself had explained it by saying to me: "I hate to give up the old boy. If I had a nice fast-trottin' horse, I'd just idle along and get fat and die quick. We all got to get exercise, and dog-gone me if I ain't so old and so ornery that the only way I'll take exercise is to club that old fool horse along."

That was like Doc. You could depend upon it that he would not have a reason like any other man's. But this horse that I saw him on in the valley, there, was a different matter. It was a blooded bay. You didn't need to look it over, inch by inch. One flash of it was enough to convince you that here was the real article in the way of horseflesh. He had the action of a fast wind skipping across the surface of a lake. And he blew across that valley and up to me as easily as you please.

When he came close, he made my pinto look like the shady side of nothing. He even transformed his rider, and old Doc sat there in the saddle, looking actually graceful and much above me.

"I said: "Doc, damn your old hide, what are *you* doing out here where only the bad boys come to play?"

He said: "Well, Mister Sherburn, when a gent gets as old as I am, folks don't much care where they go, and I thought I might as well skedaddle out here and have a look at things, you see. And here I am."

"And here is a horse for you, too," I said. "Where did you buy that horse?"

"A dog-gone' queer thing that happened," said old Doc, "was that, when I was ridin' down this here valley on that old skate of mine, I seen this here horse go gallopin' along. . . ."

"Without a rider?" I suggested.

"Exactly."

"So you called to it, I suppose, and it come right up to you . . . because you never could've come inside of a thousand miles of it on that broken-down old skate of yours."

"Young man, young man," said Doc, shaking his head at me sort of sad, "I see that you ain't got no spirit of belief in you. And what might you be doin' out here?"

"Don't change the subject," I said. "I'm plenty pleased just to talk about *you* for a while, because I got an idea that you're as dog-gone' an old rascal, Doc, as ever come out of the state of Louisiana."

"Sir!" said Doc.

"The devil, man," I said, "don't you see that you've got to tell a better lie than that about that horse belonging to you before I'll believe you?"

He looked down to the ground for a minute and he rubbed his knuckles across his chin, and in that pause I had a sudden flash into the truth of the thing and I shouted at him: "Doc!"

"Well?" he said, a little irritated. "Well, Mister Sherburn, have you got some more mean names that you want to call me?"

"I've got one thing more to tell you about yourself. You're the owner of that horse because you're on the payroll of Red Hawk. Damn my eyes if you're not one of his rotten tribe."

You would have thought that the old man would drop out of his saddle, I suppose, when he heard me accuse him like that, but he didn't. He just looked at me with a grin, and he said: "All right, Mister Sherburn. I hear what you say, right enough, but before I start in denyin' it, I'd like to know why *you* are in Cricket Valley at this time of the day?"

Chapter Thirty-Two

I gave the old fellow another look. If what I had guessed was true, I couldn't do better than to confide my purpose in him. But if I were wrong, then I was putting a rope around my neck by telling him. I had to do a little fencing, and I tried to do my best for him.

I said: "Why haven't I a right to be out here?"

"Only that you'd need an early start," he said.

"And how about you?" I asked him sharply, to show him that I was driving him into a corner as fast as he might be driving me.

"I often come out here in the hills," he said, "and sleep out with my blankets. Folks don't bother old gents at my age. We're figgered out to be pretty harmless, take us by and large."

"You're figured wrong, then," I told him.

"But maybe you was startin' on a trip?" he said. "Maybe you was aimin' for some town?"

It seemed like an outlet for me, and so I nodded at once and said: "Of course. That's it."

He didn't change his expression, just kept on watching me as a cat watches a bird that's not quite in the reach of its claws.

"I only wanted to know," he said, "because, of course, there ain't any town that this here valley points toward."

"No?" I echoed, a little dumbfounded at this.

"It leads you to nothing but trouble, they say, and hard cash," said old Louisiana Doc.

"You old rascal," I said. "What is that to me?"

"Sure," said Doc, "it's nothin'. Nothin' at all. So I guess you were just havin' a little pleasure ride . . . ain't that it? Up the valley, and then down again . . . just for the fun of it?"

"I told you that I was starting. . . ." And then I changed my mind and stopped.

Doc did not seem to notice the pause. He was reminiscing. "When I first seen you," he said, "I made up my mind right off that you had come up the valley to join Red Hawk."

"You damned old rascal!" I barked at him, but without being able to work up a very convincing amount of heat.

"Oh," he said, "I didn't mean that you were crooked. But I recollect a mighty fine young gent that I knowed three years ago. He was a promisin' 'puncher, he was, by the name of Morganson. He up and decided that the punchin' of cows wasn't work enough for him and he figgered that he would get himself famous like the young Napoleon, or something like that. You see? So away he goes and slides off up Cricket Valley because he wanted to pretend to join up with Red Hawk's gang. And when he had joined up with them, he figgered he would find out all he could about them, and, when he had a good chance, maybe he could sink a bullet in the heart of Red Hawk and then bust away into the clear on his fast horse.

"Well, sir, that was how he started out, but, in the end, they found him lyin' on the hot sands of the valley lookin' at the sun with wide-open eyes, and the buzzards was sailin' through the sky and all of them makin' eyes at him."

"You old villain," I said. "Who told you that he wanted to spy on the gang? Did Red Hawk pick you out to confide in?"

"It was just a whisper that went around. Gossip and talk, that don't mean nothin' to me, but whispers . . . well, they're different, and you can put a little trust in 'em."

It was rather hard to corral that old man. He was as tricky as any wise old mustang, and just as wayworn.

"All right," I said. "You may think that you're out of my bag, but you're not. You're in it. And as for me, you've made a pretty smart guess, but not quite smart enough. Guess again, Doc."

"But," Doc said in a tone of really holy horror, "there ain't no room in my head for the idea that you might *really* have come up here to join with Red Hawk and go around robbin' and murderin' and. . . ."

"Shut up," I hissed. "You talk like a parrot. Where did you learn that piece and who asked you to speak it?"

He didn't say anything back, just watched me with his old eyes puckering to points of light.

"I'm riding up the valley," I said. "Which way are *you* riding?"

"I'm keepin' you company for a while, maybe," suggested Doc.

"I haven't asked you to."

"I wanted to go along and tell you that I thought I seen a gent on the edge of the valley, over yonder, with a rifle in his hand."

"On that side? Then ride over that way and call to him."

"But there's one on the other side, too."

I looked, and thought I saw a gleam of sun, as though flashed from the barrel of a rifle as a man sank among the rocks. But I could not be sure.

"And behind you, and before you," said Doc with a grim tone. "You're in a little trap, Mister Sherburn, it looks like to me."

"And you, too," I said.

He grinned at me, and there was no mirth in his grin. "Oh," he said, "I'm such an old fish that, if they caught me, they'd probably throw me back into the water."

It was a pretty annoying thing. No matter how much you may have determined that you will walk right into the lions' den, after you have gone inside, it is a mean thing to hear the door click behind you and know that you can't get out until somebody else turns the key. That was how I felt—but more so—because the men of Red Hawk had a reputation that would have made a man-eating lion tuck his tail between his legs and hike for the woods. Besides, there was something about the self-satisfied way of Doc that bothered me a good deal. Frankly I didn't like the way in which he doddered along, smiling at me as though he knew a great deal that I should know.

As we rounded the next turn of the ravine, riding on, I distinctly saw the tail of a horse as it swished out of view among some rocks in the distance. I turned. There was no need of asking any further questions. Behind me came two men, riding softly, side-by-side. There were no masks upon their faces, but I did not need to be told that they belonged to the band of Red Hawk. The style of the horses they rode was eloquent and told me as much as I had already guessed from the type of horse that old Doc was riding when I first saw him in the valley.

Those fellows were coming at a soft dog-trot. But the slowness with which they were drawing along, somehow, suggested an infinite speed. A great horse always looks greater when he's in slow action than when he's slashing along. And so it was with that pair of beauties.

"If I wanted to run away," I said to Doc, "I don't think I would have much chance, unless I tapped you on the head and stole your horse."

That canny old villain had an instant answer for me. "It wouldn't do you no good, Mister Sherburn. He's all broke down in front, and, besides, he's tender-footed. On the rocks, he just curls up and can't go at all, but he manages to keep his head up pretty well when he's slitherin' along through the soft sand."

I looked at Doc and could not help laughing. "You're a grand old liar, Doc," I said. "What a man you must have been when you were young."

He regarded me blandly and mildly. "Why, Mister Sherburn, d'you think that they'd waste one of their real horses on an old crippled good-for-nothin' like me?"

I turned my back on him. That last speech was a sufficient confession, if I had wanted any, that Doc was a member of the list of spies that Red Hawk maintained. I had had enough of him. I only feared that, if I kept facing him, I might be tempted to put hands on him and wring his withered neck for him, my Louisiana patriot.

I made my ten thousandth resolution never to trust any man until I had known him for ten years—but I suppose that even ten years aren't long enough. Your best friend, who had never been tested by finding you in adversity, doesn't even know that he isn't devoted to you until the time comes when the call is to be made upon him, and then he weakens. And sometimes the fellow who merely likes you in a casual way, comes through like a hero when your back is against the wall. Well, I can never hope to know a lot about human nature. The extent of my learning in that school is just enough to convince me that I'm a poor student and a bad observer. I would have sworn by Doc, as I was saying a little while before. And here I found him turned into a crook by a wave of the hand. Magic—black magic!

I say that I turned my back upon him and let my pinto walk back toward the two gents that were riding up. They were on chestnuts—that favorite color among thoroughbreds—and when I came up pretty close, they drew up their horses as though they were thinking with one mind. And one of them held up his hand to stop me, in my turn.

They made a pretty rough-looking pair, take them all in all. They were about as far from parlor lizards as anything you could imagine. Nothing of the half-breed or the Mexican or the Indian about them. They were simply hard-boiled American roughnecks. And, take them by and large, I suppose that there hasn't been a species invented that is any tougher than the American tough. This pair was a hand-picked couple to win a prize.

They looked like brothers. Oh, you see the general type anywhere on the desert, but these were n^{th}-power duplications of the type. They had pale blue eyes—or gray, maybe—that looked at you as if you were empty air, or a mile away. They had high cheek bones without much flesh over them, and thin, drawn cheeks. The skin was drawn pretty tight over their noses, and their mouths were straight lines, without any of the lips showing—none of the lining of the lips, I mean. They had red necks with ragged-looking bandannas knotted around them. And they had old felt hats stuck on their heads—old black felt hats, turned sort of purple with so many layers of dust on them. And they were finished off with a quid of tobacco stuck in the cheek of each of them and with four or five days' growth of blond, sunburned whiskers all over their faces. They had on old flannel shirts that had rubbed out at the elbows and been cut off there, and showed the old red-flannel undershirts running down close to the wrist. They had dirty boots on their feet, and wore overalls, and they had a good cartridge belt apiece, all loaded around with shells, and holsters hanging low in what anyone who has seen a gunfight would have called workman-like, shipshape fashion.

They had repeating rifles stuck in long holsters under their right knees. And to finish everything off, those rough boys were mounted on horses that a prince would have been proud to have in his stable. I knew what they were; I had lived and grown up with that brand of man. I waved a hand and grinned at them, and one of them grinned back.

Chapter Thirty-Three

They said nothing. They sat their horses and waited, but they stared at me every instant and I stared back, because it is easy to understand your own kind. These fellows knew that I was their own kind. And, if all the wrong things I have done in my life had been heaped up together in one pile, I suppose that it would have made a blacker mass than their own bad accomplishments. Still, there was a difference. I had never taken an advantage, never so much as stuck up a man for the sake of getting his wallet. And yet I think that I didn't look to have that much virtue in me.

Three other men now came drifting up. Indians? Half-breeds? No, they might have stood as blood brothers to the first pair. Their bandannas might be of differing colors, but that was about all that distinguished them. They all were riding on those same long-legged horses with a great stretch of neck and small heads set well on the end of them and the look of speed in their eyes. With old Doc, I had a congress of six men.

They didn't consult me. They consulted one another. Imagine being tried for your life by a gang of Chinese pirates. Except that here I could understand the pleadings back and forth. I knew, of course, that these men would as soon shoot me out of the saddle as they would bite off a plug of tobacco. There was nothing that would keep them from that act—since I had seen them and their faces—except the strong feeling that I might make a useful member of the organization.

They talked me over deliberately, rolling their cigarettes and smoking them, and looking me up and down. Some were for and some were against me. The very first speech was a blast for me. I think that it was the oldest man of the lot—except Doc—who began by saying: "This gent ain't for us. He ain't our meat. In the first place, he's a hound for the booze, and old Red Hawk hates the booze chasers. Then again, he's stepped out and raised all sorts of trouble in Amityville and give us a bad time. He would've kept the cork in Juniper, for one thing. And Juniper might've handed out the news about all of us. He was about to do it. I say, let's finish this boy off, and I'm willin' to take the job."

Old Doc began to speak hastily: "Sammy," he said, "you got a good head on your shoulders, but I want to say that I've been watchin' my friend from Louisiana for quite a spell. I've seen him fightin', tryin' to go straight, and I seen that he couldn't do it. Well, we all want to go straight someday. Can you blame him for that? He tried to go straight and he thought that he'd get in solid with the straight men by makin' a play ag'in' Red Hawk, but all the time he was with the big chief . . . he was drawin' toward him. He wanted to be ridin with us and not against us. And. . . ."

"Wait a minute, Doc," broke in Sammy.

I made my own speech then, and it was the only speech that I made on the occasion. I looked Sammy in the eye, and I said: "Boys, I got just this to say. While you're talking me over, go back there a yard or two and talk low, because I don't want to hear you. There ain't any danger of me running away, because this pinto couldn't run one yard against your two. But if I hear any more of you braying against me the way my flat-headed friend, Sammy, has been doing, I'm going to hold it against him. Maybe this here argument will wind up with me getting a dose of lead through the brain. But if you take me into the gang, I tell you plain that I'm going to be rough on the ones that put any rocks in the way of me getting in."

I said that, and then I turned my back on them and lit a smoke for myself. It was a fairly bold play, though I was scared almost to death, and it brought a snarl out of them that you could have heard a quarter of a mile away. I suppose that half of them were for shooting me down on the spot, but the other half had their doubts.

You see, my idea was that I'd make them feel that I had a right to expect that I would make the gang. And that was why I talked rough, as though I were already in it. At any rate, they took my advice and drew back a little where I could only hear a mumble, and two voices rattling on top of the mumble like pebbles on a board—Sammy, who had already let me know what he thought, and Doc, who was doing his best for me in his own beknighted way.

It was sort of tense. You talk about the fellow who waits for the jury to say whether he's guilty or not—when guilty means hanging—but that fellow feels nothing compared to what I felt. Because a jury is made up of twelve honest men trying to find out the truth, and, if they can't find the truth, as they feel, they'll disagree and save the crook's life. But here I was being talked over pretty casual by a lot of thugs, and at any minute one of them might get tired of the argument and decide to end it by planting a slug of lead in the small of my back. No, it wasn't so pleasant.

After a while I judged that I was getting a better chance. I could hear Doc talking more, and when Sammy piped up, there was a sort of snarl that drowned him. I thought the boys were deciding that I would do. And I was right.

Because pretty soon somebody shouted: "All right, kid! You're with us."

I twitched the pinto around on his hind legs—lifting him off his front hoofs by tickling him under the chest with a spur, and I barked at them: "Who called me 'kid'? I'm old enough to play grandfather in this here party, except for Sammy, yonder, and Doc, who's too old to count. Lay off of that 'kid' talk. My name is Sherburn!"

And I jogged my horse straight up to them. They scowled at me as I approached. But then the scowls straightened out and they began to grin. I knew that I had won. They wanted hard-boiled men in their crew, and they were beginning to feel that perhaps I was an ideal recruit.

Well, it was a great relief, but I sashayed right up to Sammy and I said to him: "Sammy, you and me may turn into friends. But if we don't, we ain't going to mix. I give you a warning now. I'm watching you. If you see my back again, I give you leave to take off the back of my head. And if I see you make any funny passes, I'm not going to ask any questions. That's all."

It wasn't all bluff. I didn't like Sammy. Partly because he had tried to get me butchered without a trial, and partly because he had a bad pair of eyes in his head. He was about thirty-five or -six—just a little older than me, and every one of his years was chiseled into his face, and every year was worse than the one before.

He said: "All right. You chatter now. I'll have the last word to say, though."

And I more than half believed him.

Well, after I was taken into the crowd they didn't step up and shake hands with me and they didn't crowd around and say that they were glad to have me, or anything like that. They just kept right on watching me out of the corners of their eyes—none too cordial. I was one of them, but I still had to prove my right.

There wasn't much talk of any kind in that lot. No, they were such a hand-picked lot of rough ones that they didn't waste much effort trying to be entertaining. They were with Red Hawk for one thing only—and that was the coin that floated around his camp and the sure, quick ways that that red-skinned villain had of getting the stuff.

We drifted up the valley, and it wasn't long before we dipped into a wide rip through the cañon wall. Then we wound into another, and side-stepped into another, and so from place to place until I couldn't have found my way back with an interpreter.

I could see why Red Hawk had picked this place more than any other in the mountains. It was simply plain impossible to get at a crew of men in those valleys. Pretty soon a voice rang out above us. And I looked up and saw a fellow leaning out over the edge of a cliff with a rifle in his hand. We had ridden into a long, straight channel, and he could have dropped every one of us, shooting at his leisure, if he felt like it.

"I see we got a little stranger with us," says this fellow on the rock. "Howdy, Sherburn."

I recognized him—a man who I had seen twenty times in the streets of Amityville where he was known as a prospector. He had lost $8,000 in dust at one whirl of faro. And I had seen him lose it and I had heard him say with a laugh: "Well, there's plenty more money where that little pile come from."

And here he was—and this was his way of "mining". I began to feel that I might learn a good deal about the real occupations of others who were prosperous, from time to time, around the streets of the town.

After a while we began to climb, and we kept on up to the crest of a plateau. It was about half a mile long and a hundred yards wide. There wasn't a vestige of tree or shade except for a ruinous tumble of rocks, here and there. And yonder some canvas had been pegged up on poles to make a shelter from the sun. Under that shelter there was some grain for the horses in sacks and there were some smoke-blackened cooking utensils. That was all. This was one of the camps of Red Hawk, and I could see that, even if he were not an Indian, he believed in keeping the equipment down to a sub-Indian normal. These fellows could sweep together their camp and become a free-swinging, fighting force with all their goods packed in half a minute.

There were not so many of them as I had expected. There were the six men who had come in with me—counting old Doc, who really didn't matter as a fighting force, I supposed. And there were four sentinels who were scattered about on high points.

Altogether, I made the eleventh man. I said to Lefty McGruder, who was next to me as we came in and who was the only one of the lot who had introduced himself to me: "Lefty, I suppose most of the boys are away . . . eh?"

He merely stared at me. "Away? The devil, man, d'you think that we're an army?"

I stared in my turn. "Is this your average turnout?"

"Average," he snorted. "I've been with the boys for about a year and a half, now . . . barring a couple of months when I was laid up with a hole in my leg . . . and I never before seen such a crowd around."

That was news to me, of course.

"There are about five of us around, as a rule," said Lefty. "And we got to keep camp, cook our own chow, tend the horses, and stand guard. Nope, you ain't landed in no easy camp, bo, lemme tell you that. It ain't nothin' but work, here. Nothin' but work, I tell you."

"And pay," I suggested.

He favored me with a twisted grin. "Sure," he said. "And the pay is pretty sweet, at that."

Yes, he was a tough mug, was Lefty. Peace be to his bones.

"When do we get an airing?" I asked.

"You're in luck, Sherburn," he said. "We ride tonight."

Chapter Thirty-Four

We rode that night. Well, it knocked a good deal of the gimp out of me. It was famous all through the ranges that the band of Red Hawk, no matter how hard they struck home when once in motion, did not strike often. And since they had just collected a quarter of a million in hard cash, I had felt reasonably sure that, even if I were able to join the band, I should not be called upon for any sudden service. And here was notification that we were to ride that same night. It was pretty hard to have to play the part of a crook so soon.

I said: "That's more luck than I thought I'd have. After that Ludlow haul, I thought that you boys might idle around for a while."

He shrugged his shoulders.

"I should think," I went on, "that you fellows would have enough coin to satisfy you for a while."

"I suppose you would," said Lefty. "Well, there was the twenty percent that went to the chief. That was fifty thousand bones. Then the crook at the bank that the chief bribed . . . that was twenty-five thousand more. That left a hundred and seventy-five or eighty thousand to be split up among fifteen of us."

"Were there fifteen then?"

"There were. Not all together, but scattered around. But there was a little fracas around here that evening, and four of the boys cashed in."

I was pretty much surprised, of course, and anybody else

would have been. I had thought that Red Hawk must have maintained a regular iron discipline. And I said so to Lefty. "Look here," I said, "how does Red Hawk keep all the boys together if he lets them play around like this and fill each other full of lead?"

"Easy," said Lefty. "You figure the way folks usually would. But Red Hawk works by opposites. You figure that he treats us all like an army. But he don't. You'd figure, for instance, that the reason you got into the gang so easy was because he knew about you, maybe, and told us that he wanted you in whenever he could get you. Nope . . . that ain't his way. He gives us a free rein. We're the bosses and we can do anything we want. This here is a democracy, I tell you. We was sent out to elect you or shoot you. We had the whole responsibility."

I shook my head at this. It was more than I could understand, because it dynamited all of the preconceptions that I had formed about Red Hawk.

But Lefty opened up. He had taken a sort of fancy to me, as he told me a little later, because Sammy was his chief enemy, and because I had taken Sammy down a peg or two in the presence of everybody.

I got from Lefty the whole constitution of the gang, just as I intend to relate it to you, and, when you have finished hearing about it, you'll understand that Red Hawk was a genius. Because I suppose he was the first crook in the world who guessed at the possibility of a democracy of crooks.

The scheme was this. The band was responsible to no one in the world for its conduct. Neither did it have anyone to apply rules of discipline. The band made all of its own laws. And therefore when its members broke those laws, each person was more willing to inflict a penalty upon the criminal. Those penalties were all of one nature: death!

This was the single rule that Red Hawk himself insisted upon.

They could do as they pleased. Either pay no attention to offenses—or else when they did pay attention, pay it with guns. He did not care the slightest how many men he had, but he wanted to know that those men were, none of them, disaffected. He wanted to know that he could depend upon every one of those fellows to the very utmost in a tight pinch.

I want to tell you about the liberties of the gang first, before I get down to the laws of what they had to do. I want to tell you what they could do as well as what they ought to do. And this is the astonishing truth.

A member of Red Hawk's gang could ride or not ride on any expedition as soon as he heard its nature explained to him. And the chief had to state exactly what he hoped to do on each occasion. When he had made that statement, his ruffians could go or not go.

As a matter of fact, they were laws unto themselves. If a member had a grievance against another member, he did not have to ask the permission of the chief to take redress. Neither could he complain to the whole body of his treatment. Each man stood upon his own feet. If he were injured, he was at liberty to avenge that wrong when and how he saw fit. If he pistoled his enemy in the middle of a campfire meal, he was simply required to take his victim away and bury him. On the other hand, these fights might arouse the anger of other members of the party. And the result was that there was a continual feud going on.

Another liberty, and this a very grave one, was attributed to every member of the gang. When any man chose, he could simply mount his horse and ride away to enjoy his money as he saw fit. He was limited in time only. If he were away from the camp for more than six months, then he was liable to death the instant the band could apprehend him. Furthermore, no member of the band could be asked to perform servile duties by the chief or by the band itself. Each man looked after himself and no one else.

To take a bird's-eye view of the situation, you will see that Red Hawk, when he rode out to his camp, never knew how many men he could find there ready for an exploit, and of those who were present he never knew how many would be willing to undertake the task that he desired to accomplish.

You may think that this scheme was absurd, but I believe I can show you that it was not absurd at all. The very fact that the bondage in that organization was so slight caused it to be the stronger in its holding power. Because every member of the party felt perfect liberty except on one point—he had no deeply implanted desire eventually to break away from his work. And that, of course, was exactly what Red Hawk desired.

I want to consider the reverse of this matter of privileges. Each man could leave the camp whenever he chose. And the result was that, when their pockets were filled, they usually scattered very soon and the proceedings of the illegal gains disappeared at faro games, roulette wheels, and a thousand other devices. Come easy—go easy. The money came on wings and departed in the same fashion. And the liberty of the members of the gang kept them poor, and poverty made them keen to ride again on adventure, and that keenness made them eager to obey their chief.

Consider the matter that seemed most like madness to me—the freedom of every man to shoot down his enemy when he had a good chance. The result of this was that there was never a hidden strife. When men hated one another, they killed one another. And there was the end of it. No one felt that some other member of the crew was the favorite of Red Hawk, or received better chances. Because if any man had that feeling, all he had to do was to take a gun and hunt for the favorite.

As a matter of fact, if you will consider the thing carefully, you will see that when Red Hawk got to this free camp of his, he usually found it filled with a small group of empty-pocketed men who were hungry for money and adventure.

He did not select the new men who came into the band except that on very rare occasions he would make recommendations. And even then the band was at full liberty to override his recommendations if it chose to do so. The result of this was that, if a member was a traitor or a weakling, they could blame themselves, but not their chief. Usually, therefore, the new candidates were given the strictest sort of an examination of their nerve and their skill with weapons, from all of which I had been excepted, partly owing to the stringent recommendation of old Doc, and partly owing to the little reputation that, by the aid of Sam, the bartender, and a great deal of bluffing, I had worked up in Amityville.

Consider, on the other hand, the few binding laws of the gang—and even these were not laws proposed by the chief. The most important of all, and that upon which the gang was based as upon bedrock, was that, once a member, a man must be a member the rest of his life. However, as has been said before, it was possible for a man to remain away for a whole six months at a time, and then report, and there were actually four members of the crew who had retired with their plunder and gone to live in towns and had married and begun the formation of families, each one of them. They still reported every six months, and they refused to ride on any expeditions, and so all went merrily with them.

"Why don't more do the same thing?" I asked of Lefty.

"Because they can't keep their money long enough," said Lefty. "It comes in too easy. We spend it too fast. And there you are. Besides, you've always got to remember that we live a happy life, right enough. There's always chuck and a good horse to ride in our camp . . . good guns and good pals, if you want 'em.

And what more can a man ask? I've had a dozen good times in the last year and a half . . . better times than I ever had before. I'm contented, and so are the rest of them."

"But suppose a man wants to take his loot and slide out for Italy to settle down and to live there?"

"A couple have tried that. There was one that even got as far as Mexico City. Then he was stabbed in the back. They say there was one that got to Paris. But he was poisoned, they say. I ain't so sure about him. However, the boys know, all of 'em, that the chief has a long arm. It's him that tends to enforce that one law . . . and that's the only law that he insists upon . . . that when a gent had tried to duck away, he gets a knife between his ribs."

There were a few other rigid rules. One was that a wounded companion should never be abandoned in a raid except at his own request.

"And there ain't been a single one of the boys that ever asked the rest to stand by and help him," Lefty said with enthusiasm.

Furthermore, each man was expected to bear himself dauntlessly in the midst of a raid, and, while actually riding with Red Hawk, obey implicitly every direction that the leader gave to him. If not, he was punished with certain death.

You will see that this loosely formed organization was really bound together by forces stronger than brass.

Finally, as to Red Hawk himself. He never appeared at the camp except when he was on the verge of starting on an expedition. Sometimes he would send no warning. Sometimes he apprised them beforehand that he was about to arrive. But he came so seldom—he was so rarely seen—his words were so few—his plans were so dexterous and his bearing so daring—his skill as a contriver and as a warrior so great, that he was held in the strongest awe by the band, and his share of twenty percent of the total loot was considered, if anything, too meager by the rest of his men.

Chapter Thirty-Five

I wish that I had had more time to observe the most unusual crew of outlaws that was ever gathered together. Why no other leader in the West ever attempted the same scheme I cannot tell, but it was an excellent thing for the lovers of law and property that they did not. Almost always the larger bands were destroyed by internal dissension, but the crew raised by Red Hawk fought out their own quarrels long before an enemy had a chance to come near to them.

They had existed for five years, and they might have gone on forever if it had not been for the almost accidental destruction of their great leader, as I am about to narrate. Had it not been for that, Red Hawk and his men might still be leading fat lives in the great Western desert. Accident beat the great leader and not any courage or any skill of mine.

I had one other question to ask Lefty, and that was whether or not Red Hawk was really a white man or an Indian; his answer was perfectly surprising to me, because I had made up my mind that he must be the former.

He said: "I've seen him as close as I see you now. I've seen him by firelight and by sunlight. And if he ain't an Indian, I'm not a white man."

There was enough conviction in that to have satisfied any man. He was an Indian, then, after all—it was an Indian's brain that had contrived to defy organized white society for these five great years.

I had something else to do that day besides wait for the appearance of Red Hawk and study my companions, however. For there was Sammy to consider, and Sammy put himself right into the foreground of the picture.

It had come to suppertime, and, while coffee was steaming over the fire and there was a fine fragrance of hot pone and frying bacon, Sammy took up a position opposite me. The fire was big in the center. Someone had thrown on wood that burned too high, and was being thoroughly cursed by the rest of the party for his pains. And little side fires had been drawn out from that central mass. Still, they could not be taken too far from the central mass, and the heat of that, at the fag end of a very hot day, was enough to cause a very universal cursing.

But I forgot about the heat when I saw Sammy take up his place opposite me. I knew in half a second just why he had come there. I don't know how I knew. It was a sort of inborn instinct such as most of us are touched by, here and there, and now and then. There was a swelling danger in Sammy that turned his face red and made his eyes glare. I felt it, and I knew that he was there because he intended to stay face-to-face with me until we had fought out the fight that was predestined since our quarrel of that day.

Before my talk with Lefty I had surmised that we might end our differences by a mere fist engagement. But after Lefty explained to me the laws of the band, I could easily understand that halfway measures would not do. Shooting was the order of the day, and shooting was the means that I should have to adopt eventually, in order to defend myself.

So I began to eat my supper—sandwiching bacon strips between chunks of delicious, moist, crumbling pone, eating with my left hand, and keeping my right hand free all the while.

I sat on my heels, because that is a position from which an athletic man can leap to either side, or up, or back, or forward.

The flames in the central fire were now dying away to a red welter. Across the tangling lines of the heat waves, I watched my enemy. The malice in the face and the eyes of Sammy had not altered. He was eating his supper slowly—as I was eating mine—and not a move of my hands escaped him, any more than a move of his escaped me.

I'm not a believer in telepathy. I suppose telepathy wasn't needed and that our attitudes were eloquent enough, and the manner in which we eyed each other. But in a few moments every member of the gang saw what was in the air, and the talk and the laughter died away.

It had been a jovial party. These were fellows inured to the desert life and the desert sun. And besides, in all hot, dry climates the coming of evening is a joyful time. The moment the sun hangs low in the West, big and yellow and with its fires banked, a new life begins to rise in every heart. And when night itself arrives, it is so cool and so beautiful—so beautiful in its sudden coolness, you might say—that it is like wine in the body of a man.

Night was not here yet, but the cool of the evening was coming, and voices that had been subdued snarlings during the day were now fresher and higher, and old jokes were remembered, and it was quite a festive occasion. Also, they were to ride that night. But now the laughter died away like a fire under a blanket. And when the men spoke it was only to mutter. They had seen enough of Sammy and of me to understand that there was real trouble ahead. I don't mean to say that they waited apprehensively. No, they were accustomed to battle in that camp, and they looked forward to a fight with a quiet, keen joy. Every one of them knew that his own life was apt to come to a sudden end that same night. And men in that frame of mind are not peculiarly tender in their regard of others.

I heard one voice just between a whisper and vocalization

say: "There's the poison in old Sammy's fangs ag'in."

That made it apparent that he was well known for his conflicts. In fact, I learned afterward that he had been with the band from the very beginning. For five years he had kept his place, and, during that time, few could say how many had fallen under his hand.

However, I did not have to be told that he was a dangerous fellow. He carried all the signs of it about him. If there had been no more than the worn and battered look of his holster and the well-thumbed appearance of the handles of his Colt, I could have guessed that he was one in a hundred when it came to pot-shooting at other men.

Supper was pretty well ended. But nobody got up to clean his dishes. Cigarettes were rolled here and there, very quickly, by men that didn't budge their eyes from us, because men will have their smokes in spite of the devil.

It had been the golden time of the late afternoon when we began and when Sammy had taken his place on the far side of the fire. Now the sun was ducked behind a western peak, and the sky was filled with rose except for one towering cloud that was all a sheet of rolling flame. It was not the heat waves of the fire that rose between Sammy and me now; it was the glow of the embers. Now and then one of the brands crackled. Sometimes a little stir of sparks rose. It was darkening fast. Already there was more light from the fire than from the west. And now I was conscious that Sammy, instead of reaching for his gun, had thrust out his chin a little and was staring straight into my eyes.

I've seen a man broken, like that. Heroes are supposed to break down their enemies that way. But I'm not a hero. I picked out the uppermost button on his coat and I frowned at that as hard as I could. Somehow, above the level of my own glance, I could feel his eyes grabbing for me, like invisible tentacles. It wasn't very pleasant. I tell you, that fellow was a devil. I could *feel* the devil boiling in me. He hated me like poison. And I began to be afraid, in spite of the fact that I wasn't looking him in the eye.

All at once he said in a very cold, level sort of a voice: "You yaller-bellied coward. Look me in the eye."

I was within the wink of an eye of weakening—he had taken that much of a hold on me. I got myself into a tantrum to keep from turning cold, and I yelled at him: "Grab your gun and say good night! You're through, Sammy!"

He didn't wait to be asked twice. He made a pass for his gun that was pretty fast, and he flicked it out of the leather in the best style you could imagine. It was almost fast enough, but not quite. I thought that his gun was looking me straight in the eye just as I fired, but it wasn't. I guess the muzzle of his Colt was about an eighth of an inch off the level that he wanted when I fired. An eighth of an inch at the muzzle, but that was multiplied enough by the time his bullet got across the fire to me, so that I heard it flash past my ear and I quickly ducked my head, like a fool.

He didn't see me duck my head, and the reason he didn't see was because he was dead. He hadn't known a thing of what happened to him because the slug landed him fair between the eyes and he just lay back on the ground and looked up to the stars without seeing them.

Cool? Well, I wish you could have seen that crew. They didn't so much as grunt, except one fellow who said: "Well, Sammy had it coming to him for these long years."

And another chap who said: "Very neat."

He was a man who looked a bit different from the rest—the one who said that. He had a sort of clean, cool, washed look. He was very young. He looked twenty, but I don't think that he was more than seventeen. He talked good English, and what he said had a lot of point to it. He was as handsome as they come, and there was something in his pale blue eyes that was worth watching. He was thin and straight, and supple as a rawhide lariat and just about as tough, and he was just a mite faster than a lightning flash. Oh, he was a fine-looking gent, he was. It had pleased him, the nice way in which that bullet was placed between the eyes of Sammy. Had it had been a quarter of an inch to either side, he wouldn't even have said that much. Yes, they were a cool lot, and I suppose the kid was the coolest of them all.

I decided that I would be just as calm as any of the rest of them, and the first thing I did was to break open my gun and slip out the old shell and slide in a new one.

Here a chap ten yards away from me said: "While you got your right hand foolish like that . . . suppose that somebody else was to make a play at you, stranger?"

"I'd still have the left," I said, "and I'd talk right back with that and make him take his hat off."

You see, I was nervous, and that crack of his sort of unsettled me. I snapped out my left-hand gun and shot the sombrero right off his head. That sounds a good deal more than it really was, because he had the hat pushed high on the back of his head and it made a big target. But it looked pretty neat, hearing me make a remark like that and then seeing his hat fly off. The boys raised a roar and a laugh, and the other fellow didn't do a thing but reach out and scoop up his hat and sit there for a while studying the hole going in and the hole coming out.

I went around to do my duty and cart Sammy away, and the kid helped me. He came along without saying a word and took the legs while I took the shoulders. We buried Sammy quick but proper. We put him in a crevice in a rock pile a hundred yards away that the kid knew about, and then we pried loose the key rock and tumbled about ten tons of loose stone junk down on top of him. Then we started back toward the fire.

"Look here," the kid said, "were you born left-handed?"

"I wasn't," I said.

"You mean that you taught yourself all of that?"

"I did," I said.

"About how long?" he asked.

"I started when I was eight years old," I answered.

I heard him gasp.

"But I learn slow," I admitted. "And besides, I didn't know some of the things that I learned later."

"What's that?" he asked.

"That you shouldn't try to make your left hand act the way your right hand does. Each hand has its own way of doing things, and you got to favor them both. But you wear two guns, kid, yourself."

"They're a show," he said. "Would you teach me?"

I figured that I wouldn't be with the gang very long and I wouldn't have time to make him a much safer bet as a gunfighter than he was already.

"I'll teach you."

He walked ten steps without saying so much as thank you. Then he said: "My name is Caddigan. You'll never regret giving me a hand like this."

Somehow, I believed him. But the time was to come when I was to see that that was the best investment I ever made—that promise of mine.

My wife says I shouldn't mention the name of Caddigan at all, because he's become so famous that everybody knows about him, and because, as soon as they see his name, people will begin to forget about me and the fix I was in at Red Hawk's camp and just think about what a flash Caddigan was. Well, let them think. I'm glad to have them think. I'll never envy Caddigan.

As we came in view of the campfire, we saw the men on their feet, and off to one side there was a huge man wrapped in a blanket and sitting on a huge horse, with feathers sticking up out of his hair. I didn't need anyone to tell me that I was looking at Red Hawk at last.

CHAPTER THIRTY-SIX

I could feel the kid prick up his ears, too. "If you don't object," he said in his quiet way, "I'll ride beside you tonight. This job must be something choice, or the old devil wouldn't be back here so soon after the Ludlow affair."

"Did you ride in that?" I asked him.

"Yes," he said, and in a way that shut off all questions. "I rode in that."

Of course we hurried in, and on the way I saw that Red Hawk was not near to the fire, but sat his horse back in the shadow. The men of his band were busy reading a paper. That paper was passed from hand to hand, the boys shaking their heads as they read it—some of them. And others simply frowned and looked down on the ground.

I read it in my turn. It was a queer-looking paper, at that. It was drawn up like a child's essay, all under headings. It was printed, too, in a sort of clumsy, childish hand. It read like this:

Purpose: To stop the Jessamy stage, with $100,000 in gold in the boot.
Manner: By blowing up the Fulsom Bridge after the guard crosses and before the stage gets to it.

That was all there was to it. And I admit that I couldn't see much hope in a job like that. I hated to ride as one of the party. I knew the Fulsom Bridge, and I knew the Jessamy stage. The bridge was a mighty solid wooden one. Well, the Fulsom River has cut out a gorge five hundred feet deep and not more than ninety feet wide at the place where that bridge is built. To get the timbers across those ninety feet was considered a great job, in the days of which I write. That explains the bridge to you. Now about the Jessamy stage.

I suppose it was the only stage in the old days that had never been stuck up by some fool or other. The reason that it was never stopped was because it usually did carry a lot of gold shipments down from the mines. The men in the mines knew that it was a risky thing to send the gold out and they were willing to pay big for safe carriage, and so the company that ran that stage could afford to keep a mighty fine guard of men. Every three days the stage left the mines and started for Jessamy. A day down and a day back and a day's rest in between. That took men who could ride like the devil. Nobody but a tough man could stand that work for many days at a time. About two weeks and most of the new recruits said they had enough.

You can see that the guard consisted of picked men when I tell you that wages of $25 a week—equal to a hundred now—were offered and yet they never could keep more than nine or ten men on the job, it was such terrific work. But those nine or ten—they were worth fifty. They were veterans. They could shoot straight from any angle. They rode like devils, of course. And the half dozen times that bands of crooks had tried to get at the stage, those fighters had simply eaten the crooks alive.

I was busy thinking about the difficulty of this proposal when old Doc, primed by some of the other boys, stepped out and began a sort of a speech to Red Hawk, stating how much the rest of them wanted to do whatever Red Hawk proposed and that he had been a fine leader, and all that, but that this one time they rather doubted his idea, because it would be hard to blow the bridge at just the right moment. A man would have to blow up the bridge with a fuse, and a fuse took a little time to burn, and before it hit the powder, the stage itself might be on the bridge, and then there would be a lot of destruction, but no profit. Or the guards themselves might still be on the bridge, and, hardy though those fellows were, they hesitated a little at the thought of murdering ten men in that cowardly fashion. But if anything went wrong, as seemed very likely, those guards would be so many fighting, tearing wildcats, and the band would suffer a lot before they got through with the scrap.

Doc had gotten this far in his speech when Red Hawk put an arm out, and off of that arm slipped the whole blanket that had been enwrapping him. And there he sat in the dead light of the sunset and the brighter glow of the fire, a glistening, wonderful red figure of a man. He looked as though he were made out of beaten copper. I never have seen such muscles, such poise, such terrible power in the look of a man.

He wasn't ugly after the Indian fashion. I would have called him an extremely handsome fellow if his skin had been white, and he was not so very old, either. I could not have put his age over thirty-five by any stretch of the imagination. There was only the one mar on him, and that was the big leather patch that covered one eye. He put out his arm, as I was saying, and the blanket slipped off of him, and then he sent his horse into a gallop from a standing start by some mysterious sort of horsemanship. Away he went sailing into the evening, without a word to any of us.

I never saw so many shamed men, and then the kid sang out suddenly: "He's heading toward the bridge trail, and he's going to try the job single-handed!"

That had an immense effect upon the rest of the party, for they seemed to recall on the instant all of the affairs in which Red Hawk had led them in the past, and I suppose that shame stirred them, too. For my part, I have never seen anything much more impressive than the disappearing form of the chief as he rode away through the rose of the evening. There was a sudden swarming onto their horses. Only old Doc remained behind them—I suppose, to secure the camp and hide everything that was left there. Watching the sweeping strides of the horses as they started off on the trail of the chief, I knew that poor little pinto could never keep pace with them and I was thinking that this would give me a good excuse for falling behind and then purposely losing my way, and so avoiding the unpleasant work of the night. But just as that thought was forming in my mind, and while I was putting foot in the stirrup, a rider swept up to me with a led horse.

I looked up into the face of young Caddigan. "Here's my extra horse," he said. "Shift your saddle, partner. It'll be worth your while . . . it'll save you time in the first half hour of riding."

There was no doubt about that. It was an ugly-headed brute of a horse that he brought to me—a creature with a Roman nose and an ugly ewe neck, but behind the neck he was all that anyone could ask—the bone of a giant and the cut of a real flyer. There was no way for me to refuse courtesy like this. I cursed Caddigan in my heart for dragging me into the job against my will, but I snatched the saddle from the back of the pinto and swung it onto the new chestnut. A moment more and he was heaving me over the ground with a great stride like the swing of a ground swell in the mid-Pacific.

We kept hot at it for a full six or seven miles before we got up with the main party. Such was the speed at which Red Hawk's band moved along that even the single delay to change saddles put one almost helplessly out of the race. However, we were up with them at the last, and after that for some time the little procession struggled on behind the leader. The leader was Red Hawk. In spite of his great weight, such was his skill in horsemanship and such was the magnificent quality of his black horse, that he kept his position at the head of the column and we had the huge outline of his shoulders ever looming before us through the night.

We were climbing through the last half of the ride. It was full night now; we had no moon to show us the way, though at the end there was a faint looming of light toward the eastern horizon that gave promise that she was about to rise. For the rest, there were the stars, the wonderful white-and-golden stars, of the mountain desert. They have changed now. They are no longer what they were in the old days. For now the railroads have netted the land thickly everywhere. And now automobiles are grinding or whining over the roads and whisking their dust clouds at fifty miles an hour into the sky behind them. And they have run our irrigation sections like green hands into the white of the desert, and the desert, being no longer terrible, is no longer beautiful. But there was a day when we loved the stars that shone on the Rockies because we had to live by them and travel by them. And in those days, so it seems to me now, the stars alone could throw a light that was greater than the shining of the moon nowadays.

It was by starlight, then, that we climbed up to the stage road that had cost three years and a ridiculous quantity of labor and money for the building, and we came down the road to the bridge. It was a good, bulky, heavy-built structure, with beams that would have pleased a ship's architect. But stretched out its ninety feet of length and spanning the black gulf of the cañon, it looked slender enough.

When we got to it, Red Hawk leaped down from his horse and went to work by the light of a pine torch that he had brought with him and that he now kindled. What he did was to pack in dynamite under the huge cross-beams that supported the near end of the bridge. Then he attached a short length of fuse. We helped him to cover the trail of the fuse, so that the man who was chosen to light it would not instantly be betrayed by the crawling worm of fire as it ran sputtering toward the dynamite. It was sure to be a dangerous bit of work for the fellow who lit the fuse, for, in the first place, that fuse was very short, and, in the second place, there was apt to be a shower of rock fragments, and while he was running away from these, he was apt to be drilled at by the guns of the guard.

Of course we picked lots to see who was to get the prize. They were straws held in the dark hand of the chief, and, when the measuring to find the shortest straw commenced, the first man ruled out was young Caddigan—lucky devil!—who had a whole grass stem for his lot. And finally it was brought down to the chief and me. We stood face-to-face, looking each other in the eye. And then it seemed to me, as I stood there before him, searching his face, that I had known him before, some place. Perhaps among the Apaches, because I had mixed a good deal with that tribe.

We opened our hands, and when the straws were placed side-by-side in the palm of a neutral judge, it was discovered that my straw was a scant eighth of an inch shorter than the chief's. It was to be my part to blow the bridge.

I turned into a pretty sick man, I can tell you. But I swore to myself on the spot that, no matter what happened to me at the hands of the gang, I would not touch the fuse until I was assured that no living creature, horse or man, was upon the bridge. As for the robbery of the stage itself—that was nothing to me—absolutely nothing. Because if from this work I could gain the information that was necessary for the destruction of Red Hawk, or if I got the chance to send a bullet into his black heart, it would be a job worth ten times $100,000 in gold.

I sat down beside my fuse with a bunch of soft sulphur matches ready for lighting it, because sulphur scratches without a noise and a skillful man, used to lighting matches in a wind, can cup them so that no light will show from his fingers. I sat down there to wait, and I had barely taken my place, so it seemed to me, when I heard the rattling of hoofs on the distant road.

CHAPTER THIRTY-SEVEN

That rattling grew into a broken volleying, dying out when the road that the guard and the stage followed sank deeply into the side of the mountain, and swelling again when the way edged out on a shoulder and the sound could fling straight across at us. Someone stooped above me, and I heard the sympathetic voice of Caddigan saying: "Too bad, old-timer. I saw your face when you got the pick. I know . . . it's a dirty business . . . blowing men to hell when their backs are turned."

He went on. Another form stood above me, and I heard a deep, heavy, husky bass voice saying: "When the right time comes . . . just before the horses of the stage pass that dead tree . . . you light the fuse, or else. . . ." I felt him leaning above me, and the cold, round lips of a revolver pressed lightly against the back of my neck.

A pleasant chap was this Red Hawk. He went away, making me feel that I was already more than half dead. I tried the lighting of a sulphur match. It seemed to me that there was enough flare and light to attract the attention of a whole army, and as I whiffed out the flame in haste, I heard a deeply murmured—"Good!"—out of the darkness above and behind me.

It was the chief, waiting there and watching me. I had all sorts of wild impulses as I stretched out on my belly, close to the end of the fuse. I thought of trying to leap up and get to my horse and away through the darkness. I thought of rising and sauntering casually in that direction. No, I knew that it was too late now for me to reach the horse or even to stir from my post. And I had another feeling—that the chief was constantly reading the hidden thoughts as they drifted through my mind.

My mildest thought was that I might be able to swing myself at the critical moment over the edge of the precipice and clamber down into the darkness for shelter, clinging to the chance ridges of the rock that I might find there. I had merely to move my body a few feet in order to glance over the edge, but what I saw there was quite sufficient to discourage me. It was a face of polished rock along which the highlights of the stars made little paths as across water, until they showered the last of their soft silver upon the distant flowing of the river beneath me. No, my nerve was not up to such a freaky undertaking as that. I let myself relax and decided that I should not think any more or nerve myself any more until the crisis actually was there upon me. I fixed my attention on that dead tree of which the chief had spoken.

All that mountainside had been cut many years before and the logs flumed down the river beneath toward the sawmills. There had sprung up a second-growth forest of lodgepole pines, a mere unimposing thicket, you might say, that hardly rose to the knees of the great lightning-blasted, fire-girdled hollow trunk that stood by the roadside. This was the dead giant left standing there as a relic of the greater days in that forest. Its broken top stood up against the stars like the battlements of a great tower of masonry. It seemed more than wonderful that mere vegetation could ever have reached such a height. And this was the landmark that Red Hawk had selected for me.

It showed how calmly calculating and wise he was—wise as a white man is wise, and cunning as an Indian, also. For Indians are not supposed to make such fine deductions as the relation between the speed of stage horses coming downhill and the running of fire along a powder fuse. However, one was soon prepared for anything from the lips of Red Hawk.

Very suddenly I heard the screaming of brakes, loud enough to be almost at my ear. The stage had swung above the head of the grade and was now descending. And in front of the shrieking brake, there was the pounding of the hoofs of the stage horses, throwing themselves heavily back to check their impetus, and then the crashing hoofs of the mounts of the guard as they whirled along in the front.

An outsweep of the road, and there they were all before us, sweeping in a dark procession against the forest. Closer and closer, and my heart sank in my breast. For instead of swinging away well ahead of the stage, as one might have expected, the guard was reining well back toward that swaying, groaning vehicle.

I suppose the horsemen were riding with less vim than usual. For it was about 11:00 P.M., and Jessamy was only a scant eight miles away—most of the eight miles being downhill. It seemed, besides, a most unlikely place for a hold-up. The road was not narrow, and all was well. And so, becoming a little drowsy with the thought of safety and warm comfort in their beds in another scant hour, the nine or ten guards who rode before that stage rode carelessly and let their horses crowd back toward the stage itself.

But, no matter what the guard did, my orders were most precise to fire the fuse when the head of the lead team of the coach came opposite to the blasted giant of a tree. And again I swore to myself that I would not do it. Because, from the present appearances, that would send the whole guard crashing down to their deaths from the bridge to the waters of the Fulsom River so far below.

A very acid moment for me that was. Some luck came my way, however. One of the horses of the leaders of the guard was a restless colt, with some spirit left in spite of the long march that lay behind it, and now it stretched forward into a rocking gallop down the slope. The rest of the mounted party lurched away, sleepily following that example. Instantly a gap opened between the riders and the stage itself, and then the gap widened. How I prayed that the horses might have wings and the riders might drive their spurs deep. How I prayed for that.

But it seemed far too slow a pace to save their lives, for yonder the heads of the lead team of the coach were nodding past the big dead tree, and already I had overstayed my time limit. Overstayed it—and still the bullet had not come.

There was not a whisper out of the deathly darkness around me. All those keen eyes, like the eyes of wolves, were waiting and watching for the signal that I was to give in thunder. It seemed to me that all my senses became terribly awake and alive. I lived an hour in every second. There was a year of life to me in the joy that I felt as the gap between riders and stage opened foot by foot. Now the leading riders were beating the bridge beneath the hoofs of their horses. The brakes of the stage shrieked just a bit to the left of me. And it seemed that the hand of Red Hawk was drawing steady aim behind me to punish my treachery.

At length I could endure it no longer. I lit the sulphur match with all the skill that I possessed—a skill born of having to ignite cigarettes in the midst of desert winds, or of cherishing the cigarettes themselves through the surging and sweeping of a wet storm. I lit the soft-headed sulphur match and it seemed to me that the sound of the friction against my coat sleeve was as loud as a warning scream. But not a head turned toward me among the guard or from the coach, where the driver on his box was swearing sleepily at the lead horses and cursing them out of the way of the team in the swing. Now, in the hollow cup of my hands, there was a brightening flame, and that flame I touched to the end of the hidden fuse. The fire began at once. It sped down the line of the fuse, and it left a dull red line behind it, though fairly sheltered by skillfully disposed rocks and brush from the sight of those on the road.

Aye, but it never could reach the bridge in time to head off the stagecoach itself. I swear that I had made up my mind that coach and all were about to be blown to eternity, and I was about to leap up and spring on the fuse and tear it from its place when luck struck in my behalf again.

In spite of all the care and the wisdom of the chief, he had bought a faulty fuse. And, after burning at a steadily regular speed for a distance that brought it almost up to the head of the bridge, the fire reached the flaw and faltered a winking moment, and then flashed across through almost free powder the rest of the meager length of the fuse and to the cap itself. That flash, as the free powder ignited with a flare, caught the attention of the leaders of the guard as they turned from the end of the bridge safely onto the road beyond. And instantly there was the crackling of a pair of revolvers and a voice that shouted loudly: "Watch out on the coach! Speed up!"

If they had sped up, they would have rushed to their own destruction. But the sleepy driver, waking to hear such a warning, did what most startled and unprepared men will do. He dragged at all his reins with one hand while with the other hand and his right foot he jammed on the brakes. And the stage halted with its leading span of the team only a very scant distance from the bridge head. In the meantime, the last of the guard rushed across the bridge at the first token of the spurt of fire, and as they scampered onto the firm ground beyond, the dynamite cap was reached, and the whole charge detonated at my ear.

Yes, I thank heaven that I can say that not a living creature was on the bridge when the mine was exploded and the famous Fulsom Bridge lifted one end awkwardly, almost slowly into the air. There was a shrieking and a crackling of great splintered timbers, half drowned as the thundering echoes of the explosion poured roaring back upon my ears. And then the bridge end rushed back toward its first lodging place. It was so strong that it had been unseated, but not actually broken to bits by that powerful charge. I heard the heavy structure strike with a crash and a jar. I thought, at first, that the bridge would remain intact and that the next feature would be a headlong charge of the guard back against Red Hawk and his crew. In that case I was determined that my guns should be turned first on the spot where I felt Red Hawk himself to be in hiding.

But there was no chance for that. The bridge struck, rebounded a little, and then slipped with a groaning sound. And after that, the whole edge nearest to us slipped off the embankment and then sagged out of sight into the cañon. The next I saw was the sudden upward fling of the farther end of the bridge as the fall of the long structure pried it loose from its moorings. And so the whole ruin went smashing down into the cañon, battering and crashing against the walls on either end, and finally splintering to bits on a projection somewhere near the bottom—splintering with a sound that came hollowly back from the heart of the big ravine, and spilled out over the mouth of the precipice.

And there was the work done. From the farther side the guard was pouring an ineffectual fire into the trees beside the road. But they were separated by ninety feet of thinnest air from their coach, and Red Hawk's grip was already fastened, as you might say, on the treasure.

It was another miracle accomplished.

CHAPTER THIRTY-EIGHT

It was ridiculously easy after that. At the first glimpse of the big body of Red Hawk, some woman in the stagecoach screamed his name, and the gunfire from the other side of the bridge ceased by magic. What they feared, as it developed afterward, was that if they kept up their shooting, the Indian would murder and scalp every person with the stage.

For the rest, there was no thought of resistance. We came swarming up in our masks and backed the driver and the guard and the passengers in a line on the side of the road. Two of the boys searched them. They got half a small sackful of wallets and some jewelry like watches, and such stuff, together with a little off of the two women passengers. But, when they had finished their work, Red Hawk in his queer, husky bass voice ordered all of that stuff to be returned, for he had found the gold itself.

A little later, with $100,000 divided into ten parcels, we were scooting through the darkness as fast as our horses could leg it.

All very simple, you'll think. And I suppose that it *was* simple, once you had the key move in mind. Once you suggested to yourself that the bridge be blown up, all the rest was like a first-grade reader. A child could almost have done it.

But the blowing of that bridge I shall never forget to my death day. It comes whirling across my mind in the middle of the day a thousand times, and I see the great timbers lift, and I hear the rush and the smashing of the rock detritus all around me, as the fragments came showering back out of the air. There were fifty- and hundred-pound bits of rock that would have smashed me like an egg, but the luck was with me, and, when luck is on your side, a miss is as good as a mile, and no mistake. The ground around where I was lying was dented good and plenty, but I lived through those few seconds of hell, and afterward I felt quite cool about it.

It was not until later that my knees began to give way. Perhaps you've noticed that. Some things are too big for your eyes and your brain and your nerves to inhale at one whiff. But afterward you taste the horror little by little and the thing begins to grow on you and your hair begins to stand on end. It has kept growing on me.

Most of all, however, I see two things in retrospect. I see the lead horses of the stage team huddled back and squatting toward the ground with their ears flattened in terror too great for bolting, and I see the last horses of the vanguard stepping off the farther end of the bridge, just as the inferno of smoke and fire flared up before me.

The boys seemed to think a good deal of me for firing the bridge in that way. They came around and shook hands with me and said a few pleasant things, after we had put a couple of miles between us and the spot of the stage robbery. Only Red Hawk didn't say a word to me.

Something told me, by the squaring of his shoulders, that he didn't like me, that he too nearly saw through me. The rest of the boys seemed to feel it, too. But Caddigan was the harebrained fellow who demanded an explanation. He took my horse by the rein and carried the pair of us up where old Red Hawk was riding by himself.

Caddigan came up, then, and cried out: "Look here, chief, you act as though Sherburn had been playing hooky, when he's the fellow that has kept school together. Why not loosen up and tell him that he deserves a stick of candy?"

The big Indian turned his great head toward me and said in that odd, deep voice, that seemed to start in vibrations at his toes: "I had his life in the curling of my finger. Sherburn, you nearly died, and you know why." With that, he lifted his big black stallion away from us at a rattling pace and we fell back.

Caddigan was cursing softly. "He doesn't like you a bit," he said. "It looks as though he's down on a member of the band for the first time in history. It sure looks that way. I'm going to talk it over with the boys."

In another five miles we all came piling up to the place where Red Hawk had halted his horse and stood, waiting. I suppose that, altogether, the big brute had not said more than fifty words during the entire affair, and he did not need to speak now. As the men came up, they piled off their horses and the gold was brought all together. I don't know which one of them had a scale, but the scale was there, and a set of balancing weights.

For half an hour, very carefully, the boys worked on the division. They balanced down to the weight of a hair. I found myself mounting my horse with $8,000 in stolen gold—enough to make half of the men in the West try to murder me for the profits—for one evening's work. No wonder men flocked to Red Hawk as fast as they were used up in his work.

The chief, as I said before, had not a single word to say. He took his share and wheeled his big black around and was gone like a shot into the darkness, while I remembered Doc and suggested to someone that we would have to make up a share for him out of our cash. But Lefty told me that Doc was the only one of the gang who was specially provided for by Red Hawk himself and never put his hand in the general pile. He was the only member of the gang who did not take a share in the gun work and the adventures by night.

I was interested in what they said about Doc. The old Louisianan appealed to me as an amusing sort of crook. He was just mellow enough to have his villainy appear sort of different from the bad things that men in the prime of life do. And yet I suspected that Doc was really the worst of the lot. It was probably through him that the chief drew the most of his information about the affairs of the town of Amityville. So I rode on toward the camp, feeling more than two thirds queer about old Doc, and firm on having a talk with him when I saw him again.

After that, we jogged on quietly through the night, as mild a looking lot under the stars as you ever saw in your life. And still there was something stirring in us that would have made a hard fight for any posse that overtook us on the way.

We had gone whirling up through the mountains like the wind. But we came back so slowly that the dawn of the spring day was beginning when we got to the old camping grounds, and somebody began to shout out for Doc.

"Get up, you old rascal!" yelled two or three. "Where's the hot coffee that you promised us? Where's the bacon and the pone? Where's Doc?"

"He's gone back to his soft bunk in town," growled Lefty. "Why should he care how we feed before sunup?"

"I'm going to have him out," swore the first inquisitor, "and, if he's around this camp and ain't worked up a little reception party for us, I'll take the hide off of him an inch at a time."

And then someone yelled in a queer voice: "Hey . . . what the . . . why, here he is!"

Something in that voice startled the most calloused of us and brought us swiftly in a group around the designated spot, and there we found what had been asked for—old Doc indeed, but how changed. He lay flat on his back with glassy eyes fixed upward and with a patch of crimson along his breast and running down the side of his coat. And his white hair, falling in a film back from his head, gave an odd sort of nobility to his face. He looked like one of the best old men in the world.

"And who stuck that old pig that's too tough for eating?" asked a brutal voice from the group. That was the epitaph that was spoken for the death of Doc.

"Old Red Hawk got tired of giving the old loafer a split, I suppose," yawned another, "because there don't seem to be no other explanation."

"Either Red Hawk done it or else somebody else has been here in our camp, and maybe they're waiting by for the rest of us right now."

It made them scatter with a yell, and, while they were swooping about through the dull gray of the morning, I had kneeled close to the side of Doc and took his feeble old head in the palm of my hand. I was sorry for him from the bottom of my heart, old scoundrel though he undoubtedly was. And then it seemed that a miracle was affected by sheer sympathy. Life and light glimmered faintly for a moment in the depths of the eyes of the veteran. And then a vague recognition came into his face.

"Grip, my boy," he said gently.

At that touch of gentleness from the dying old man, I tell you that a flame of rage went through me and an overwhelming desire to avenge his death. And I breathed close to his ear: "Doc, old-timer, who did it? Will you tell me who did it?"

He seemed to have forgotten his pain until that instant, but now a wave of agony swept across his face and turned it gray. And he could only breathe to me: "Amityville . . . keep clear. . . ." And he died in that way, with a warning for me on his lips.

I got help from Caddigan and we buried him. And just as the grave was filled and the rocks rolled across the top of it to keep it inviolable by wolves or other animals, I looked to the side and happened to see that the sun was rising in the east—sending the first hotly burning rim of gold above the mountains. I suppose I was in an impressionable humor, but just then it seemed to me that there was a sort of a promise of forgiveness in that for Doc.

At least, no matter how many bad things he had done in the world to other people, he had tried to be square to me. And now with his last breath, what had he been trying to warn me about?

I must have presented a brow so black that Caddigan said suddenly to me: "The devil, Sherburn . . . he was just an old crook."

"Aye," I said, "but he was a kind old man, Caddigan. He was a kind old man, too."

I lay down in my blankets and gave myself a twist in them. I was too tired to do any more thinking at that time of the day, but, when I wakened with a start, all running with perspiration in the midmorning heat, I knew what I was going to do. I was going to let the warning from old Doc slide, and I intended to go into Amityville and see what was what.

I rested through the day in the coolest places I could find. But as soon as the sun began to drop westward a little and the day had cooled off a mite, I saddled the pinto, who was as fresh and as lively as a wildcat after his rest, and I started jogging along toward the town.

Caddigan ran after me a step or two, and sang out: "D'you want any company, old-timer?"

I shook my head and jogged on slowly across the desert.

Chapter Thirty-Nine

I didn't go straight to Amityville, at that. I got headed pretty close to it, and then something pulled me to one side, the same way that the needle pulls toward the lodestone. I headed for the house of old man Langhorne before I knew it, and I was jogging along down the trail when I saw Jenny herself turn out into it. I gave her a regular Indian yell, I was so glad to see her, and, when she heard me, she turned around and her horse stopped, and she sat like that in the saddle, not stirring a bit. When I came up to her, confound my eyes if there weren't tears on her cheeks.

"Darn it, Jenny," I said, "what sort of a way is this to carry on . . . just like a girl, and not like you, at all."

"He said you were never coming back," said Jenny. "And I . . . I was pretty near believing him. But I'll never believe him about anything again. I . . . I hate him now. The liar!"

"Good Lord," I breathed. "Are you speaking about Pete Gresham?"

"I am," she said.

"But he . . . ," I began, and then I had to admit, "but I let him think, when I left, that I likely would never come back. I didn't expect to."

"I don't want to talk about him," said Jenny. "And I don't want to think about him. He . . . he doesn't exist any more."

I didn't have to ask her who *did* exist. I put my arms around the girl who thought I was a bigger man than Peter Gresham and I told her the first couple of chapters of the story about how she was made the finest woman in the whole world, and why. She seemed to think it was a pretty good story, at that, and I don't know how long the foolishness would have kept on when I saw a couple of her father's cowpunchers heave in sight over the hill, and Jenny and I broke away. We went on down to her home and there I stayed only long enough to hear Major Langhorne explain a part of a great scheme that had just come to him for revolutionizing the power problem in the world. His scheme was just to construct some enormous burning glasses that would focus the rays of the sun on the desert and with those concentrated rays he would make steam and with the steam he would make electricity, and that electricity he would wire to all parts of the country that needed power. I asked him what would happen when the night came, and he pointed out that there were a lot of industries that could get along fine without power at night. He even had the cost of the burning lenses figured out, and he had everything fine until I asked him where he would get enough water in the desert to make the steam.

He hadn't thought of that, and I left him rubbing his chin and looking grave. Not beaten, but checked. Then I gave Jenny a foolish look and she gave me another, and I started off toward Amityville in earnest.

When I reached the town, I was a considerably bigger and more important man than I had been before I saw Jenny. I had started for the town, feeling that the problem was probably a lot too big for me. And I got to Amityville with the feeling that there was nothing in the world that was really too hard for me to tackle. Jenny was one solved problem behind me, and no other problem was half as important as she.

I was glad that it was the thick of the evening before I got to the hotel. I slipped around to the back entrance and slid up to my room as quickly as I could. I mean, I got to the room that formerly had been mine. And I sat down in the familiar place to get my wits together, and think over the thing that had brought me here.

The first thing to do would be to see Gresham, of course, and let him know everything that had happened to me since I had left town. Or no—would it be right to confide even in Gresham? I decided that I would know that when I looked him in the face. And yet I was filled with my achievement. I had gained a place in the band. I could come and go as I chose, and it would really be hard if I could not arrange a manner of scooping in the entire band with the assistance of a score or so of the honest gunfighters of Amityville, with big Gresham at their head. The more I thought of it, the more certain I was that I would have to tell Gresham everything. But I was foolishly sensitive about showing myself to him again after having announced my departure so determinedly and such a short time before.

I was turning these matters in my mind, back and forth, when I was startled by the sound of the lock in the door turning.

"Well?" I called in a guarded voice.

For answer, there was the rustle of a paper and a folded bit was pushed through the crack beneath the door. It made the hair bristle on my head, even a small thing like that—which shows you how thoroughly my nerve had been shaken. I jumped up and scooped up the paper. If I had been cold before, I turned to ice when I read the contents.

For there I found, printed out in the childish, sprawling hand that I had seen the night before, the following notice: *Leave Amityville at once. You are wanted!*

That was all, and that was enough. Red Hawk himself had printed out that missive, if there was anything in the similarity of handiwork. Had Red Hawk's own hand passed it under the door? No, that was impossible. I tried the knob of the door; the lock was fast. It seemed strange to think that the key had been on the outside. And yet here I was, cooped up, unless I could get through to the room of Gresham, which adjoined mine. I tried his door softly, but it was as I feared. His lock was also turned from the outside, and if I wished to leave the room, I had nothing left but the foolish expedient of climbing through the window and so down the side of the building. Of course I didn't like that, but the saying runs that beggars can't be choosers.

I had gone back to the window, then, and examined the false balcony that ran along the side of the building—the same balcony from which the knife must have been thrown at me on that other historic night, when it seemed to me that I heard a slight noise in the room of Gresham. I hurried back to his door and tapped lightly upon it, to be answered instantly by the surprised and cheerful tone of Gresham himself:

"Well, hello there. Who's there?"

"Sherburn," I answered.

I heard a muffled exclamation. The door was unlocked and opened, and there was Gresham himself, his face a study in bewilderment, and yet a study in apparent pleasure, also.

He swore that he was very glad to see me. "If you were to cut loose from me like this," he said, "I hoped that you would give me a chance to pay you off for your share of the partnership. . . ."

"It was too short a job to be worth any pay," I assured him.

But he wouldn't hear me. He vowed that I had been a great drawing card and that cowpunchers and prospectors were still pouring in every day, hungry to see that celebrated whiskey-shifter, John Sherburn. We had a laugh together over that. And the next thing I knew, Gresham was asking me anxiously if I could really come back and stay on the job with him.

"Do you want me?" I asked him, filled with curiosity. "Do you really want me, Gresham?"

He answered me slowly and honestly, with a cloud on his face. "I'd like to say yes," he told me. "But there's one thing that prevents me from saying it. And I think you know what it is."

"It's Jenny," I suggested.

"It is," he said. "You stick like a bur in her mind. You've taken her fancy. And frankly I'd like to have you a thousand miles away. I'd pay money to have you that far off." He covered that with a laugh, but the laughter rang flat and short.

"There's no danger," I vowed to him rather hypocritically. "I've come back for a short stay only. I have a little news to give you. And a good deal of advice to ask."

"Then," he said, "let's have the news first. Advice is cheap, but news is worth something."

"Doc is dead," I told him bluntly.

I was sorry for it as soon as I spoke. I had not realized that the old fellow meant much to Gresham. But now he lifted stiffly half out of his chair, and then sank back, limp.

"Doc is dead?" he echoed me heavily.

"Dead," I said. "And murdered. And before he died, he said something to me about Amityville . . . urging me to keep away from it."

"And that's why you came back?"

"Of course."

"There is a queer sort of logic in the things you do, Sherburn," he said. And, as he spoke, a faint smile played upon his lips. "And now for the matter of the advice, if that's all the news you'll give me . . . if you won't tell me when and where and why poor old Doc went west. . . ."

"That news I can't give you now. But I want your advice

about this. . . ." And I laid the paper before him.

He spread it out and pored intently over the childish printing. "This is interesting, Sherburn," he said. "Where the devil did it come from?"

"It was passed under the door of that other room . . . just after the lock had been turned on me."

He began to chuckle. "Somebody is playing a little practical joke and trying to see how good your nerves are."

"Are they?" I asked him savagely. "But let me tell you, Gresham, that I have good reason to know that the communications that Red Hawk sends out to his men are printed in exactly the same manner."

He had taunted that confession out of me, although it was a good deal more than I had intended to say. However, at least it served the purpose of wiping the smile from the face of my friend. He stared very gravely at me, and then he shook his head. "Is it possible?" he asked me gently. "Are you really sure about this?"

"As sure as I am that I sit here and see your face."

He pondered it a moment. He asked no questions. He didn't try to break through any reserve that remained to me. There was a world of dignity in big Gresham, and he liked to leave the dignity of others intact as well as his own.

"It sounds a bit weird," he said, "but I can't doubt you. As a matter of fact, I suppose it is about the way an Indian would write. What do you make of it?"

"I am ordered out of town at once, as you see."

"And?" asked Gresham earnestly.

"Gresham," I said, "I don't have to read in the rest of the message. It's implied. If you had ever seen Red Hawk face-to-face, as I have seen . . . close almost as you are now . . . you would know that he's the sort of a fellow who does what he threatens to do and does it pretty thoroughly. The part of the message he has left out is simply this . . . if I don't leave at once, I'll be murdered!"

Chapter Forty

I thought I could see Gresham stiffen a little under the shock of this. At length he got up from his chair and stood over me with his big arms swinging loosely. What a giant of a man he was.

"Look here," he said. "I'm not going to say that you're superstitious. I just want to ask you to remember one thing . . . you are in my house. Do you mean to say that you would fear for yourself even here?"

I could not help saying: "A knife missed my life by a hand's breadth in the room next to this, Gresham."

Here he flushed angrily. "It is true," he admitted. "I wish to heaven that I could have located the scoundrel who accomplished that. But isn't this a little different? Do you mean to say that you would still have a fear if I were to remain here in the room with you?"

I had to say: "Gresham, I know you're feared far and wide, but this devil of a redskin is more terrible than you. Yes, I would still be afraid. He implies in this note that I leave or die. And die I most certainly shall unless I leave."

"What?" cried Gresham. "Confound it, this is getting a little ghostly. Are guns to appear through the solid wall, then?" He leaned out the window, saying as though to himself: "There's nothing in sight. Don't be an ass, my dear boy. The side of the house is perfectly empty. Wait a moment. I have to run down to the game room, but I'll be back immediately."

He already had his hand upon the doorknob when I clutched

at his arm. "Gresham," I said, "if you have any friendship for me, forget every other duty that you have in the world and stay here with me tonight. I'm in a funk. I'm in a blue funk. I've got to have you here."

He turned slowly back from the door, frowning at the floor. But immediately he cleared his face and laid his big, gentle hand upon my shoulder.

"Certainly," he said. "I remember a time when I was a boy and had a touch of delirium in a fever. When my mother tried to leave the room, I would break into a screaming fit, for it seemed to me that, if she left me, devils would have me in their grips in no time. I don't accuse you of being delirious or a boy. But I think you will confess a little later that this affair has gotten on your nerves."

"You may call it anything you like," I told Gresham. "But just now I am in terror of my life. And I intend to fight for my life . . . fight for it!" I backed into a corner. I felt the wall behind me. I sounded the floor there with a tap of my heel. "Now," I said, "the danger cannot get in behind me. Let it come from in front . . . and particularly through that cursed window . . . and I'm ready for it." I had both guns in my hands.

Gresham leaned at the open window, his arms folded across his breast.

"Get away from that place, Peter!" I begged him almost hysterically. "I tell you a gun may appear there at any moment!"

But Gresham merely laughed. "Why, my friend Sherburn," he said, "I think you're so far gone with nerves right now that you couldn't hit the side of a barn. Why don't you put up those guns, then?"

It was true, too. My hands were quivering and jerking in the most foolish fashion, and the guns wobbled awkwardly. In fact, I was in the sheerest panic. I followed his advice. I dropped the guns back into their holsters, and then I beat my cold hands together, trying to work warmth and strength back into them. And, as I worked, I said: "I thank the Lord for you, Gresham. I would feel like a naked soul in the world if it weren't for you here."

"No doubt," he said. "No doubt."

It made me jerk up my head and stare at him in another fashion, for I cannot tell you how much grimness there was in that voice that I heard from the lips of Gresham. I looked up and I saw that he was still smiling. But it seemed to me that the mirth was gone from his mouth and there was nothing but a deadly menace there. I looked upon him, I swear to you, as one looks upon a frightful thing in a nightmare—a loved face turning into a hated one.

"I am glad," said Gresham sneeringly, "that you put your trust in me."

And then I knew. Then the horrible, the amazing, the unbelievable truth rushed upon my mind. I still cannot believe it. It was a thing that turned my hair gray in a fortnight, and still it drives a shudder through me. I knew the whole truth, and, thrusting out a stiff arm, I pointed to Gresham and I cried faintly: "Gresham . . . oh, my Lord . . . *you* are the man!"

He still smiled—still stood there and smiled like a devil at me.

"Why, yes," he said. "I am the man. And you, Sherburn, have looked fairly well into the truth of the matter. I intended to get rid of you a long time ago. I intended that that knife should have split your thievish heart. But luck helped you out. And now, Sherburn, I have the exquisite pleasure of reading the certainty of your death in your face even before you die. It is worth waiting for. I only wish that your girl, Jenny, could be standing by to see this." And he added, while I stood mutely, looking at that terrible and handsome face of his: "But she will forget you in a little while. She is not the sort to remember very long. Not the sort at all."

"You lie," I said. "Draw your gun, Gresham. Eternal heaven, was it really you who murdered old Doc?"

"The old fool was tired of working as my spy on you. He was even beginning to plead with me on your behalf."

"Tell me this . . . did Doc know?"

"He knew too much . . . as you know too much. And. . . ." His voice snapped in the midst of the sentence; his gun flashed out from its holster. And I, dragging mine out with nerveless fingers, knew perfectly that I was a dead man for any strength that lay in me. I was beaten—beaten utterly so far as big Peter Gresham was concerned.

What happened I hardly saw. But there was a faint glimmer of something at the window, and then a ripping, jagged explosion. A bullet grazed my cheek. But still I stood there, unhurt, and watched big Gresham topple forward on his face. And, in the window, I saw young Caddigan, sitting astride of the sill. He was a little white and drawn of face, but still his voice was steady.

"I guessed you were not one of us. I guessed that from the start. But what I *didn't* guess was that anybody in the world could be such a nightmare as this devil." He waved to me. "I hear them coming, old-timer. So long. Remember me in your prayers. I deserve it."

And he was gone, and I stood there, looking down on the last of the man who had played a double rôle so well and so long.

When they came in on me, they found me standing there like one in a daze. And dazed I was, and helpless. They took the guns out of my hands. They raised the big fellow from the floor. They stripped away his clothes, and then they received their first shock. His body, below the neck, was covered with a rich copper-red stain.

There was a close search of everything. And what they found

was enough. They found an eye patch, such as Red Hawk wore. They found a quantity of stain. Just what it was, I don't know, but I think that black walnut juice was the foundation of it, together with a strong cleaning fluid that he had compounded and that would take off the stain quickly, though water would not effect it.

They found these things, but that was only the beginning of the search. And, before it ended, they discovered in his safe stocks and bonds worth over $400,000. So thrifty was this clever devil!

But I, for my part, have never been able to get out of my mind the first picture that was in it of the big fellow as he rode into my ken on that hot spring day when I was dying for water on the desert, and that thing for which I am eternally thankful is that the bullet which slew him was not fired by my hand.

And yet people have never stopped saying that I was the man who finished him. Caddigan, though he became so famous for other reasons later on, was never mentioned in the great general humor. And so it comes down to the present day and I suppose that, if anyone remembers my name at all, it is solely as the person who ended the great Red Hawk.

I suppose the explanation of his career was simple enough, though he died before it could be verified. He had run down Red Hawk early in his effort to avenge his murdered brother. But, when he laid the chief low, he must have seen the astonishing resemblance between his own physical dimensions and those of the marauder. The rest was soon hatched, out of his imagination. The endless trail he was supposed to follow in pursuit of the Indian gave him the opportunity to escape from Amityville often, unsuspected, and, while he was away, he appeared in the part of the chief from time to time, and then appeared again in Amityville in his proper skin and color.

Well, big Peter Gresham is dead, but to this day I cannot but think that there were two natures in the man. The one was the kind and honest gentleman I first saw. The other was the inhuman fiend—Red Hawk. And there was only one place where the two natures joined hands—wherever Jenny Langhorne came into his life.

Jenny will never speak freely about him. But I have gathered since the day she became my wife that Jenny from the very first was held back from becoming the wife of big Peter Gresham simply by an odd instinct. Something, she felt, was wrong with the man. She could not tell what. It was like a shadow cast by an invisible body. But she trusted that instinct and that instinct saved her.

We still live near Amityville. Major Langhorne is still alive. And once or twice a week that very ancient man comes driving over to see us and sit on our verandah and he confides to me some great scheme that will change the destinies of the world.

As for me, I ceased from the part of the ruffian at once and forever. I became a quiet and hard-working rancher. Not overly prosperous as far as worldly possessions are considered, but very happy.

And for a long decade now, I have looked back to my other self as to something found in the pages of a book, interesting but unreal.

Jenny has one theory that she will sometimes talk about. I cannot tell what has brought it into her mind, and yet it fascinated her and it fascinates me. She thinks that, had it not been for her, my partnership with big Gresham might have developed into a real affection between us. I might have drawn him back to honesty, and he might have drawn me up from ruffianism.

But that would have been too good to be true.

ABOUT THE AUTHOR

Max Brand is the best-known pen name of Frederick Faust, creator of Dr. Kildare, Destry, and many other fictional characters popular with readers and viewers worldwide. Faust wrote for a variety of audiences in many genres. His enormous output, totaling approximately thirty million words or the equivalent of five hundred thirty ordinary books, covered nearly every field: crime, fantasy, historical romance, espionage, Westerns, science fiction, adventure, animal stories, love, war, and fashionable society, big business and big medicine. Eighty motion pictures have been based on his work along with many radio and television programs. For good measure he also published four volumes of poetry. Perhaps no other author has reached more people in more different ways. Born in Seattle in 1892, orphaned early, Faust grew up in the rural San Joaquin Valley of California. At Berkeley he became a student rebel and one-man literary movement, contributing prodigiously to all campus publications. Denied a degree because of unconventional conduct, he embarked on a series of adventures culminating in New York City where, after a period of near starvation, he received simultaneous recognition as a serious poet and successful author of fiction. Later, he traveled widely, making his home in New York, then in Florence, and finally in Los Angeles.

Once the United States entered the Second World War, Faust abandoned his lucrative writing career and his work as a screenwriter to serve as a war correspondent with the infantry in Italy, despite his fifty-one years and a bad heart. He was killed during a night attack on a hilltop village held by the German army. New books based on magazine serials or unpublished manuscripts or restored versions continue to appear so that, alive or dead, he has averaged a new book every four months for seventy-five years. Beyond this, some work by him is newly reprinted every week of every year in one or another format somewhere in the world. A great deal more about this author and his work can be found in *The Max Brand Companion* (Greenwood Press, 1997) edited by Jon Tuska and Vicki Piekarski. His next Five Star Western will be *Sun and Sand: A Western Trio.* His Web site is www.MaxBrandOnline.com.